The
Broken
One

ALSO BY RUTH CARDELLO

Up for Heir
In the Heir
Royal Heir
Hollywood Heir
Runaway Heir

LONE STAR BURN

Taken, Not Spurred
Tycoon Takedown
Taken Home
Taking Charge

THE LEGACY COLLECTION

Maid for the Billionaire
For Love or Legacy
Bedding the Billionaire
Saving the Sheikh
Rise of the Billionaire
Breaching the Billionaire: Alethea's Redemption
A Corisi Christmas (Holiday Novella)

THE ANDRADES

Recipe for Love (Holiday Novella)
Come Away with Me
Home to Me
Maximum Risk
Somewhere Along the Way
Loving Gigi

THE BARRINGTONS

Always Mine
Stolen Kisses
Trade It All
A Billionaire for Lexi
Let It Burn
More Than Love
Forever Now

TRILLIONAIRES

Taken by a Trillionaire
Virgin for a Trillionaire

TEMPTATION SERIES

Twelve Days of Temptation
Be My Temptation

BACHELOR TOWER SERIES

Insatiable Bachelor
Impossible Bachelor

The Broken One

RUTH CARDELLO

Montlake
Romance

Published by Montlake Romance, Seattle

www.apub.com

Amazon, the Amazon logo, and Montlake Romance are trademarks of Amazon.com, Inc., or its affiliates.

ISBN-13: 9781542009706
ISBN-10: 1542009707

Cover design by Eileen Carey

Printed in the United States of America

This book is dedicated to everyone who helped my daughter find her stuffed wolf when we lost him. We posted him on all of my social media accounts and the outpouring of support from friends as well as strangers was heartwarming. A week after losing him, he was back in my daughter's arms and all was well in our household again.

To learn more about the true story of Wolfie, visit www.ruthcardello.com.

Don't Miss a Thing!

www.ruthcardello.com

Sign Up for Ruth's Newsletter:
https://forms.aweber.com/form/00/819443400.htm

Join Ruth's Private Fan Group:
www.facebook.com/groups/ruthiesroadies

Follow Ruth on Goodreads:
www.goodreads.com/author/show/4820876.Ruth_Cardello

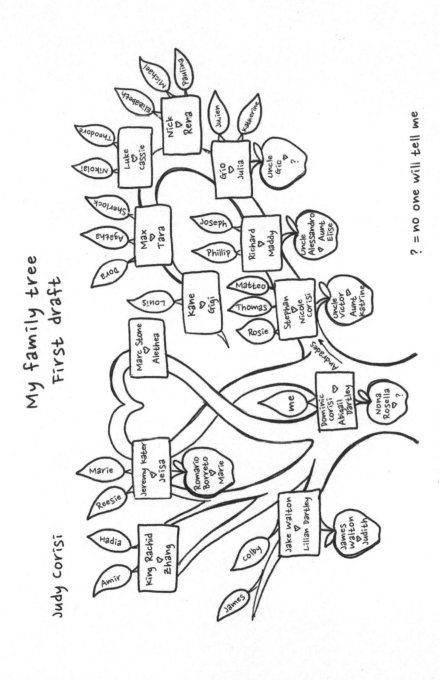

My family tree
First draft

Judy Corisi

? = no one will tell me

CHAPTER ONE

JUDY

Barefoot and dressed in white, fluffy, hooded unicorn onesie pajamas, Judy Corisi spun in the high-backed leather chair behind her father's desk. He didn't like her in his office, but she remained secure in the knowledge that there was no bite behind his growl.

And she had an important reason to be there.

After one final spin, she pulled the chair closer to the desk, opened her school folder, and took out a piece of paper. Even though it was a first draft, she'd put a significant amount of time into it. She'd hoped to get a quick okay from her teacher so she could move on to the next step. Instead, her teacher had met with her and asked for a major overhaul of the assignment.

Frustrating.

I worked hard on this.

Harder than normal, because I wanted to make Dad smile. Usually her father loved hearing about school. He often came home late from work, but always made time for her. They'd curl up on the couch, read together, and she'd tell him about her day. Over the years, she'd gone from reading to him to reading next to him. No matter how busy he was, he was hers for that window of time. Her life was full with friends, soccer practice, and schoolwork, but time with her father was something special.

Not that time with her mother wasn't. According to her friends, Judy had the sweetest, most attentive mother ever. She attended all of Judy's games, volunteered in the school, and made Judy's friends feel special whenever they visited. *Perfect* was how everyone described Abby Corisi—which often made it hard to live up to her expectations.

I have too much of Dad in me to always follow the rules.

Dominic Corisi—his name alone commanded attention. Her mother joked that he'd been a rascal before they'd met. Judy never did get what that meant, but Uncle Jake said her father had as many enemies as he had friends.

And he certainly had a lot of friends.

Judy looked around her father's office. The mahogany shelves that lined the walls were full of photos and every award Judy had received since preschool. She couldn't imagine anyone not liking her father. He didn't even have a temper.

Which was why she had been shaken by his reaction when she'd said her teacher had asked everyone to make a family tree.

He'd been angry.

And something else.

When she'd asked him why, he'd said he was tired.

Her father didn't get tired.

When she'd pushed for him to explain, he'd gotten a haunted look in his eyes and walked away. She'd chased after him, but he'd brushed her off and closed himself in this very office.

When asked about his response, all her mother had said was that she would talk to him. About what? Judy didn't know. Whatever their talk had involved, it hadn't changed her father's feelings toward the project. She'd made the additional mistake of asking him about his own father the next day. She'd never forget the look on his face. So much pain it had sent a flash of panic through her.

Her father had always been invincible. Nothing could hurt him—no one could scare him. Yet Judy had glimpsed a dark memory in his eyes and knew that someone had.

Imagining anyone hurting him brought out a protectiveness in Judy. More than anything, she wanted the smile back in his eyes. A full family tree, one that included all the people who loved him, had felt like the perfect way to do it.

Her first draft had been time consuming, but exciting once she'd started it. On the trunk of her family tree, she'd written her grandmother's name in an apple, then her parents' above in a box, with herself represented as a leaf. A long Andrade branch wove around one side of the tree with all their children and grandchildren. Smaller branches balanced the other side, representing her mother's family as well as offshooting branches for the Katers, the Borrettos, the royal Hantan family. In the middle, two branches wove both sides together, a beautiful tangle of love. It was a first draft, but one that she'd been excited to share. This was the family her father had built. She'd planned to transfer the information onto a canvas and give it to him for his birthday—until she'd shown it to her teacher.

Apparently her diagram needed to be pruned. She hadn't followed the directions carefully enough. It wasn't that Judy had misunderstood the assignment; it was that her definition of family didn't match her teacher's.

Revision was normally something Judy was okay with.

Uncle Jake says the secret to true genius cannot occur until one is willing to acknowledge that very little that is accepted as known actually is.

Mistakes often lead to incredible discoveries.

She ran a hand over her diagram.

I don't see how my teacher's version could be incredible. Less is not better.

Despite how full the paper was, only a small number of names listed were circled with a yellow highlighter. Mrs. Chase had been very clear that every name not circled had to be removed.

Judy texted a request for her aunt to come to the office and looked over her paper again while waiting. Every single person she'd listed felt like family—how could they not be? More than that, the trimmed tree wouldn't have the effect Judy was looking for. Rather than cheer her father, it would look small and limited.

Not what I want to give my father.

"Are you supposed to be in here?" a female voice asked from the door.

Judy turned her paper over. "Thank you for meeting with me."

"Not a hardship since I'm technically *babysitting* you." Dressed in a casual but chic pantsuit, Alethea floated across the room. Her red hair was tied back in a sophisticated, loose bun. She could have been a model. Everyone said so, but instead she ran a security company with her husband, Marc Stone. Safety was serious stuff.

Being born to a family of wealth came with perks, but Judy had learned early that it also had a cost. Her father was internationally well known and, by default, so was Judy. She didn't know what it was like to go to a playdate without a security detail. She'd never gone for a walk without the same.

Marc and Alethea made sure Judy was safe, and she couldn't remember a time when they hadn't been part of her life.

According to Mrs. Chase, that doesn't make them tree-worthy.

Alethea took a seat in the chair in front of the desk, crossing one leg gracefully over the other. "What can I do for you?"

Tapping her fingertips lightly on the desk, Judy leaned forward. "I'd like to hire you for a project, but absolute discretion is imperative."

"Absolute discretion." Looking as if she were holding back a smile, Alethea nodded. "Of course."

"I'm serious." Loving Alethea as she did didn't mean she was blind to her aunt's reckless history. "I can't get grounded again—not right before summer vacation."

With one eyebrow arched, Alethea asked, "Grounded? I don't know what you're planning, but it already sounds like I won't be able to help you. I would never go against your parents' wishes."

Judy rolled her eyes skyward. "Oh, please. Trouble is your middle name."

Looking unfazed, Alethea shook her head. "Perhaps once, but not anymore. Ask your uncle Marc. I'm rather boring lately—just a happily married woman who spends most of her time in an office."

That was true and had been the topic of more than one conversation Judy had pretended not to overhear. It was time to lay that card on the table; a new challenge was just what Alethea needed. If riding lessons had taught Judy anything, it was that falling off didn't define a rider, but getting back on or not did. "Auntie Lil says you haven't been yourself since you botched a job for Delinda Westerly."

Alethea frowned. "Really? I wasn't aware she felt that way."

Whoops. "She didn't say *botched*. I'm summarizing."

Her aunt pursed her lips. "I appreciate the clarification."

This wasn't going how Judy had imagined. Time to refocus. "If you're too scared to help me, I'll ask Uncle Jeremy. Or maybe Auntie Zhang."

Alethea's eyes narrowed. "Aren't you a little young to already sound like your father?"

Judy sat up straighter. "Age is a number."

"You're *nine*."

"Will you help me or not?"

After a quiet moment, Alethea uncrossed her legs and leaned forward. "What do you need?"

"First you have to promise to keep this between you and me."

"Keep what?"

"First promise."

Concern filled Alethea's eyes. "If someone at school is bothering you—"

"It's not that."

"Honey, you know I can't promise to keep anything from your parents." One hand went to her temple in what looked like an attempt to massage away the start of a headache. Her other went protectively to her stomach.

Her stomach. "Are you pregnant, Auntie Alethea?"

"Why do you ask that?" Alethea's hand fell to her lap, and her face went white. For a long moment she looked more uncertain than Judy had ever imagined her supersleuth aunt could.

"You're married. That's when people start having babies. Unless they don't know about condoms, then babies just happen."

Shaking her head, Alethea said, "Judy, I'm not ready for you to grow up yet. Where did you learn about babies?"

"School and the internet."

Rubbing her hands over her temples again, Alethea took a deep breath. "You know you can ask me anything. Even about . . . sex."

Judy shook her head vigorously. "Ew. No. Sex sounds gross. No. Stop. It's not about that."

Looking relieved, Alethea lightly slapped her own cheeks twice, then crossed her legs again. "Well, then, let's talk about this job you want to hire me for."

According to her father, the art of negotiation involved standing firm, because nine times out of ten the other person would cave in the face of unwavering confidence. Back straight, shoulders squared, she looked across her father's desk and calmly held her aunt's gaze. *She already knows my condition—all I have to do is wait.*

"You're good," Alethea said with a chuckle of resignation. "I promise I won't tell anyone unless I feel that you're in danger."

"Okay." Judy nodded and turned back over her school assignment, then leaned over her desk toward her aunt. "My teacher asked my class to make a family tree. I have to redo mine."

Alethea stood and moved beside Judy so she could see the paper. Her expression revealed her displeasure as she looked it over. "What did your teacher say when she circled *some* of the names?"

Judy lowered her gaze. She didn't want to say it, because she didn't want to hurt Alethea's feelings, but the truth was there for her to see. "Mrs. Chase said my family tree should only include people who are biologically related to me." An emotional lump clogged Judy's throat. "No Andrades, no Katers . . . no Stones."

"What a bitch," Alethea growled. "I'm sure she'll explain family to you differently after I speak with her—if she's even employed at your school when I'm done. Your family tree is perfect just the way it is."

Judy rose to her feet. "You can't have Mrs. Chase fired."

Fire spit from Alethea's eyes, but she smiled. "I believe I can."

Judy knew that look. She put her hands on her hips. "Auntie Alethea, you promised."

Alethea held her gaze for a moment, then sighed. "Did I?"

"Yes, you did. And Mrs. Chase is a very good teacher."

"That's a point we'll have to agree to disagree on."

Maybe this was a bad idea. Judy sat back down. She looked down at the highlighted names again. "This isn't about my teacher; it's about Dad. Ever since I told him about the project, he's been different."

"Different?"

"He looks—sad. I asked him to help me with it, and he said no. He never says no. Look at the circled names—just me, Mom and Dad, Nona, Auntie Nicole and Auntie Lil, their husbands and kids. That's not a lot. I can keep Uncle Stephan because he's married to Nicole, but not his father—Uncle Alessandro . . ." Judy stopped herself. "Should I just call him Alessandro? He's not actually my uncle, is he?"

Alethea's hand tightened on her shoulder. "He is in every way that matters."

"I know." She looked down at the diagram again. "But Dad's biological family can't end with his sister and his mother. He has to have more family out there. So I was thinking . . . what if I find them and surprise him with a family tree that has more of his relatives on it? One of my friends has a new half brother because her father had a DNA test done."

Her aunt's eyebrows rose and fell. "How did your friend's mother take the news?"

Judy frowned. "She was happy, I think."

"I'll take your word for that." Leaning forward, Alethea said, "Let's focus on your family. If your father wanted to find someone, they would already be found."

Judy shook her head as she remembered her father's expression. "I don't think so. I think he wants a big family like Uncle Alessandro has, but he's afraid."

"Your father? Afraid?"

Remembering the look in her father's eyes confirmed Judy's resolve. After scanning the room again, she said, "I'm going to do this with or without you."

"Have you run your idea by your mother?" Alethea sat on the corner of the desk.

Judy shrugged. No reason to ask when one already knew the answer. "Her favorite word is *no*."

"That's true." Alethea laid a hand on her stomach again. "Judy, there was a time when I would have been all over this. I thought the truth mattered more than how anyone felt about it. I hurt a lot of people with that philosophy."

"Mom told me you've saved as many people as you've annoyed."

Alethea averted her eyes. "That's . . . one way to put it, I guess."

There was something different about Alethea in that moment, and it was unsettling. She seemed—*unsure of herself?* No, that couldn't be. "Are you afraid you'll botch this too?"

"No. Of course not. That's the most ridiculous thing I've ever heard." Alethea tapped her forehead lightly with her index finger. "Okay, yes. I'm scared. I can't fuck up right now. I'm going to be a mother. I don't want my baby to ever be on the outside of the family looking in."

"Auntie Alethea?"

"Yes?"

"You just said the f-word."

"Oh. Sorry. Don't tell your mom."

"I won't." Judy stood up and hugged Alethea tightly. "I'm sorry. I shouldn't have asked you. I just thought if anyone could find my father's family it would be you."

"And I appreciate your faith in me." Hugging her back, Alethea asked, "It's never that simple, though. If we did find them . . . then what? They might be horrible people. Opening any door is always a gamble."

"Yes, but . . ." Judy stepped back and studied Alethea's expression. "We could watch them for a while . . . Then, if they aren't nice, we just don't tell him about them."

"Why am I considering this?"

"Because family is important, highlighted or not"—Judy shot her most persuasive smile up at Alethea—"and you love me."

"I do love you." With a reluctant answering smile, Alethea said, "I'm in, but we end this if I come across anything shady. Deal?" She held out her hand.

Judy shook it. "Deal." She turned and folded up her diagram again. "You need to watch me again soon so you can update me on your progress."

Alethea laughed as she stood. "Absolutely. Good meeting. Now how about we go downstairs and watch a movie so I can maintain my cover as your babysitter?"

After gathering up her work, Judy followed her out the door. Alethea went with her to her bedroom so she could deposit her papers. They were walking down the grand staircase when Judy asked, "Auntie Alethea?"

"Yes?"

"You already know where my father's family is, don't you?"

Alethea smiled—neither confirming nor denying.

So cool.

I'm going to be like that someday.

CHAPTER TWO

HEATHER

It wasn't my best moment. Not much used to shake my confidence. In college my housemates had consistently put me forth as the spokesperson whenever our landlord was upset with us—which happened more than I care to remember. People in authority don't intimidate me; I learned how to take care of myself early . . . and that life was a lot easier when one didn't break the rules.

If I had to claim a weakness, I'd say it was that I had a problem saying no. I knew what it was like to have no one to turn to, and I couldn't knowingly leave anyone else in that situation.

That was how I'd ended up running with a wild crowd in college. Brenda and I had shared a room freshman year, and she had been a hot mess. If I hadn't woken her, she would have slept through every one of her early-morning classes. She had been gorgeous, though, and that explained many of her problems. She had been constantly invited to parties, and there had always been a man trying to be her very special friend. It had looked exhausting.

Despite how different we were, or perhaps because of it, we had gotten on well. When she'd moved out the following year, I'd gone with her into a crazy, bed-hopping-coed situation. One I had been part of and not at the same time. I hadn't been a drinker and had spent most of my days in my room studying, but I still smiled when I looked back at that time. Brenda and I had needed each other. She'd kept me laughing, and I'd made sure the bills were paid on time. Oh yes, and I'd talked the landlord back into liking us each time he'd threatened to toss us out.

That was me—the fixer.

After college I had become one of the rare tax preparers who enjoyed poring over people's prior returns for errors. I was not above doing some pro bono. Nothing felt better than finding a few extra dollars for those who needed it the most. That kind of attention had brought me enough clients to start my own accounting business.

I've also always been a bit of a prepper. If an asteroid hit the planet, I knew where the global seed banks were located, and I had a plan for how to get there—just in my head. *Writing it down* would be crazy. I just knew that life had a tendency of sucking big-time, and the better one prepared for those bumps, the easier they were to survive.

I hadn't prepared, however, for the heartbreak that came along with parenting. My four-year-old daughter was sobbing in my arms, and I didn't know how to make it better. "I want Wolfie."

"We'll find him, Ava," I promised, even though I had no idea where he'd gone. It had been a good day until I'd pulled into our driveway. None of the parenting books I'd read had instructions for what to do the moment she'd looked frantically around the back seat of my car and announced that her stuffed wolf—the one she slept with every night, the one she didn't get into the car without—wasn't still with her.

I'd torn my car apart, unearthing stale french fries, melted crayons, and sticky things that had me instantly reaching for hand sanitizer, but no Wolfie.

"I want Wolfie," she said again in a broken voice that tore right through me.

When it came to crunching numbers or knowing tax law, I was confident with my skills, but this was bringing me to the edge of a panic attack. What would Brenda have done? Would I ever feel like I knew what I was doing?

I wasn't supposed to be a mother . . . not this young.

A few years after we'd graduated, I'd held Brenda's hand in the delivery room and welcomed Ava into the world. I'd signed a paper agreeing to take care of Ava if anything ever happened to Brenda, but I'd never imagined that she would die from an infection she'd caught in the hospital or that Ava's father would have been so eager to sign away his rights to her.

In her short life, Ava had already lost so much—I should have tied Wolfie to her arm . . . or to the car . . . I don't know. Something.

I took a deep breath. "I know you do, hon. He's not in the car, but I remember putting him next to you. At least I think I do. Do you know where he went?"

Her dark hair was plastered to one side of her face when she raised her head from my shoulder. Tears spilled from her deep-blue eyes. "He wanted to stick his head out."

My chest tightened. "Ava, did you open the window?"

"Maybe."

I shifted her higher on my hip, so we were eye to eye. How had I missed that? I'd received a call from a client whose question had turned out to be more complicated than I'd anticipated, but I hadn't spoken to her for long. *It only takes a moment.* That was a lesson I'd only learned about a thousand times since taking Ava home from the hospital. She was gifted at proving that life was full of surprises no matter how well I planned. "I won't be mad. I just want to find Wolfie for you. Did he fall out the window?"

Her face crumpled. "Yes."

"How long ago?"

She shook her head helplessly.

I took another deep breath. "Okay, let's get you back in your car seat, and we'll look for him."

Her thin body shuddered against mine. "I can't go in the car without Wolfie. It's not safe."

"It's safe. Mommy's a very careful driver." I stepped toward the open back door of the car and kept my voice calm. I probably shouldn't have told Ava that Brenda had loved wolves or that she'd bought the stuffed animal for her. I'd wanted Ava to always know she was not only loved by me but had been loved by her biological mother as well. Somewhere along the way Ava had begun to think Wolfie protected her like some kind of guardian angel.

I thought it was sweet.

Harmless.

I never imagined she'd throw him out the window.

Ava's arms tightened around my neck. "I need Wolfie."

I swayed gently back and forth. "We'll find him, Ava, but you need to help me. I can't look for him if you don't get in the car."

"I can't without Wolfie."

I hugged her to me and told myself this would someday be a story we'd look back and laugh about. Right then, though, it didn't feel funny at all.

I pride myself on being independent, but I wished I had a partner—male, female, anyone I could hand Ava to. I had friends I could call, but I needed help right then. Wasn't the first twenty-four hours the most important when someone went missing?

No, that was for an actual kidnapping, not for a stuffed animal. Don't judge me; I believe there is a direct correlation between how clearly someone can think and how loudly the child in their arms is crying.

I got her back into her car seat. *How* will probably one day be discussed in a therapy session, but I was desperate, and she had cried through all of my initial nonwrestling-technique attempts.

I played her favorite songs and sang as I drove back to the supermarket I'd taken her to after picking her up from preschool. When she didn't sing along, I lowered the volume and stretched my arm between the seats to offer her my hand. She clung to it while scanning the side of the road for her friend . . . so young, so brave.

We didn't see him in the parking lot, so I called inside.

No luck.

Drove around the parking lot a few more times.

Nothing. We went through a drive-thru for a treat, but it wasn't enough to cheer her.

On the way home, I drove slowly and pulled over several times to let cars pass. Wolfie wasn't worth anything to anyone but us. I couldn't imagine anyone else wanting him. So where was he?

Ava helped me carry in the food, shoulders hunched, looking like she'd just lost her best friend—because she had. Dinner was painfully quiet. She burst into tears twice during her bath. I made funny faces and voices for her other stuffed animals, but she didn't want any of them.

Story time didn't happen, because she refused to go to bed without Wolfie. I fielded each of her questions the best I could.

"Do you think Wolfie is scared?"

"No, wolves are brave by nature."

"Are you mad at me?"

"Of course not, Ava."

Her bottom lip stuck out. "I didn't tell you he went out the window, because I didn't want you to be mad."

"You didn't mean to lose him."

"I opened the window. It's my fault. He's gone and I did it."

"Oh, baby. Accidents happen."

"Do you think he's in heaven with my first mom?" Her eyes filled with tears.

I blinked back my own. "I don't think so. I bet he's out there having a great time with all the new friends he's making. When we find him, he'll have quite a lot of stories to tell you about his adventure."

"You're sure we'll find him?"

I bent down to look her in the eye and flat-out lied. "I'm sure."

There was no convincing her to go to her bed alone, so I carried her to the rocking chair we'd spent many nights in when she was younger and rocked her to sleep. Only once she was fully out did I tuck her into her bed.

Standing at the door of Ava's bedroom, I felt ridiculous praying about a stuffed animal, but my heart was heavy. In my experience, prayers didn't work. They'd never brought my mother back after she'd left my dad. My father had said she'd wanted to start over without either one of us. I don't remember my father ever being happy, but he was miserable after she left.

Sometimes life just sucked.

Hoping for a happy ending only led to disappointment.

But that wasn't what I wanted Ava to believe. For her, I'd move heaven and earth to make the improbable happen.

I took my laptop to the living room and wrote an email to my assistant, telling her I would be late to the office. I uploaded a photo of Wolfie from my phone to my social media accounts, along with a hundred-dollar reward and a description of where we'd lost him. Most of my "friends" were clients, but I knew some of them had children and many lived in the area.

The more eyes looking, the better the chance we would have of finding him.

I called the store again.

Still nothing.

I closed the laptop, looked up at the ceiling, and sighed.

Everything's going to be okay.

I'll make it okay.

I'm just saying—I wouldn't mind a little help.

CHAPTER THREE

SEBASTIAN

"I'm looking at it right now," I said into my phone as I waved for my driver to remain in the car and let myself out. I didn't hire him to open my door or impress anyone. I also didn't consider him a luxury. Time was money, and I could get more done while stuck in traffic than most could in a day of meetings. Not that there was much traffic in Durham, Connecticut.

"What do you think you'll see in an empty lot that our people didn't?" my brother Christof asked. If Mauricio had asked the question, his voice would have been heavy with sarcasm. Christof genuinely wanted to know, which was the only reason I entertained the question.

"Timing is important. On paper the town looks like it's verging on expanding, but will it? An area has a certain feel to it right before it explodes. So far, I don't see what would lure anyone here."

"So back to the drawing board?"

"I didn't say that. The price is right. The competition would be easy enough to crush. I'll take a look around, talk to the planning board tomorrow, and see how eager they are to have us."

Christof chuckled. "I love how you gloss over the idea of wiping another grocery chain from the map like it's no big deal. Do you have any sympathy for the people who will be shaking in their shoes when they see our 'Coming Soon' sign go up?"

"Nothing lasts forever. Nothing. No one escapes that lesson." I hadn't meant to say it as emphatically as I had. May 20 never brought out the best in me. I didn't have to explain that to Christof—he knew. It was probably why he'd called in the first place. Not that we would discuss it. He knew me too well to even bring it up.

"If you want a second set of eyes, I can be there tonight."

"All set."

End of conversation.

"Mom asked if we'll see you this weekend. She's making her seafood scampi."

I almost smiled. Every Sunday I stepped out of my role as head of the family company, put aside the fast pace of meetings, and became a grown man who allowed his mother to ruffle his hair and kiss his head. "I should be. Talk to you then."

I ended the call, stepped away from the car, and tripped over something soft. A filthy, gray-and-white stuffed animal—a husky, maybe—lay at my feet. A memory of another stuffed animal tore through me—a little brown teddy bear my mother had bought the day Therese had told me she was pregnant. My child would have been her first grandchild.

Should have been.

Fuck.

When the doctors had asked me if I wanted to know what the gender of the baby had been, I'd said no. I didn't want one more thing to torture myself with. Already every little girl made me wonder what mine would have looked like. Every little boy made me hate myself more.

I kicked the stuffed animal away. It came to a rolling stop, facing me. I looked into its blue glass eyes and saw my pain mirrored. I should have gone with my wife to her doctor's appointment. I didn't, because how much could one appointment matter? I had thought there would be a hundred more, and the deal I had been negotiating was important to secure a financial legacy for my family.

I walked over and picked up the stuffed animal, gripping it so tightly in the middle that it flopped back on either side of my hand. Five years. The wound shouldn't feel as fresh as it did. Bile rose in my throat. I scanned the field, but all I could see was my wife's face done up with more makeup than she'd ever worn, eyes closed as if she were sleeping.

When I realized I was still holding the stuffed animal, I raised my hand to toss it aside—then didn't. Couldn't.

Still holding it, I climbed into my car and told the driver to take me back to my office. I threw the stuffed animal across the seat and stared out the window, emptying my mind as I went. There'd been a time when I'd wanted to die right along with my wife. I had drunk myself to sleep, woken up, and drunk more. Mauricio and Christof had taken over the family business while my father had stayed at my side—despite how many times I'd told him I didn't need him or any of them.

They'd stayed with me and pulled me through the darkest time of my life. Eventually I surfaced, sobered up, and took back the reins from my brothers. Some say what doesn't kill you makes you stronger. Bullshit.

It had made me more successful, though. All joy had left my life the day my wife and child didn't return to me, and although it didn't make anything better, every one of my competitors had paid for that loss.

Ruthless? Maybe.

Life was ruthless.

I no longer wanted a family of my own, but I did glean a certain satisfaction from knowing my parents and brothers would never want for anything. Nothing beyond that mattered.

I asked the driver to stop at a liquor store.

I paid for the bottle of Crown Royal without exchanging a word with the clerk. I was giving in to a weakness and hating myself for it. I could have gone back to my apartment, but I knew I wouldn't sleep that night.

In the garage of our headquarters, I shrugged off my jacket and wrapped it around the bottle. Although the elevator I walked toward was a private one, I didn't want security footage of my transgression. There was no need to worry my family. The past only haunted me one day a year, and it would soon be over.

"Mr. Romano?"

I turned at the sound of my driver calling after me. He trotted up and held out the stuffed animal I'd found on the side of the road.

"You forgot this in the car."

"Throw it away."

"Sir?"

"I don't want it."

"Oh. Are you sure? I saw you find it. I bet some child is missing it."

I hadn't thought of that, but the last thing I wanted to do was start thinking about children again. "Does that sound like my problem?"

"No, sir. Sorry, sir." The driver took a step back, and I almost snapped at him again. If he wanted to keep his job, he'd need to toughen up.

I rubbed a hand over my face. "Rick?"

"Rob."

"Whatever." The last thing I needed was my family to hear I was running around picking up stuffed animals off the streets. They'd think I'd lost my mind again. "Just dispose of the fucking thing, and don't tell anyone about it. Got it?"

"Dispose of it?" Eyes wide, he looked down at the stuffed animal like it was evidence I was asking him to make disappear. "Here or somewhere else?"

Oh my God.

I ripped the thing out of his hands and growled, "Forget it. I'll get rid of it."

Still looking freaked, Rob stammered, "Should I wait, sir? Will you need a ride home?"

"I'll call if I do," I said as I walked away. New drivers were a pain in my ass. Had I said that to my youngest brother, Gian, he would have told me I wouldn't have that problem as often as I did if I wasn't such an asshole.

Asshole.

I didn't even mind the label anymore. Like so much else, it didn't fucking matter.

I let myself into my office, tossed the stuffed animal onto one of the chairs, opened the bottle, and took a long swig. While loosening my tie, I walked over to my desk, sat down, and propped my feet up on it before taking another generous gulp. The burn felt good on the back of my throat.

Oblivion couldn't come fast enough. I raised the bottle again.

The more I drank, the sadder the stuffed animal looked. "Don't look at me like that," I said with a slur. All glassy-eyed, it just continued to stare back at me.

I slammed my fist down on my desk.

"I don't care if there is some kid looking for you. Let the little bastard learn now that if you don't take care of something, it disappears like that."

I snapped my fingers in the air.

"Throwing you away would be doing a favor for that kid. A fucking favor."

I tipped the bottle back again.

"You picked a really shitty day to show up. You know that?"

The blank stare mocked me.

"I bet you do. The universe loves to fuck with people, doesn't it? Well, the joke's on you. I don't feel anything. Nothing. You should have taken me along with them, because whatever good there was in me died with them."

The door of my office opened. "Yep, he's in here."

Oh, fuck.

All three of my brothers walked in. Technically, Gian is my cousin, but my parents raised him as one of their own—and, as far as we're concerned, he's our brother.

Mauricio smoothly removed the bottle from my hand and placed it on the table behind him. Christof hovered beside him. Gian plopped down in a chair in front of my desk and said, "Why do you never invite us to the party?"

"How did you know I was here?" I growled.

With two fingers, Mauricio picked the stuffed animal off the chair and studied it as he answered. "I bribe all your drivers to tell me where you are when you go off the grid."

I dropped my feet to the floor and wagged a finger at Gian. "See, they deserve to be fired. Damn snitches."

"He's wasted," Christof said.

Gian nodded. "Let's get him home."

"What is this thing?" Mauricio asked, still holding the toy out in front of him as if it might bite.

"Nothing," I said. "I found it near the Durham site. I couldn't just leave it there."

All three of my brothers looked at me with visible sympathy in their eyes, and my temper rose in response. "I'm not doing this. Does it look like I want any of you here?"

Christof folded his arms across his chest. "I call shotgun. I'm not sitting in the back seat with him again. Last year he slept on my shoulder the whole way home."

"I did not," I instantly denied, then remembered doing it. Like a werewolf, one day a year I turned into someone I didn't recognize. Every year I thought I would handle it better, that I wouldn't turn, but there I was again—drunk in my office, not wanting to go home because there was no place I considered home anymore.

Mauricio stepped closer. "Come on, Sebastian. Let's get you out of here."

I covered my face with both hands. If life was fair, I would have been the brother mine deserved. I would have faced tragedy, pulled myself together, and shown them that Romanos could survive anything.

I stood and swayed on my feet. They were right—it'd be better for the business if I kept this side of myself out of the office. "Thanks."

My brothers flanked me as we walked through my secretary's office. As we approached the elevator, I heard Mauricio ask Christof, "What should I do with this?"

Christof answered, "Leave it here."

I didn't turn to see what they did with it; I had more important things to think about: walking straight and not throwing up.

CHAPTER FOUR

HEATHER

Late the next morning, dressed in a dark-blue skirt, matching blouse, and sensible flats, I zipped Ava's lunch box closed. "Ready?"

She looked ready. Ava was particular about how she looked. Her hair needed to be neatly braided. She liked dresses with matching tights and owned more pairs of shoes than I did. I smiled. It was easy to forget we didn't share the same gene pool. She was a mini me, but a more colorful version. "I want to help you look for Wolfie."

"No, hon, you need to go to preschool."

"Why? I'm good at finding things."

"Yes, you are, but I'm going to be in the road. It's not safe."

Wrong thing to say. Ava teared up. "Not safe?"

"For small children. For you. I'll be fine. I'm taller." I hugged her, then picked up her lunch box. "Come on—the sooner you go to school, the sooner I can look for him."

Bottom lip quivering, she placed her hand in mine. "Can you drive the long way? Maybe he's on the road waiting for me."

Doubtful, but I agreed. People said miracles happened every day. I didn't have firsthand experience with that, but Ava's concern for him was so pure—that had to count for something, didn't it?

Silly me, since she'd shown determination to find Wolfie, I had expected her to climb into her car seat without protest. The inner workings of a child's mind were more complex than that. I pleaded. I warned.

If I'd had a million dollars, I would have considered bribing her with it. Eventually I turned and leaned against the car, shaking my head.

She stopped crying and looked at me. "What are you doing?"

I shrugged. "Giving up. I'm not going to wrestle you into the car seat again. If you don't get in on your own, I guess we're never going anywhere again."

Sniff. Frown. Sniff. "We have to look for Wolfie."

"I want to look for him, but I don't really have a choice, do I? If I can't get you in the car, how can I go anywhere? Luckily I have the kind of job I can do from home." I pushed away from the car. "I can probably find someone to come over and watch you. Let's go back inside."

"No." She put her hands on her hips and planted her feet.

"I suppose I could bring my laptop out here and work in the driveway."

She squared her shoulders. "No. I'm getting in."

Please. Yes.

I opened the back door. She walked toward it, then stopped. Those big blue eyes of hers met mine, and my heart twisted in my chest. "I'm scared."

I put a hand on her shoulder and hugged her to my side briefly. "But you're also very brave. Brave doesn't mean never being afraid. Brave is being stronger than what scares you."

She nodded. So solemn. So much like me when I was that age. My father always said I knew how to put on a brave face no matter what I was up against. I'd definitely made my share of mistakes raising Ava, but I needed to believe I had done as much right. Watching her climb into her car seat and secure herself went a long way to reassure me I had.

We drove down the road we'd lost Wolfie on, but there was no sign of him. I didn't promise her again that I'd find him, because I was beginning to doubt I would. Drop-off went surprisingly smoothly. I spoke to her teacher on the side and rushed out of there before Ava had a chance to remember that she didn't want to stay.

Two hours later I was sitting at my desk in my small office, trying to motivate myself to dig into emails I was sure were waiting for me. Fighting a headache, I released my hair from its clip and ran my hands through it.

"Knock, knock," Teri, my assistant, said as she walked in. "Hey, you should wear your hair down more often. It's really pretty."

I forced a smile. "Thanks. Now what can I do for you?"

Her smile was much brighter than mine; she'd probably slept the night before. "You have a package. A courier brought it over. It's light."

My heart was thudding in my chest. She handed me the box, and it was indeed light. I shook it, and the contents sounded like they were something soft . . . could it be . . . had someone found Wolfie? I read the card. "Hope this is what you were looking for—Mr. and Mrs. Eddy."

Barely breathing, I tore off the ribbon. Blue glass eyes looked up at me from the face of an exact replica of Wolfie—a perfectly clean, beautiful copy. My shoulders sagged as I put the box down on my desk. "What a beautiful gesture."

Teri pulled the stuffed animal out of the box. "Is it the exact same wolf?"

I nodded. "That's what he used to look like."

"You could tell Ava you gave him a bath."

"I'd also have to tear up one of his legs, sew it back together, and mark up the bottom of his feet with nail polish"—I sighed—"then lie to her."

"Everyone lies to their kids. I would to mine if I had any."

"There's enough in her life that will be confusing as she gets older. I want to be a person she knows she can trust."

"It's just a stuffed animal."

"Thanks for bringing the package in to me, Teri." She accepted the gentle dismissal in my tone. It was okay that she didn't understand. I didn't need her or anyone else's approval—not when it came to Ava. If I had listened to well-meaning friends, I wouldn't have taken on the responsibility of her in the first place. A friend, one who had drifted out of my life soon afterward, had told me I would regret adopting Ava—and it had been wrong for Brenda to ask me to, since her child wasn't my problem.

Problem? Of all the things Ava was to me, she'd never been that.

No matter how she'd come into my life, she'd become part of me just as I was part of her. Family wasn't a concept I considered myself an expert on, but Ava had given me a second chance at getting it right. I didn't regret a single sleepless night or missing out on whatever people my age did when they didn't have children.

I took the package off my desk and set it on the floor. The Eddys had been clients of mine almost from the first day I'd opened my doors. Their kindness warmed my heart. I took out a piece of stationery and wrote a thank-you note, then put it in my pile of outgoing mail.

My attention returned to the stuffed animal they'd sent. Trying to pass it off as the real Wolfie was tempting, but I knew I couldn't do it. Others might handle the situation differently or better, but right or wrong, all I could do was the best I knew how to.

I decided to give the wolf to Ava with the truth about where he came from. It was the same brand—that had to make it Wolfie's cousin or something.

I dug into answering emails and updating files for my clients. Time flew by, as it always did when I lost myself in work. There was a certain satisfaction from knowing I was good at what I did and that what I did mattered. I'd been offered jobs at a few big financial-planning firms, but I wouldn't have felt comfortable giving up control like that.

It wasn't that I didn't trust anyone—just that I trusted myself and my instincts more. Having the rug pulled out from beneath my feet early in life had taught me the value of owning my own damn rug.

"Knock, knock."

I came back to the present to see Teri standing at my office door again. "I have something you should see."

My stomach did that funny flip again even as I told myself to stay off that roller coaster. I sat back and stretched my arms above my head. "What?"

She walked over to the side of my desk and turned her phone so I could see the screen. "Your post about Wolfie has been shared five thousand times."

I took her phone so I could see it better. "You're kidding." No, there it was—five thousand shares and hundreds of comments. I scanned the first fifty or so. "Did anyone say they'd seen him?"

Teri pursed her lips. "No. Sorry."

I handed her phone back to her. "That's incredible, though. I'll show Ava tonight. I'm sure it'll make her feel better that so many people are looking for him. Thanks for bringing it to my attention."

I wasn't actually sure that the shares would help at all—but there was a chance they might. I wasn't looking forward to telling Ava I hadn't found him. One almost-Wolfie and hope . . . that was all I had.

Pocketing her phone, Teri continued to look down at me. "Some of my friends are meeting me after work. We thought we'd look for him before we go out. Ask around at gas stations and stuff. I'll text you if we find him."

A lump rose in my throat. "Thank you."

Teri didn't move. She looked like she had something else she wanted to say. I waited. Finally, she said, "Ava's lucky to have a mother like you."

I blinked quickly and smiled. "Are you angling for a raise?"

Her smile beamed. "No, but if that's where gratitude takes you, I'll have my friends look for Wolfie all night."

"Find Wolfie, and you'll have earned a raise." I chuckled and checked the time. "It's four. I'll see you tomorrow."

Alone again, I leaned back in my chair and let out a long breath. Five thousand shares. I had expected only a handful of people to care. I took out my phone and read the messages with a growing sense of wonder. Friends, clients, people I didn't know, were sharing stories of their own childhood "Wolfie." Some still had them. I wiped tears from the corners of my eyes.

I didn't know if it was the simplicity of a child loving a stuffed animal or the connection people were making to a more innocent time in their lives, but their responses restored some of my faith in humanity. The comments came from people of all ages, races, backgrounds. Even men were saying that they had shared my post on pages and groups they belonged to.

Someone had even shared it on a page for active and retired Marines.

When all else fails—send in the Marines.

I smiled.

Why not?

Earlier that day, I'd been ready to give up, but the outpouring of support for Ava was bringing something back to life in me.

I was beginning to think that maybe, just maybe, this time there'd be a happy ending.

CHAPTER FIVE

SEBASTIAN

As I walked into my office building, I missed the days when I cured a hangover with a good, stiff drink. Thankfully, a headache was all that was left of the day before. If I spoke to any of my family, they would act as if last night hadn't happened.

My reflection in the mirror beside the elevator didn't show me anything unexpected. My suit was crisply pressed. My black hair was perfectly in place. I looked every bit the successful business shark I was.

Every hint of weakness had fled. Gian joked that I had a resting don't-fuck-with-me face.

Good.

It's best not to mess with a man who has nothing left to lose.

I strode through my secretary's office, sparing her no more than a perfunctory "Good morning."

Miss Steele had worked for me for almost three years. Mauricio liked to joke that she'd quit at least once each of those years, but she'd never handed me a resignation or said a word about wanting to leave to me. He claimed it was because he kept talking her into staying. Was it true? I never cared enough to ask her. She was efficient and reliable. I paid her a generous salary.

Our encounters didn't require more depth than that.

"Mr. Romano," she said in a rush as I passed.

I halted and turned. "Yes?"

"I found this on my desk, and I was wondering if there was something you wanted me to do with it." She held up what I had completely pushed out of my thoughts—the stuffed animal I'd found on the side of the road.

It rocked my mood like a sucker punch to the kidney. No part of May 20 was ever allowed to bleed over to the next day. My fury must have shown on my face, because she took a step back.

"Throw it away. I don't want to ever see it again. Is that clear enough for you?"

"Yes, sir." She hid it behind her back. "Consider it gone."

"Good." Chest tight, glaring even though my issue was not with her, I snapped, "Is that all?"

"Yes."

I turned, walked into my office, and slammed the door. Fists clenched, I took several deep breaths. One day. I could concede one day to the past, but that was all I would allow. Slowly, I regained control of my mood and pushed everything else out of my head.

First on my docket was the decision of whether or not to purchase the lot in Durham. I made several calls, brought some reluctant officials around to agreeing to more than they wanted to, and decided that moving forward with the deal would be lucrative. I signed the paperwork and sent it on to my lawyers.

One of the town officials had warned me that the current store was owned by a family closely tied to the community. Close ties with influential people.

Was that supposed to intimidate me? Instead it made the project more appealing.

Let the battle begin.

I drew up some initial plans, then hit the gym for an hour. After a light lunch, I felt better. Hell, I almost smiled at Miss Steele as I walked past her desk, but I didn't want to set a new precedent for our exchanges.

I came to a sliding halt when I saw that I had company in my office. My mother rose as soon as she sensed my arrival.

"Mom, is everything okay?"

She came toward me. "Does something have to be wrong for me to visit my son?"

"No, of course not." I closed the door to my office. Something in her eyes told me that my mood was about to take another hit. "If this is about yesterday, I'd rather not talk about it."

She cupped the side of my face with one hand. Tall and proud with dark-brown eyes and shoulder-length hair that was just beginning to be peppered with gray, Camilla Romano looked every bit the strong Italian mother she prided herself on being. "Another year, Sebastian. Your brothers said this one was rough."

I covered her hand with mine. "Sometimes they say more than they need to."

"Only because they love you."

"I know, Mom."

"Love is a strength, not a weakness, Sebastian. You used to understand that."

I gently removed her hand from my face and stepped back. "I can't do this, Mom. I'm sorry."

She reached into her oversize purse. "After talking to your brothers last night, your father and I decided it was time for you to take something back."

I knew. A part of me knew what she had in her bag. Time slowed. My vision narrowed to her bag and then to the brown bear she pulled from it.

She held it out.

I stood frozen. "No," I said in a hoarse voice I didn't recognize as my own.

She took my hand in hers and placed the teddy bear in my hand. "Yes. Five years, Sebastian. You've tortured yourself enough. Don't tell me you've moved on and only think about them one day a year. I'm your mother. Even if you lie to yourself, you can't lie to me. You hurt every day. You're angry every day. Denying it won't change it—all it does is stop you from moving on."

"Is that what you think I should do? Move on? Forget about them?" I could barely get the words out.

Her eyes misted with love. "No. No. Remember them. Let yourself honor them the way they would want you to. Be the man Therese loved."

"That man died with her."

My mother shook her head and laid her hand on my chest. "He didn't. He's right here. You think you're the only one who lost someone that day? I lost them, too, and my son. But he can come back—he just has to want to."

I hated the tears that filled my eyes, but I couldn't hate the woman before me. "I fall apart when I remember."

She took my hand in hers. "Because you push the memories so far down, they come back with the power of a volcano." We stood there for a long moment without saying anything. "I have something else to show you."

I wouldn't have stood there for anyone else, but there was no doubt my mother was acting out of concern for me. She was the kind of woman who loved with her whole heart and without condition. On my worst day, I would never so much as raise my voice to her.

She fiddled with her phone for a moment, then held it out toward me. "A friend of mine shared this post with me. I know this sounds crazy, but when your brothers told me about what you found last night . . . I couldn't help thinking that it might be what this woman is looking for."

It was a post that offered a hundred-dollar reward for the return of a missing stuffed animal. The post described how it had been lost along the same road I'd found it on and that her little girl was missing him terribly. A hundred-dollar reward? Her child must be pretty attached to it.

I groaned. Wolfie? Yes, I knew those glassy blue eyes and that his fur was every bit as sticky as it looked in the photo. "I had him, but I told Miss Steele to throw him out this morning."

Because I'm an asshole.

My mother smiled. "I bet she still has him."

"I'm sure she doesn't."

"How sure are you?"

"Why?"

"Sometimes things are not as lost as we think they are. If Miss Steele threw the stuffed animal away, I promise to leave and not bring it up again."

"I like the sound of that."

"But if I'm right and she still has it, you have to promise to do something."

"Why do I get the feeling you already know she has it?"

My mother's eyes rounded with innocence. "Are you suggesting I'd cheat?"

"Never." Think it—yes. Suggest it? No. I'd never hear the end of it.

"Okay, then, if Miss Steele still has this Wolfie, you'll personally deliver it to the child who lost it."

"If she still has it, Miss Steele is welcome to leave early to deliver it herself."

"No, you, Sebastian. You need to do it." She gave my hand a squeeze. "The Sebastian I raised would have, and he would have done it gladly."

"I'm not that man anymore."

"Then maybe it's time you start acting like him. One act of kindness to bring a smile to a child. You owe this to yourself and to the memory of your family."

I shook my head. "I can't."

"I know what it brings back, but one day your brothers will have children. Will you avoid them too? Do this one thing for me."

My answer was a curt nod.

She dropped my hand, walked over, and opened the door. "Miss Steele, could you come here, please?"

"Of course," my assistant answered before appearing in the doorway. My mother turned to me.

I cleared my throat. "Miss Steele, that thing that was left on your desk last night?"

"Yes?"

"Did you throw it away?" I asked with more growl in my voice than I meant to.

She looked from me to my mother and back. Her hesitation was telling. I could have let her sweat it out, but I decided to be kind. "If you haven't, we appear to have located its owner and would like to return it to her."

Only then did I realize I was waving my child's brown teddy bear around as I spoke. *I have finally completely lost my fucking mind.*

Red-faced, Miss Steele said, "Oh, good. I thought you were upset I hadn't thrown it away yet. I was going to, but I didn't have the heart to. I had a stuffed zebra, Harvey, when I was little, and, I don't know . . . this toy looks like it is loved by someone. I'm so glad I trusted my gut. You found the owner? That's amazing."

"Yes," I said curtly.

"Oh, I'll go get it," Miss Steele said before rushing back to her office.

"She has it," my mother said, smiling.

"So it seems."

Back in a flash, Miss Steele handed me the wolf. I stood there with a toy in either hand, feeling like I'd completely lost control of the situation. I held them up. A pristine teddy bear and a wolf that had known a much more active, child-rich life—one that had apparently required sewing one of his legs back together.

Miss Steele made a smart and hasty retreat.

My mother returned to my side. "There's a phone number on the post. Christof did a little checking into them for me. The mother's name is Heather Ellis." My mother pulled a piece of paper out of her purse. "This is their address."

I took it in the same hand as the damn stuffed wolf. "I don't have time to do this today."

"You promised, Sebastian."

Did I? Fuck.

"Fine. I'll drop it off on my way home. Is there anything else?"

"We'll see you Sunday?"

"I wouldn't miss it for anything."

She gave my cheek a warm pat. "I know you'll tell me it doesn't matter, but there's one more thing I think you should know."

I was already a tangle of emotions, but there was no escape. "What?"

With a Mona Lisa smile, my mother said, "She's single." Then she walked out of my office and left me standing there with a pounding headache, two stuffed animals, and the address of a woman I had no desire to meet.

CHAPTER SIX

HEATHER

Between rinsing off our dinner plates and placing them in the dishwasher, I kept glancing over to the area where Ava and her friend Charlotte were playing with dolls. Whoever thought of the open concept for homes was brilliant.

When my phone beeped, I wiped my hands, answered it, and turned so I could watch the children.

"How are they doing?" Erica, Charlotte's mother, asked. Erica was a stay-at-home parent who lived one block over, and meeting her at the park when Ava was still in a stroller had felt like winning the lottery. Even though Erica was my age, Charlotte was her third child, and Erica therefore had a wealth of experience I often took advantage of. Is this a rash or hives? How do you get dirt out of a skinned knee? Help, Ava has decided vegetables are evil. Erica either knew the answer or she had a story that made me feel better about not knowing.

Pure gold.

When I'd told Erica that I hadn't found Wolfie, she'd suggested a playdate with Charlotte. Charlotte had been with me when I'd picked up Ava, and Ava had been so excited to see her friend she hadn't asked me about Wolfie. She'd gotten in the car without hesitation, and we'd even enjoyed a pleasant dinner. While she'd been distracted, I'd stashed the box with the new wolf in the other room. Eventually

Charlotte would go home, and I was doing my best to prepare for the tough questions that would surely follow.

"Great. You're a genius," I said in absolute appreciation. "Really, I can't thank you enough."

Erica chuckled. "Stop. It's as much a favor to me as to you. I played outside with the boys, then actually got to hear about how their days were. I love my daughter, but she is a chatterbox. Bob is home. Should I leave the boys here or bring them with me?"

"I can drop Charlotte off if you want."

"No, don't worry about it. It gives me an excuse to take a walk. If I'm lucky, Bob will have the kitchen cleaned by the time we get back."

See why I worship her genius?

"Bring the boys. Ava loves them."

"Tyler and Kevin get a kick out of her too. They tell Charlotte that's what a girl is supposed to look like."

"Ouch."

"Brothers."

"Yeah," I said, even though I'd always wished I'd had one. "Charlotte is a beautiful little girl and so polite." She really was. Dark-blonde hair down to her waist. Striking hazel eyes just like her mother. Her brothers could say what they wanted, but one day they'd be beating admirers away from her. For now, though, she was rough around the edges from trying to keep up with the twins.

"Not to her brothers this week. Bob keeps thinking we need one more child, but I already feel like I'm a lion tamer. Three kids under the age of seven. He's lucky he gets any sex at all."

I laughed, glad I hadn't chosen speakerphone. "Well, we're here when you want to pick her up."

"I'll head over now."

A few minutes later, after a knock, my door opened, and all quiet vanished. Tyler and Kevin were wild six-year-old twins no mere mortal could contain. They bounded through my house like puppies, chasing each other up the staircase that led to our bedrooms, then back down.

Erica closed the door behind her, then called out, "Boys, stay downstairs." Her smile was apologetic as she crossed to where Charlotte and Ava were still playing. "I did offer to leave them home."

I didn't mind. They were high energy, but good outside of that. As they ran past again, I said, "How was school, boys?"

Kevin made a face at me. "*School* is a bad word."

Tyler danced back and forth in front of him in a playful manner. "You're a bad word."

They chased each other around my couch. *Pop*—one went up and over the back of it. The other followed like it was a vaulting competition. "Easy, guys. No one is allowed to break their neck until summer vacation."

Kevin stopped and smiled. "*Summer*. Now that is a good word."

Tyler tackled him. "Got you."

As they wrestled on the floor, Erica met my gaze and shrugged. "I can yell at them, but my guess is someone in their class had a birthday party today. They came home like this."

"They're good," I assured her. My childhood had been a quiet and lonely one. I didn't want Ava to have the same memories. A little chaos was a positive in my mind.

"Charlotte, get your shoes on." To me, Erica said, "You're a saint and the only babysitter they like."

"They're always good for me." They ran past again. "I just don't ask them to sit down. I'm sure they've had enough of that by the time they get home."

Erica laughed. "When they're like this, I imagine years of uncomfortable parent-teacher meetings."

I smiled. "I see future track stars. Possibly Olympic gold with their stamina."

She nodded, looking pleased. "That's why they love you."

My doorbell rang.

"Do you mind watching them while I answer that?" Still in my clothes from work, but barefoot, I answered the door.

The first thing I saw was his tie. I had what could almost be called a fascination with them. Ties said a lot about a man. Some refused to even wear them. Some lacked the discipline to tie them with precision. Don't even get me started on knot types. Some men's education stopped with the four-in-hand their fathers had taught them. Others sported Full Windsors like peacocks fluffing their feathers. The one before me was a crisp Neapolitan knot, an international, old-world preference. Done wrong, a tall man might end up with a tie that was too short, but whoever this man was, he was too sophisticated for such a faux pas.

His jacket was expensive and expertly tailored. He was tall with broad shoulders. Strong. Powerful. He filled my doorway like a linebacker. My guess was his shirt concealed a delicious set of muscled abs. Whatever he was selling, I'd take one—maybe two.

I slowly made my way upward. Nice jaw. Clean cut. Square with just the beginning of dark stubble. I indulged in a quick fantasy of how that stubble would scrape a tantalizing path as he kissed his way from my jaw down to my . . .

The stern line of his lips brought me back to reality. His mind didn't appear to be going where mine was.

My eyes flew to his. Striking, dark, but not black. Gray? Long lashes I'd kill for. Too bad he was glaring at me. Whatever had brought him to my door, he was not happy about it. He oozed power and authority. Not a politician. Too well dressed to be a police investigator. Government official? Was one of my clients involved in something I didn't know about?

I instantly pictured being handcuffed . . . then being handcuffed naked . . . then how *he'd* look handcuffed to my bed. Hey, I was a woman in my prime who hadn't had sex since I'd brought Ava home.

Four years is a long time. Still, I gave myself a mental shake. "Can I help you?"

He looked me over, and my body warmed everywhere his eyes wandered. Sadly, he didn't look any happier when his gaze met mine again. "Miss Ellis?"

"That's me." I smiled. He didn't smile back.

"I found something—"

When he brought his hand around, I saw the most glorious thing. Everything else fell away as relief swept through me. "Wolfie." I couldn't help myself; I launched myself at the man and hugged him so tightly I'm pretty sure the sound I heard him emit was the air I'd crushed out of him.

The sheer joy of the moment consumed me. I didn't realize how uncomfortable I was making the man until he set me firmly back from him. I couldn't even be offended; I was that grateful.

We stood there for a moment, me smiling ear to ear, him looking as happy as someone having a tooth extracted. He held Wolfie up. "Well, here it is."

I was about to take him when Ava squealed from behind me. "Wolfie!" She snatched him from the man and hugged the stuffed animal to her chest, closing her eyes to savor the feel of him. She breathed him in. Spun with him. Laughed. Cried a little.

I nearly burst into tears watching her, even though I was still smiling.

"Everybody," Ava called out, "Wolfie is home."

Charlotte came running, along with her two brothers. She and Ava danced in a circle while Kevin and Tyler hooted and cheered. Above the mayhem, I said, "Ava, you didn't even say thank you. This nice man found him and brought him home to us."

Ava walked over and looked up at the towering man. I was about to prompt her a second time when she tugged on the sleeve of his jacket.

He frowned down at her.

41

She tugged again.

The boys raced back into the other room. Erica appeared and stood beside her daughter. She looked from my unsmiling visitor to me and wiggled her eyebrows, mouthing the word "Yummy."

The man bent a little, and at Ava's insistence bent further. She studied his face. "Thank you."

A real sadness glimmered in his eyes as he answered. "You're welcome. I'm glad he's back where he belongs."

"Can I hug you?" Ava asked, cocking her head to one side.

See, a better version of me. She at least asked.

Now that I'd had more time with him, I regretted my earlier impulsiveness. Nothing about him looked the least bit huggable. Fuckable, yes. Fantasy fuckable, but not more than that. Life was hard enough without looking across the breakfast table every morning at a man who didn't know how to smile. I'm pretty sure that was why my mother left my father. It was why I had distanced myself from him. He always focused on what he didn't have rather than what he had. There was no pleasing him, because in his core, he was not a happy person.

I swore I would never be like that.

Happiness doesn't just happen. It's a decision. Like anything else, it needs to be tended and protected. Negative people had no place in the new life I'd built for myself.

"Ava—" I hadn't gone on more than first dates since bringing Ava home; they didn't meet her. Normally she was shy around men, but not this one.

Of course, no one else had ever returned Wolfie to her.

His nod was all she needed. Still holding Wolfie, she wrapped her arms around the man's neck in a way that mussed his hair. I half expected him to set her back from him as he'd done with me, but he just stood there, hands on his knees until she released him.

"My name is Ava."

"Hello, Ava. My name is Sebastian," he said in a decadently deep voice.

"Sebastian." She said his name slowly. "My hero."

He straightened, looking strangled in a way that pulled at my heart. He wasn't angry. He was hurting. I put a hand on Ava's shoulder and moved her back from him.

"Thank you," I said, giving him the out he wanted.

Erica stepped forward. "What a nice thing—to deliver Wolfie yourself. You don't look like someone who would want the reward, though."

"The reward," I said in a rush. "Of course. Oh my God. I don't have cash on me, but I could write you a check. Hang on."

"No," he said with such authority I stopped. "No reward necessary." He looked down at Ava, who was hugging Wolfie happily again, then back up at me. "Good night."

"Wait," Erica said. "Are you married?"

I gasped and shot a look at my friend. *Stop.*

She shrugged, shamelessly delighted. She was constantly trying to find a man for me, but we didn't have the same taste. Her husband was a mechanic. Hardworking. Jean-wearing, barbecue-making kind of guy. My type was . . . Okay, on the surface, this guy was my taste, but it was painfully apparent that I was not his.

Kevin came running up with the replica of Wolfie I'd brought home. "Look what I found! Ava, you have two Wolfies."

Ava spun, accepted the second wolf, and held them up to compare them, then pulled them both to her chest for a hug. "Mommy, Wolfie wasn't lost; he went looking for a girlfriend. I'll call you Wolfina." She smiled up at Sebastian. "We're going to have puppies. Wolf puppies."

He almost smiled. "Cute." He stepped back. He looked like he was about to turn and leave when Kevin and Tyler burst by him, nearly knocking him off his feet.

"Mom, Tyler took my doll," Charlotte yelled as she also sped past Sebastian.

"That's my cue to go as well," Erica said, chasing after them. She stopped just behind Sebastian long enough to shoot me a double thumbs-up, then disappeared down the stairs.

Ava lost interest in Sebastian and brought the two stuffed animals to the rug where she'd been playing. He watched the children go, then turned back to me. The heat to his look sent my heart racing. My hand tightened on the doorknob.

I couldn't invite him in.

I wasn't about to try out my rusty flirting skills on someone like him.

So I did what any woman would do when she found herself with a gorgeous man at her door who didn't look like he knew if he was coming or going. I just stared at him.

He looked back as if lost in his thoughts.

When the silence dragged on to an awkward length, I said, "Thank you again for bringing Wolfie back. Where did you find him?"

My question seemed to shake him back to the present. "He was on the side of the road near an empty lot."

"You have no idea how much his return means to us. We're so grateful." When he frowned, I joked, "Don't worry. I'm not going to hug you again."

A flush spread up the man's neck. "Whether I'm married or not doesn't matter. There's nothing here I want."

It was my turn to flush. Thanks, Erica, for making him think I'm desperate enough for a man that he has to clarify that. "Okay. Good talk. Thanks again."

I closed the door in his face and leaned against it.

Asshole.

CHAPTER SEVEN

SEBASTIAN

I'm an asshole.

I stood on the porch of the woman I'd insulted for doing nothing more than thanking me for returning something to her child, reasonably certain that wasn't how my mother had imagined that going.

It wasn't how I'd thought of it either.

Ditch and run. That had been my plan.

No conversation. No real engagement.

Nothing stupid coming out of my mouth.

My hand hovered over the doorbell. I should apologize. And say what?

You're a beautiful woman with an adorable child and a house full of laughter. I almost had that. Neighbors dropping in. Children underfoot. That was how I once pictured my life.

I don't want that anymore.

I turned away and walked down the steps to my car. My driver opened the door for me. I slid in without exchanging a word with him.

When he was behind the wheel, I barked, "Take me back to my apartment."

"Yes, sir."

The painfully long ride gave me far too much time to think. I did my best not to. I craved the oblivion I'd allowed myself the day before, but that was a once-a-year indulgence.

My phone rang. I welcomed the distraction. "Hey, Dad."

"Your mother wants to know how it went when you delivered the stuffed animal, but she doesn't want to ask you in case it didn't go well. She's asked me about a hundred times how I think it went. Please, give me something I can tell her."

The corner of my mouth curled in a hint of a smile as I pictured my mother hounding my father until he broke down and sneaked off to call me. "I dropped it off. They were very happy to have it back. That's all there is to know."

"Your mother said the woman is not only beautiful but also intelligent. She has her own accounting business. All your mother had to hear was that her little girl was adopted. You know she has a soft spot for anyone who can love someone else's child as their own. It says a lot about that woman's character too. You could use someone like that in your life."

"I am not short on female companionship."

"I've seen the women you date. I'm talking about one you could bring to dinner. Someone you could settle down with."

"I have zero desire to ever marry again."

My father was quiet for a moment. "Do you want company? I could sleep in your guest room."

"I'm fine, Dad."

"We all loved Therese—"

"Don't, Dad."

"I worry about you, Sebastian. Nothing that happened was your fault. You made a decision you thought was best for your family. Accidents happen. You didn't kill your wife."

Since there was nowhere for the conversation to go, I changed direction. "So I signed the paperwork to purchase the Durham lot. We'll be moving forward aggressively with that project over the next few months. I've been crunching the numbers. The local competition is a chain store. I see a full buyout or bankruptcy in their future. With potential profit even higher than we saw in Maine."

"You know how many stores I had back in Italy?"

I sighed. *Here we go.* "One."

"Exactly. And I was happy. I had your mother, you kids, and home-made wine. That's all a man needs."

"Well, I don't exactly have any of that, do I?" I snapped, regretting the words as soon as I voiced them.

"Because you hold on to the pain, Sebastian. Therese wouldn't have wanted you to."

"No one knows what she would have wanted."

"She loved you, Sebastian. When you love someone, their happiness is where you find your own. You have always been a good son. You were a good husband, but you are an awful widower."

I rubbed the bridge of my nose. "Thanks. I didn't know there was a rating system."

"Was she beautiful, Sebastian?"

"Who?"

"This Heather Ellis."

"Yes." Her face was too easy to picture. Big brown eyes. Long, loose curls—perfect for a man to bury his hands in. Her conservative attire paired with bare feet had made it too easy to imagine how she would have looked sprawled across my desk. Losing Therese didn't mean I was dead from the waist down. I still found women attractive. I just made sure I chose partners who were okay with nothing beyond sex. Heather didn't come across as a woman who would agree to those terms.

Not to mention, I didn't date anyone with kids.

No exceptions.

"And her child? How was she?"

"Sweet. They seem like a nice family."

"Did you get the sense that the woman liked you?"

I remembered the look of outrage on her face right before she'd slammed the door in mine. "I wouldn't go as far as to say that."

"That's a shame. She sounded like someone we would have liked to meet."

"Sorry to disappoint you, but if you have enough intel for Mom, can we talk about something else? Anything else?"

CHAPTER EIGHT

HEATHER

Midmorning the next day I pushed back my desk chair and stood. I didn't like what was distracting me from my work, but it was time to admit to myself that the day before was still very much on my mind.

Sebastian had gotten into my head. And not in a good way. I walked to the window of my office and decided to face the issue head-on.

There were certain indisputable truths: I hadn't had sex in years, and he was gorgeous.

Anything I may or may not have done with him in my dreams last night was due to that, along with the yogurt I shouldn't have eaten right before I went to bed. Everyone has sex dreams. Dreams like that are normal. Healthy.

I closed my eyes as a particular scenario from mine brought heat to my cheeks. Shaking my head, I chuckled. No way he would actually be that good in bed anyway. God had wasted a perfectly good Adonis face and body on a man with no personality.

I opened my eyes and scanned my office absently while I remembered the way he'd dismissed me, us, as nothing he wanted. That had stung. It still stung.

Breathe. He didn't hurt me; he'd hurt my pride. There were thousands, millions, of men in the world who probably didn't find me attractive, and I didn't care about them. My self-image wasn't contingent on male approval.

He's not part of my life. He doesn't matter. Focus on the good that came from last night. Ava happily slept in her own bed with Wolfie and Wolfina in her arms.

All was back to normal.

My pep talk didn't improve my mood, so I dug deeper. I didn't want to brag, but I'd always been my own best psychologist. I had discovered the skill in college when Brenda had suggested that I needed to shed my anger with my parents before it made me just like them. It was probably the deepest thing Brenda had ever said to me, and though she was stoned when she'd said it, it had resonated.

Rather than seeking professional counsel, I read books on choosing happiness and changing mental habits. They taught me to judge everyone less—myself and those around me—to forgive if only for my sake, and to keep my focus on the positive I wanted in my life. The philosophy had served me well in my professional as well as my personal life.

I loved my job. I had a good circle of friends. Ava was my family unit, but I didn't need more than her, did I?

Four years without sex. Maybe it's time to let Erica set me up with someone again. Just because I hadn't liked the ones she'd suggested so far didn't mean I couldn't find someone that way.

Or I could use . . . Tinder?

I shuddered. Not my style.

Get a babysitter and sit in a bar until some guy buys me a drink?

I tipped my head back and rubbed a hand over my forehead.

I don't just want sex.

I walked back to my desk and sat down.

What do I want?

What was it about Ava hugging Sebastian's neck that kept the scene popping into my thoughts?

What did it represent?

What do I feel like I'm missing?

A happy, successful man who gives me butterflies just by showing up. A man who sees me as his partner in and out of bed.

Someone who would love my child as much as I do.

I'm wishing for a unicorn.

I stretched my arms above my head.

The positive?

I had admitted something important to myself: I wanted more than Ava in my life.

A healthy step.

It also made Sebastian's rejection easier to work through. It wasn't that I cared about him not wanting me. I'd let him represent my ideal, and that had given my exchange with him more importance than it warranted.

Deep breath.

Inner peace returned.

Thank you, Mr. Romano, for returning Wolfie to us. For me, not you, I forgive you for your rude parting comment. I hope you find something today that makes you smile.

"Knock, knock," Teri said at my doorway. "Erica is here and asking if you have a moment."

"Send her in."

Smiling, Erica entered, placed a brightly wrapped package on the corner of my desk and said, "I had an epiphany this morning."

Teri hovered near the door. I stood and waved her in. I might need the moral support. "An epiphany. Sounds interesting."

Erica turned to Teri. "Did she tell you about the man who brought Ava's stuffed animal back?"

"She did not." Teri's eyebrows arched in interest.

I put a hand on one hip. "He was above average in the looks department, but not big on pleasantries."

"He was hot," Erica said, fanning the air. "H. O. T. And she practically wet herself just looking at him."

51

I rolled my eyes. "It wasn't like that."

Elbowing Teri, Erica nodded. "You should have seen the look on her face. She wanted to eat him up. And he was looking at her the same way. I should have offered to take Ava with me so they could have gotten it on right there."

Hand to heart, Teri said, "How romantic is that? What a great way to meet."

I pinched an inch of air. "Erica is exaggerating just a little bit." I separated my fingers. "By that I mean a lot. He dropped off Wolfie, we barely spoke to each other, then he left. End of romantic story."

Laying her hand on the package on my desk, Erica said, "Only if you let it end that way. This morning you said you had Ava write him a thank-you letter. Do you have it with you?"

I glanced at the pile of paperwork on the corner of my desk. "Yes, but I have no intention of actually sending it to him. I just wanted her to take the time to express her gratitude."

Erica tapped the top of the wrapped box. "That's so wrong. Take her note, add one of your own, and send him this package. I guarantee you'll have a date with him by the weekend."

"Trust me, he doesn't want to hear from us again."

Lifting a shoulder and cocking her head, Erica said, "I never knew you were a coward. Did you know that, Teri?"

"I'm not in this," my assistant said wisely.

Mirroring my stance, Erica continued, "Since I met you, Heather, you've described a certain kind of guy you could imagine yourself with—but when he actually shows up at your door? What do you do? Write him off? Do you know who gets married by giving up that easily? Um. No one."

My eyes narrowed. "Have you ever heard of false advertising? His packaging might be what I said I wanted, but I'm not bringing anyone into my life—into Ava's life—who isn't as together on the inside as he looks on the outside."

"You talked to him for two minutes. You don't know what's on his inside."

"Trust me, I got a glimpse of it. I saw it in his eyes. He's not happy."

Erica looked to Teri, then back at me. "Oh, sorry, I didn't realize you were also looking for perfection in a man. Let me amend my advice. Forget about this guy and stock up on vibrators, because you're never going to find someone who doesn't have some kind of issue."

Teri coughed and excused herself from the room.

I stood taller, temper rising. "He literally looked right at me and said he didn't want me."

Erica's eyes rounded. "I don't believe that. Did he use those words?"

"I'm paraphrasing."

"No, you're reading into what he said because you're afraid you might actually have met a man you could like. You're scared. Admit it."

I plopped into one of the leather chairs in front of my desk. "Do you think he actually looked like he wanted to eat me up?"

With a chuckle, Erica took the seat next to me. "Oh, hon, he was a starving man, and you were an all-you-can-eat buffet."

I laughed. "It felt like that for a second, but then it didn't. He did actually say it didn't matter if he was married or not because there was nothing there he wanted."

"That is odd."

"Isn't it?"

Erica called out. "Teri, can you see if you can find anything online about a Sebastian Romano? Tall. Black hair. Gray eyes. Successful. You'll know him if you see him. Drop-dead gorgeous. Kinda broody."

"That's not going to work."

"Everything is online now. Everything. Just wait."

A moment later, Teri called out, "I think I found him. Yee—ow—za. If you don't want him, could you give him my number?"

Erica stood. "Let's go see if this hunk is married."

Shaking my head, I went with her to stand behind Teri at her desk.

There were pages of photos of him, both from groundbreakings for new Romano Superstores and nightclubs with different women hanging on him. Erica nudged Teri's chair. "Stop drooling and find out if he's single."

"Oh no," Teri said as she clicked on a link. "He was married, but his wife died in a car accident five years ago." She covered her mouth with one hand. "And she was four months pregnant. The baby didn't survive either."

"That's horrible." My eyes filled with tears. Well, that explained the look in his eyes.

"Are there photos of him with her?" Erica asked.

Their search brought up photos of a much-younger version of him on his honeymoon. Laughing. Carefree. Totally in love. Not much after that.

"Doesn't look like he was as successful before she died," Teri said quietly. "There isn't much on him from then."

Erica touched my arm. "Classic. He threw himself into work. He must have loved her very much."

Wiping tears from the corners of my eyes, I said, "What a sad story."

"It's actually good news."

I sniffed. "How could it be?"

Erica pointed to the photo of him smiling down at his wife. "That's a man who knows how to love. Some don't."

I hugged my arms around my waist. "Or maybe she was his soul mate, and he has nothing left for anyone else."

"Really?" Erica asked in a sarcastic tone. "One day Ava will move out, and you're going to find yourself alone. It doesn't have to be that way. Five years, Heather. He's had time to heal. A man like that is not going to stay single forever. You're the one who always tells me the secret to happiness is envisioning what you want and going after it. This is your chance to prove that's not just bullshit you spout to make yourself feel better."

"I found his office address if you want it," Teri offered tentatively.

"I don't want to bring negativity into my life," I said.

Erica tilted her head at me. "Right now you're the only negative one in the room. Teri and I think you can land this guy. Don't we, Teri?"

"Sure," Teri said, then smiled. "I could even babysit for you when you go out. I adore Ava."

It was crazy.

It was pointless.

"What's in the wrapped box?" I asked.

"Homemade cookies," Erica said, clapping her hands together. She knew she was near victory.

"And you think that would be all it would take for him to ask me out?"

Crossing her arms in front of her, Erica said, "Men are not as complicated as you think. He's back in his office probably kicking himself for what he said. Wondering if you liked him."

"I slammed the door in his face." When they both gave me an odd look, I became defensive. "You would have too if you'd heard what he'd said."

"Now I'm sure he's thinking about you. So open that door a little. Just a crack. Nothing softens a man's heart like my Nanna's chocolate chip cookies. I still make them for Bob when he gets grumpy—that and oral sex always cheers him up. Write this Sebastian a nice message, nothing too deep. Send him Ava's note and the cookies. Then go get your nails done, because an invite is a done deal."

I couldn't believe I was considering doing it. "What do you think, Teri?"

Teri spun in her chair to face me. "Was there a spark? Did you zing when you saw him?"

I bit my bottom lip briefly. "Oh yes."

"Then I'll line up a courier. Let's get him these cookies today."

CHAPTER NINE

SEBASTIAN

I emerged from back-to-back meetings early in the afternoon and closed myself off in my office to set the next phase in our acquisition of Bhatt Markets. None of the snags that had surfaced since our purchase went public were out of the ordinary. Our competition had gone for an injunction to block any construction, completely expected. They'd rained letters from their lawyers on our office—so predictable I almost felt sorry for them. Their resistance would be a speed bump on our way to replacing their chain with our own, and in a year the community would actually appreciate the change. We were bigger. Our prices were lower. And we didn't mind taking a short-term loss as long as the outcome was the dissolution of our competition. Small businesses couldn't weather the storms we were willing to create and could afford to ride out.

Winning was one of the few things that brought me satisfaction. My father liked to say money didn't equate to happiness, but even before the company had taken off . . . it wasn't love that had gotten us where we were. I'd worked at the family store and at as many side jobs as necessary to keep our family afloat. My family had moved from Italy to the US so we would have more opportunity, but my father had struggled for a while to break into the market. He thought small, and his relaxed business plans didn't work in the land of corporate sharks.

Before I'd joined, Romano Superstores had been one neighborhood convenience store that had been teetering near bankruptcy. There hadn't been money for college—for me or for my brothers. I took out loans for my degree, then paid for my siblings via our family's store. Straight out of college, I'd taken over the business and expanded it from one store to a chain—even when doing so hadn't made sense on paper.

Sheer determination carried us through those first few years. Looking back, I don't know why Therese married me. We'd met and fallen in love in college, but my focus after graduation had turned toward my obligation to my parents and siblings. My brothers had graduated without loans, because that had been one of my priorities. My parents had moved into a house in a safer community, because providing for them was a matter of pride for me.

Sebastian Romano—provider for his family.

Therese had never complained about the long hours I worked or how little of me was left for her at the end of the day. Despite having a degree, she had accepted my preference that she not work after we were married.

I'd had an image in my mind of what my family was supposed to be and what my role was in it. I provided. I protected. She managed the house. Had she been happy with the arrangement?

I never asked her.

My arrogance and single mindedness had cost me the opportunity of rectifying that or making the changes that would have brought her real joy. She hadn't complained the day I told her I couldn't take her to the doctor. It hadn't been the first time I'd put work above going, and she'd never questioned my decisions.

What did that say about our marriage?

What did it say about me?

I'd had five years to think about it.

Five years to regret not having been the husband Therese deserved.

I read an email, then read it again, too lost in my own thoughts to care what it said. Two days past the anniversary of her death, I wasn't supposed to still be floundering.

"Mr. Romano?" Miss Steele asked via the intercom on my desk phone.

"Yes?" I growled.

"A courier just delivered a package. Should I bring it in to you?"

"I didn't order anything."

"It looks like a gift."

A gift? My birthday was months away. None of the women I'd been with recently were the gift-giving type. It was likely a mistake. "Double-check the name. It's probably for one of my brothers."

"I did. Your name is on the card."

"Bring it in." I wasn't getting anything productive done anyway.

I met Miss Steele at the door of my office. She handed me a gift-wrapped square box about twelve inches in diameter. There were two cards taped to the top of it. My name clearly printed on each: one in an adult's handwriting, one in a child's.

I didn't want it. I almost handed it back to Miss Steele.

She was smiling, though. "I bet it's from the family you returned the stuffed animal to yesterday. How adorable is that? She had her daughter write you a note too."

Adorable.

My stomach churned.

Refusing the gift would raise more questions than I wanted to field again. I thanked my secretary and put the box on a table in my office. I could always dispose of it later.

Yesterday was done and gone. All the gift had achieved was to remind me I owed the woman an apology. Was that why she'd sent it? Best way to make an asshole feel even worse about himself? Send him a gift?

I returned to my desk and forced myself to refocus on work. I was engrossed enough that I didn't notice anyone had entered until my brother's voice surprised me.

"Just checking in about the acquisition. It seems to be going as expected," Mauricio said from just inside my office.

I stood and crossed to where he was standing. "That's my take on it. I don't foresee it being any different than what we've encountered before."

"Good," he said, rocking back on his heels. Although there was no mistaking that we were brothers, he had our mother's brown hair and brown eyes. He also had her smile, which he'd used to charm nearly all the single women in our hometown of Brookfield. If he'd spent half as much time on business as he did with his endless string of lovers, he'd still be running the family company. Like my father, the ruthless business gene must have been recessive in him. He did, however, like the lifestyle having money allowed him—fast cars, wild parties, travel.

He was a good face for the company, though. He could clean up and present himself well. Men and women alike enjoyed his company. Having him around saved me from attending business-related social events.

"Hey, what's this?" he asked as he spotted the gift box on the table.

I cursed myself for not stashing it in the closet. "A thank-you from the woman with the stuffed animal." No reason to hedge, the truth was obvious from the notes still attached to the top.

"Aren't you going to open it?"

"I'm working."

He tore one of the envelopes from the box. Ava's. "You should at least read the notes. Mind if I do?" He opened it without giving me time to respond one way or the other and read it aloud: "Dear Mr. Romano, thank you for . . . I think the next word is beginning . . . no, bringing . . . thank you for bringing Wolfie home to me. Thank you for being so nice to him. You are my hemo . . . oh, hero." Mauricio laughed and waved the letter at me. "You're her hero. That is the sweetest thing. I might cry."

Mauricio had taught me early that it was possible to love someone and want to smack the shit out of them. That luxury had departed along with childhood—sadly.

He reached for the second card. "This one must be from the woman Mom says is perfect for you. Helene? Hailey?"

"Heather," I said, then groaned because his smug grin revealed he was giving me shit. I put my hand out. "Give me the damn card."

He stepped outside of my reach and tore it open. "'Dear Mr. Romano.' So formal. Apparently you didn't knock her socks off."

"Give me the fucking card." I moved toward him.

He stepped even farther away and kept reading. "'Thank you for returning my daughter's stuffed animal. You brought smiles back to our house. We hope our gift brings a smile to your office. Sincerely, Heather Ellis.' Sincerely. Not love. You're not *her* hero."

With one swift move, I ripped the card from his hands. "Are we done now?"

His grin only widened. "I can't leave without knowing what she sent."

"Yes, you can."

His grin faded a bit. "You're going to throw it away, aren't you?"

"Don't you have work to do?"

He walked over to the box, picked it up, and shook it near his ear. "What if it's something amazing?" He turned it in all directions. "Aren't you curious what a woman thinks would put a smile on your face? Let's be honest; you're not a laugh-a-minute kind of guy."

"I don't care what she sent."

He flipped the box in his hands, acting like he might drop it. My eyes narrowed, but I didn't allow myself to reach for it. "That's a lie, and we both know it. If you didn't care, you would have opened the box. You're scared."

"And you're an idiot."

"You're afraid you might like what she sent." He tucked the box beneath one arm and put his other hand over his heart. "And that, gasp, it might actually make you smile. Then what would you do?"

"Put the fucking box down."

He didn't. "Not until you admit you liked the woman. Dad said you thought she was beautiful."

I sighed. "She was."

"So you took her number?"

"No. She has a kid."

"Yeah, I know. Mom told me all about her. If you don't date her, I think Mom is ready to adopt her. She's totally stalking her on social media already."

"That's . . . unfortunate, since I have no plans of ever seeing her again."

Mauricio flipped the package in the air again. "Maybe I should look her up then. I wouldn't mind a woman sending me gifts."

I closed the distance between us and removed the box from his hands, slamming it down on the table where it had been. "She's not your type, Mauricio. This is a nice, family woman."

"I'm not getting any younger. Who knows, maybe it's time for me to find a woman like that to settle down with."

He was deliberately trying to push my buttons, and for some reason it was working. "If your goal is to piss me off, you're doing it. I don't have time for this shit."

Still smiling, Mauricio sauntered to the office door and asked, "So it's okay if I call her, right?"

I didn't dignify his question with a response. Instead I closed my office door with enough force to relay my thoughts on the matter. On the way back to my desk, I paused and reread both cards. Ava's handwriting was difficult to decipher. Some of the words would not have made sense except for Heather's addition of the correctly spelled word beneath.

"Thank you for being so nice to him . . ." Ava obviously did not know how close Wolfie had come to the trash bin.

"We hope our gift brings a smile to your office . . ." I took Heather's card with me back to my desk and read it through again. It was generously polite, considering what my parting comment had been. There was no hint in it of wanting to hear from me again.

Which was for the best.

I threw the card onto my desk and tried to dive back into work, but couldn't. My thoughts kept returning to how Heather had thrown herself into my arms when she'd first seen Wolfie. Joy filled. Uninhibited. Exactly the way a man wants to be greeted just before he carries his woman off to bed.

She was an educated woman, one who ran her own business, and it showed in the confident way she'd looked at me. Her attire might have been office appropriate, but her demeanor had been warm and relaxed. She hadn't seemed at all bothered by the chaos of the children, and her protectiveness of her daughter had been clear. It was a combination of strength and softness I found appealing.

As appealing as I'd found the rest of her.

I shook my head.

Connecticut was full of single women—many as attractive if not more attractive than she was. There was no need to spend another moment thinking about how perfectly she'd fit against me or how the scent of her had sent my blood rushing straight to my cock.

Intelligent women were not a rarity. Nothing about her was unique. I could find all of that in another woman who didn't have a child.

I remembered the feel of Ava tightly hugging my neck. Initially it had brought back nothing beyond a sadness that my own child would never hug me that way. Having read her letter, though, I had to admit it felt good to know I had returned the smile to her face.

Her hero.

She could do a lot better than me, but I didn't hate the idea that something I had done had brought joy to the child.

I ran my hands through my hair and tried to shake off all thoughts of Heather and her child. I might have brought them comfort, but they were stopping me from being able to close the door on May 20. Two days, and I was still looking back, still wasting time hating myself for things I could do nothing about.

If I wasn't careful, I'd end up at a liquor store again . . . and that was something I refused to allow to happen. At least, not until May 20 came around again.

Through sheer willpower alone, I pushed through emails and a pile of paperwork. The sun had set, and Miss Steele was long gone by the time I closed down my computer and pushed back from my desk.

I walked over to the table where the gift still sat and stood there for a moment simply looking down at it. What the hell. I tore off the wrapping and pulled back the cardboard. Inside, wrapped in clear plastic wrap, was a plate of chocolate chip cookies.

Homemade cookies. Many of them broken, but no less delicious looking.

I lifted the plate out and inhaled.

My stomach rumbled, reminding me I'd worked through lunch and dinner.

Perhaps because I was so hungry, or because I hadn't indulged in a cookie for years, I savored one bite. It was soft and chewy with a hint of nuts. Perfection.

I stuffed the rest of the cookie into my mouth, then licked the bit of chocolate that had stayed on my thumb. It tasted like childhood and laughter. Memories of wrestling with my brothers over after-school treats brought a smile to my face.

I didn't expect something as simple as a cookie to affect my mood as much as it did. Yet I was still smiling as I rode down the elevator, gift box tucked under my arm.

CHAPTER TEN

HEATHER

Every parent knows the dread of a surprise fever. Ava had been fine the night before, a little restless, but I thought it was because she was still so excited to have Wolfie home. When she refused breakfast—I knew.

A temp of a hundred was enough to keep her home, but not enough to impress our pediatrician into giving us medicine. He told me to let her rest, give her plenty of fluids, and watch for any other symptoms.

I called Erica. She echoed his advice, then apologized for not being free that day to watch her. She had her own doctor appointments set up but could cancel them if I really needed her to.

Of course I couldn't ask her to do that.

My third call was to my assistant to tell her I was working from home that day. Luckily there wasn't much I couldn't do on my laptop as long as Ava was quiet. With her snuggled up to my side on the couch, I turned on cartoons for her and went through my morning emails.

A short time later the ring of my doorbell had me sliding out from beneath a cuddly Ava to answer it. I dreaded how I looked—still in pajamas with my hair probably sticking up in every direction. What could I do? There hadn't yet been time for me to think about how I looked.

Thankfully, it was only Teri. She'd stopped by the pharmacy and gotten everything from Pedialyte to an assortment of children's fever medicine. I laughed when she accused me of trying to get her sick too with a hug.

I was still smiling when I settled back onto the couch with Ava. It wasn't that I'd needed the supplies, but I was moved by her concern for my child.

I was lucky to have good people in my life who cared about me and my family. I told myself to focus on that rather than the disappointment I'd felt when I hadn't heard anything from Sebastian.

I ran a hand lightly over Ava's hair and tried to imagine how I would feel if I'd lost not only my partner but also my unborn child. *I wouldn't be all smiles either.*

Still, I shouldn't have bought into Erica's romanticized version of our meeting. Although I would deny it if anyone asked, a part of me had wanted it to be true. I'd imagined him munching on Erica's cookies, thinking of me while mustering the courage to call.

Disappointment is a by-product of unrealistic expectations.

Unrealistic expectations are unhealthy.

I might feel hurt, but that was on me.

He could not have been clearer about how he felt.

I tried to push him out of my thoughts, but I couldn't stop thinking about how different he'd looked in his honeymoon photos compared to the brusque man who'd filled my doorway. A tragedy like he'd experienced changed someone forever. I still missed Brenda. As I rubbed Ava's back, I shuddered at the thought of who I would become if I ever lost her.

Stop.

Horrible things happen to people every day. I couldn't carry the weight of all their pain with me or live in fear that it would happen to me.

I wasn't a stranger to sadness or loss. My childhood had contained enough of it to give me a real empathy for anyone experiencing either. I refused, though, to let those dark thoughts pull me down. I'd worked too hard to make a new life for myself.

Sad from something you saw in the news?

Not sure what to do with those feelings?

Do something good for someone—anyone. You can't help everyone, but you can make someone's day a little easier.

Okay, maybe I've read too many self-help books, but before them I was lost and angry.

I made a modest online donation to a children's hospital. No, it wasn't the kind of donation they'd make a plaque for, but it made me feel better. My child only had a slight fever. There were parents out there dealing with much more, and every little bit helped keep programs funded for them.

Ava woke up. I took her temperature again—no change. Fluids. Light lunch. Then she wanted to play with her dolls, which I took as a good sign.

When my phone rang, I answered without even looking at the caller ID. It was either Erica or Teri. "She still has a fever. Looks like I'll be working from home again tomorrow."

"It's Sebastian Romano."

"Oh. Sorry." I smoothed a hand over my wild hair even though he couldn't see it. "Hello."

"Are you sick?" Only he could voice that question without a hint of warmth.

"Me? No. Ava woke up with a fever this morning, but it's nothing."

"How high?"

"Excuse me?"

"How high is her fever? Have you contacted her doctor?"

His questions weren't offensive, but his tone was. Arrogant. Demanding. Like I wouldn't know how to care for my own daughter.

Was this how he spoke to his employees? If so, I couldn't imagine many of them liked him.

You're wrong about him, Erica. I don't need this in my life. "Although I appreciate your concern, I have the situation under control. Was there something you wanted?"

He was silent long enough that I considered ending the call.

"I wanted to thank you for the cookies. They were delicious." When he finally spoke his voice was deeper, closer to the one that had inspired decadent thoughts of him growling sexy demands into my ear.

Whoosh, my body was humming. I poured myself a glass of cold water and considered pouring it over my head. "You're welcome."

"And to apologize. I was in a sour mood and should not have taken it out on you."

I leaned forward on the counter, rolling the glass across my forehead. I enjoyed audiobooks and spent endless hours listening to male voices—some even reading steamy scenes I hoped Ava never found on my Kindle—without ever feeling as turned on as I was just by listening to him. And he'd barely spoken so far.

What was wrong with me?

"You're forgiven and you're welcome," I said in a husky voice.

There was another pause . . . long enough for my heart to start beating wildly in my chest and for me to begin to believe he was just about to ask me out. No. No. No. Hadn't I just decided he wasn't for me?

I held my breath and waited.

If he asked me out . . . what would I say?

I should say no.

I wanted to say yes.

If I kept him separate from Ava, agreeing to a dinner would be harmless.

Right?

If that led to a night of hot sex . . . I could pay a babysitter to stay over . . . and didn't I deserve a little of what my body was craving . . . at least once this decade?

"Good," he said simply.

Another pause. Was he hoping I would ask him out? Was he waiting for some kind of sign that I liked him? "It was incredibly nice of you to deliver Wolfie yourself."

Nothing.

No one could accuse him of talking too much.

Across the room Ava met my gaze with glassy eyes. The bright pink to her cheeks hadn't been there before. I walked over and touched her arm. It was warm—a lot warmer than it had been. Shit.

"Sebastian? Thanks for calling, but I have to go."

"What's wrong?" His tone was intense again.

"Ava's fever is spiking. I need to check it again, start her on some Motrin, and maybe call the doctor back."

"Go take her temperature. I'll wait."

My mouth rounded in surprise. He sounded serious. I almost brushed him off, but remembered he'd lost a wife and child. Even though he didn't know us, hearing that Ava was sick might have struck a chord with him. "She's fine. Trust me, this is not our first fever."

"I'll wait."

"It'll take me a few minutes."

"That's fine."

Feeling a little ridiculous, I put my phone on the counter and went to retrieve the thermometer. One hundred one. I poured her a cup of water, gave her some Motrin, and settled her into her bed for a nap. I didn't expect him to still be there when I picked my phone back up. "Sebastian?"

"How is she?"

"It was higher than this morning. One hundred one. Still nothing to panic about. I'll see if my doctor has an opening today. Right now she's napping."

"If her doctor won't see her, you need to find another doctor."

Deep breath. His tone is harsh because he's worried. "She has a wonderful pediatrician. Really, there's no reason for you to be concerned. After what you've been through, it's natural to be—"

"What *I've* been through?" His tone went ice cold.

I cringed. "All I'm trying to say is that I understand why you'd be worried, but she's not in any danger."

"You know about my wife."

It wasn't a question.

"Yes. My friend googled you. I'm sorry. I shouldn't have mentioned it." And this is why I'm single. I'm too honest.

"You read a few articles, and now you think you know me?"

So angry. I felt sorry for him because I knew he hadn't always been that way. "I don't know you, but I do know what it's like to lose someone. It doesn't excuse bad behavior, though. I'm a good mother. I don't have to prove myself to you. I don't require your approval. If you're looking for someone who will tiptoe around your moods, that's not me. I'm home today with a sick child. I'll probably be home with her tomorrow with a very real likelihood of no sleep tonight. So sorry if I'm not up to flirting or sparring with you, but I have more important things on my mind." I ended the call and tossed my phone on the counter.

Sex was overrated anyway.

CHAPTER ELEVEN

SEBASTIAN

Once again her response had been completely appropriate. My only problem with what she'd said was that it made me face my contribution to our exchanges.

My family was right—the past still had a stranglehold on me. I told myself it didn't, but my conversation with Heather had shot that claim to hell.

I didn't normally speak to women as if they didn't know what they were doing—especially not one I was interested in. Usually I brought them pleasure, they brought me pleasure, we both moved on. I didn't struggle to find the right words or second-guess how I behaved.

I couldn't understand why it was different with Heather.

Because she had a child?

It felt like more than that.

I left my office early, deciding to drive myself to be alone with my thoughts. I wasn't surprised when I found myself somewhere I usually only went once a year—my wife's grave.

I laid my hand on top of her stone and closed my eyes. *Five years, Therese. I'm still as sorry today as I was the day I lost you. You wanted to have a child right away, but I convinced you to wait. It's my fault you never held our child, never had a chance to comfort or scold it. I thought we had more time . . .*

My family wants me to move on. I don't want to.

But holding on is turning me into someone I don't recognize.

Someone you wouldn't have loved.

I blinked back tears.

You deserved better than I gave you. So much better.

If I could trade places with you—I would.

If I could go back and do that day over . . . do our marriage over . . .
I would do so many things differently.

I went to my knees and sat back on my heels.

What do you want from me, Therese?

I don't know.

I've been with women since you—do you hate me for it?

None of them mattered.

Heather's image danced in my thoughts.

She has the potential to.

I don't know if that's a good thing or the ultimate betrayal of our vows.

I loved you so much.

*I thought I was doing what was best for our family—what was best
for you.*

I'm so sorry, Therese.

Tears ran down my cheeks, and I let them. I'd fought to hold them
in for too long. It felt good to let them out.

Eventually, I used her stone to pull myself back to my feet. When
I turned, I saw all three of my brothers along with my father leaning
against my car. I glanced back at my wife's grave. "They loved you too,"
I said aloud.

I know.

It might have been my imagination, but I would have sworn on my
life that she'd answered me. Was the voice in my head just an echo of a
memory or a real connection to her where she was? I didn't know, but I
felt lighter when I walked toward my family. Real or imagined, I'd come
in search of her permission, and I felt like I'd received it.

"We thought you might be hungry," Gian said, as if they hadn't just found me bawling my eyes out.

I nodded. "I am."

"Mom's making lasagna," Christof said while studying my expression.

"How could I miss that?"

My father pulled me in for a back-thumping hug, kissed my head in the way he used to when I was much younger, and said, "You're a good boy, Sebastian. You'll be fine."

I swallowed the lump in my throat, then looked over at Mauricio. His expression was far too serious to let it stay that way. "Stop paying people to track me."

He smiled, shrugged, then walked over to my car. "Better hurry or I'll be driving."

"Never going to happen," I joked as I crossed to the driver's side. This was our familiar banter, and it calmed me.

We all drove to my parents' house and enjoyed a multicourse meal with spirited discussions on every topic from politics to the future of the family business. Opinions differed, voices rose, then lowered again when the heat of the moment passed.

Just a regular meal with my family.

No one brought up where I had gone after work.

No one asked me about Heather.

On a full stomach, I sat and watched my brothers argue over which team would win the World Cup. Love for them washed over me. For years I had felt a distance from them that wasn't there. I had changed; they hadn't. I remembered my mother saying she'd felt like she'd lost me right along with Therese, but I could come back if I wanted to.

I finally wanted to.

CHAPTER TWELVE

HEATHER

Three days after I brought Ava to the doctor, I was lying on my couch with a bowl beside me. Every bit of fight in me had been expelled from my body, either into the toilet or into the sink.

The only reason I answered my phone when it rang was because Ava was at preschool and parenting didn't take a day off. "Hello?" I croaked.

"Is something wrong? Is Ava okay?" Sebastian growled.

I groaned and closed my eyes. *I can't do this right now.* "Ava's fine. All better. I caught a stomach bug from the petri dish of disease that is her pediatrician's waiting room."

"Where's Ava?"

I didn't have the energy to be offended. "At school. Then Erica is keeping her for the night so I can sleep this off."

"Do you need anything?"

From Mr. Gorgeous while I look like roadkill? Umm. Hell no. "Thanks, but I'm all set."

"Do you have someone there to take care of you?"

I groaned again. "No, but it's for the best. I don't want to give this to anyone."

"Someone should be there with you. I can be there in a little over an hour."

I chuckled, because if I didn't I might cry. "No. I haven't showered since yesterday, and I look every bit as bad as I sound. No one is seeing me like this. Especially not someone like you."

"Someone like me?"

Maybe it was the fever. Maybe I was just too exhausted to care, but I said, "My hair is plastered to my head. I may have thrown up organs I'll miss later, and I'm not done yet. If you like me at all, hang up, call me back next week, and let me pretend we never had this conversation."

"I'm closing down my computer now. Is there anything you don't have? Ginger ale? Soup?"

I shuddered at the thought of anything passing my lips. "I honestly don't need anything."

"I'll bring you something. My mother is good at knowing what works well in situations like this. I'm sure she'll have a good idea. Will you be able to let me in?"

My head was pounding. My stomach was churning the countdown to my next dry heave. Could I let him in? I moaned. I dropped my phone and gagged into the bowl. Nothing came up. Nothing was left inside me. That didn't stop me from making some ungodly sounds as my body tried to expel . . . my toes, I guess?

I fell back onto the couch. It was a moment or two before I remembered Sebastian had been on the phone. I picked it up, and because I was completely, utterly mortified, I joked, "I've never been good at flirting. How am I doing?"

He made a sympathetic sound. "It's a unique style, but I'm still coming over."

Whatever. There was little past survival I cared about right then. "I should shower before you get here, but I don't know if I can do it."

"I can help you with that when I'm there."

I groaned again. Was it possible to be half-dead and turned on at the same time? "I don't want the first time I shower with a man to be something I remember for the wrong reasons."

He was quiet for a moment, giving me long enough to replay my last words in my head and kick myself for saying them. "I wasn't suggesting we shower together . . ."

Oh, wait, the sound of me getting sick hadn't inspired a fantasy of us naked in the shower? He probably hadn't been celibate as long as I had been. *I'm an idiot.* "Don't come, Sebastian. This fever has me a little delirious, I think."

"Do you have anyone who can come be with you?"

Teri was holding down the office. I couldn't risk getting her sick. Erica was watching Ava for me. "No," I admitted, closing my eyes.

"Then I'm on my way."

I wanted to sleep, but I pushed myself up in a seated position. If Sebastian was coming over, there was no way I wasn't going to clean up before he arrived. I stumbled to the shower, stood beneath the hot spray long enough to endure another round of dry heaving, then pulled on checkered pajama bottoms with a buttoned-up top. Teeth brushed, hair still wet, I lay down on the couch for a moment. I told myself it was just for a second. I intended to clean up the living room a little before he arrived, but when I closed my eyes, I fell into a deep sleep and didn't wake until I heard my doorbell.

Light-headed, I made my way to the door. After opening it, I tried for bravado by putting a hand on one hip and saying, "Well, this is what's left of me."

He stepped inside and placed a grocery bag on the floor. "You're all wet," he said like a parent discovered their child misbehaving.

I closed the door and swayed on my feet. "I couldn't let you see me the way I was." I turned, stepped on the hem of my pajama bottoms, and would have gone careening to the floor if he hadn't caught me.

As if I weighed nothing at all, he swung me up into his arms and strode toward the living room.

I wrapped my arms around his neck and settled my head on his shoulder. "This is just like in the movies, except you're probably hoping I don't throw up on you."

He paused, mid stride. "Is that an imminent possibility?"

I breathed in his scent and weighed his question. "I don't think so. It's been a little while, and as long as I don't eat anything, I should be fine."

"You need to stay hydrated."

"Shh," I said, closing my eyes. "In my fantasy of this moment, you weren't nagging me."

I felt, as well as heard, his chuckle. "Well, when you feel better you can tell me about any and all fantasies you have. I'll do my best to live up to them. For now, you need to get into dry pajamas, and I'll get you some ice chips."

"Ice chips. Your mother's advice?"

"Mothers always know the best cure."

My arms tightened around his neck. "I wouldn't know. I don't remember mine."

"I'm sorry."

"Don't be; I'm not." I sighed. "It used to really bother me, but then I decided that I wouldn't be who I am today if she hadn't left me. I'm pretty incredible."

He gently deposited me on my feet near my bed. "Where do you keep your pajamas?"

"You're not dressing me."

"My fantasy of how it would be between us isn't exactly this, either, but how about I put some clothes on your bed, and you just call me if you need me?"

I sank to a seated position on the edge of the bed. "Top drawer on the left."

As he set a fresh pair of my pajamas beside me, I blushed because he'd just gotten an up-close look at exactly how unsexy the rest of my sleepwear was. He paused before turning away, and I was struck again by the beauty of his eyes. So intense. Too bad I'd probably never look into them again. I couldn't imagine him wanting to come back.

"I'll be right outside the door if you need me."

I nodded and slumped as soon as I was alone. I hesitated before removing my top. I had a man I didn't know in my home. He could be dangerous.

I caught a glimpse of myself in my bedroom mirror. My hair had dried in all directions but how I would have styled it. Dark circles under my eyes. Pale, like I was as close to death as I felt. *God bless any man this turns on. I'm sure I'm safe.*

I stripped, put my fresh pajamas on, and stood.

Then a thought came to me.

A slightly wicked, impulsive thought that had me sitting back down on the edge of the bed. It wasn't every day that I found myself alone with a man who wanted to take care of me. Was there any harm in letting him do it for just a little longer?

"Sebastian?"

He opened the door and returned to my side.

"Could you get me a brush from my bathroom?"

He was back a moment later, settling himself beside me on the bed. "Turn and I'll brush your hair."

He was so gentle, so careful, I started to wonder if I was actually still asleep on the couch waiting for him to arrive. This wasn't the man who'd dismissed me so completely the first day. It wasn't the harsh man who'd interrogated me on how I was caring for my child.

I made a sound that revealed my pleasure and didn't even care if he heard. I would use that moment, that feeling of being cared for so tenderly, as a standard for how I wanted to be treated. I didn't trust easily and always felt bad about asking anyone for anything. I naturally fell into the role of caretaker, but it felt good to not be the strong one.

When he stopped brushing my hair, I turned around and looked into his eyes. Despite how shitty I felt, there was an intimacy I couldn't deny. Under any other circumstance, I would have kissed him, and he looked as if he was thinking the same.

"I should go back to the couch," I whispered.

"I'll carry you there," he said with enough fire in his eyes that I felt sexy. He lifted me into his arms again. Strong arms. Rock-hard chest. The world would be a much happier place if we all traveled around in this man's arms.

I must have been smiling, because he said, "Feeling a little better?"

I laid my head back on his shoulder without answering. If admitting that I was meant he would put me down, I was prepared to milk my illness for a moment more.

We were just entering the living room when I heard Erica say, "Oh my God, I'm sorry. I thought you were alone."

Sebastian stopped, just holding me in his arms.

I raised my head. "Erica, you remember Sebastian. He came over to make sure I was okay."

She'd pay for that grin later. "As did I, but it looks like you're in good hands . . . literally." She winked.

Sebastian lowered me onto the couch. "Are you the one watching Ava tonight?"

"I am," Erica said, looking back and forth between us.

He walked over and shook her hand. "Sebastian Romano."

"Erica Hood. We met the other night. My children nearly mowed you down."

"I'm sure I'll see you and them again."

Erica gave me a pleased look. "I'm sure you will. Heather, do you need anything, or are you all set?"

"I'm good," I said, shoving my empty barf bowl beneath the end table with my foot.

"I'm sure you are," she joked as she walked toward the door. "I'll drop Ava off at school tomorrow morning. Call me if you need me to pick her up in the afternoon."

After she left, Sebastian headed to the kitchen, and I quickly tidied the area around the couch. He returned with a bowl of ice chips. I accepted it and placed it on the table beside me.

We looked at each other awkwardly for a moment.

"I'm fine if you want to go," I said.

"Do you want me to?" he asked.

"No," I admitted huskily.

He sat in the chair beside the couch. "I enjoy sci-fi movies."

"I do too," I said in all sincerity.

He picked up the remote for my television and said, "Want to?"

"Yes." *Yes. Yes. Yes.*

Now that he was there and not glaring at me, there were only about a thousand things I wanted to ask him. Sadly, though, my body had other plans. Five minutes into the movie, and before I had a chance to wow him with my wit, I fell asleep.

CHAPTER THIRTEEN

SEBASTIAN

And she's out.

Once again she'd delivered an entirely different experience than I'd imagined, but it was actually refreshing. Heather was real in a way many of the women I'd dated hadn't been. Was that why it'd been so easy to move on from one to another?

None of the women I'd spent time with after Therese would have worn matching flannel tops and bottoms. Their drawers were full of slips of lace designed to entice, some bought by me, some bought by the men before me. I felt no guilt when our time together ended—my gifts were likely still being worn by them while they enjoyed their next partner.

I'd have to be more careful with someone like Heather. Had she been joking about never having showered with a man before? There was very little chance that she was still a virgin, somewhere in her late twenties.

Thank God.

I wasn't looking for that kind of innocence. I didn't want someone who looked to me to have all the answers or make all the decisions. Been there, done that, and it wasn't a role I played well. I wanted someone who would challenge me, go toe to toe with me when I was wrong. My parents argued, but they made up and seemed stronger from it.

My mother was a sweet woman, but she had a temper. I don't think a man in my family would ever forget the day we'd all been so wrapped up in whatever we were doing that not one of us had called to tell her we'd be late for Sunday dinner.

When we'd finally gathered, oblivious and hungry, she'd walked out of the kitchen with a full tray of food and dumped it right on the floor of the dining room. She'd said only one word, "Respect," before she'd walked out of the room.

My father had sprinted after her.

Message received.

The following Sunday had gone more smoothly. My family didn't keep grudges. We said how we felt, yelled it sometimes, but we always came back to each other.

Heather seemed like a woman who could handle us. Restless, I tapped my hand on the arm of the chair. I hardly knew her. Was there actually a need for me to weigh how well she would or wouldn't fit in with my family?

I stood and retrieved a blanket from her bed, laying it over her as she slept. Even sick as she was, there was something about her I couldn't resist. I didn't belong there—but taking care of her felt right.

For just a moment, after I'd brushed her hair, I'd forgotten how sick she was and almost kissed her. Crazy. Impulsive in a way that didn't fit my personality.

And carrying her, I'd done it the first time out of real concern and the second time simply because she'd felt good in my arms. I settled back into the chair beside where Heather slept and decided I would give this—whatever this was—a chance.

Even if it meant I might not hear the end of it from my mother if it worked out. She already thought this woman was damn near perfect.

No one was, though.

Heather had shared that she'd never known her mother. That couldn't have been easy for her. Was her father dead? Did he live too far away to have been able to come care for her? No distance would have kept my own father from my side had I been in need.

With that thought fresh in my head, I sent a text to my father with a quick update that Heather seemed past the worst of it and was sleeping. No need to respond. Talk to you tomorrow.

I settled myself deeper in the chair and remembered that Heather had said she'd lost someone too. Had she been referring to her mother? Ava was adopted—had she been close to her biological parents?

There was so much I wanted to know about her.

She had her own business. What did she do? Was it a source of enjoyment for her or something she endured to support herself and Ava?

Her home was comfortably furnished and in a nice, suburban neighborhood. Whatever her occupation, she was good enough at it to make a decent income.

Independent.

Proud.

Says it as it is.

Not afraid to share she'd had fantasies about being with me.

Sexy as hell.

I closed my eyes and imagined how differently that night would have gone if she'd felt better and had waited to take a shower. It was a thought that had me smiling and forgetting how uncomfortable the chair was as I slipped into a light sleep.

The sky was still dark when the sound of Heather moving around woke me. Her blanket had fallen to the floor beside her, and her top had ridden up to reveal a delicate rib cage. Women revealed a hell of a lot more out in public, but that unexpected flash of skin was enough to fill my mind with all sorts of activities she wasn't healthy enough for yet.

I smiled as I remembered when Gian had first discovered how to surf the internet unfiltered by parental controls and had come to me with what he'd considered a serious question. I was twenty-seven at the time; he was eight. He'd just read an article that said men thought about sex eight thousand times a day and wanted to know if that was going to happen to him.

"Sounds about right," I'd joked.

He'd been horrified.

I made a mental note to bring that up the next time he gave me grief about something. A smart brother kept an arsenal of shit like that.

Eight thousand times?

There were only one thousand four hundred and forty minutes in a day. So what was that? One sexual thought about every ten seconds or so? That might be true of a teenager, but no man would ever get anything done if he only existed in that state.

At thirty-eight, I still had a good sexual appetite, but it had become more discerning. Like with beer, I still enjoyed a good one now and then, but I'd outgrown any desire to tap a keg. Quality over quantity.

Marriage had taught me how to take my time and that my partner's pleasure increased my own. Five years of playing the field had enhanced the variety in my skill set, but I couldn't say I'd had mind-blowing sex since Therese.

Sex could be good with a woman I wasn't in love with—but earth shattering? That required more.

Could I have that with Heather?

She rolled again, swatting at a curl of hair that tickled her nose. She was the first woman who made me think it was a possibility.

Her eyes flew open. "Sebastian?"

"How do you feel?"

She sat up, adjusted her shirt, and rubbed a hand over her face. "A little better." After taking a sip of water from the glass that had been full of ice chips, she looked at me and winced. "I wasn't sure if you were actually here or if I'd dreamed the whole thing."

"No, I'm here."

"And Godzilla? Because he was here too."

I smiled and turned the television off. "Sorry, I fell asleep with it on."

She lifted the blanket off the floor and hugged it to her stomach. "You didn't have to stay. What time is it?"

I glanced at the clock near the television. "Five thirty. I wanted to make sure you were okay."

"Thank you."

"Don't go there."

She cocked her head to the side in confusion.

"Every time you thank me, I say something stupid, and you either slam the door in my face or hang up on me. It's a pattern I'd like to break."

She looked exhausted, but when she smiled her eyes did as well. "Well, then stop saying stupid shit."

I chuckled. "I suppose I could try that."

Her subsequent laugh ended with tired, slow blinking.

"You should try to get some more sleep."

She nodded and gave me a look I understood. With the crisis over, my presence was . . . awkward.

I stood and straightened my tie. "Is there anything you need before I go?"

The look she gave me had me wondering if I was reading more into the moment than there was. I did something else that was out of character for me—I hovered over her, unsure if I should stay or go.

Finally, she said, "No, I'm fine. Thank—"

"I thought we'd agreed not to go there again."

She laughed. "Right."

I told myself that was my cue to go, but I stayed rooted where I was. "I'd like to see you again."

Her mouth rounded in surprise. "Really?"

I fought an urge to kiss those sweet lips of hers. Like the shower, though, there would be a better time and place for it. I raised and lowered a shoulder. "What can I say? I'm a sucker for a woman with a good snore."

She gave me a long look. "I didn't take you for someone with a sense of humor."

"I'm fucking hilarious once you get to know me."

She laughed. "I would call you on having an inflated opinion of yourself, but I believe I've already told you I'm incredible."

"That you did. And I'm inclined to agree. My productivity at work has significantly decreased recently. Your fault."

Her hand went to her adorably mussed hair. "Is someone paying you to say this?"

I took in the image of her, all eyes, feet tucked up beneath her, color back in her cheeks. Beautiful. "How have you never showered with a man?"

The question hung in the air.

I'd thought it but hadn't meant to voice it.

"I've had sex," she declared in a burst.

I laughed.

She groaned and smacked her forehead. "I can't believe I just said that. Why are you not running away?"

I leaned down until our eyes were level, bracing myself with one hand on the arm of her couch. "I like you." With that, I kissed the red mark on her forehead and stepped back. "I *am* going to head out, but I'll call you."

"Okay" was all she said.

CHAPTER FOURTEEN

HEATHER

I've had sex.

    Brilliant, stunning comeback.

    "I'll call you," he'd said.

    And what had I left him with? "Okay."

    Okay.

    I deserve celibacy.

    I checked the time. Another shower was not out of the question, and then, if I could pull myself together, I just might be able to get some work done that day. Phone calls could be made from anywhere.

    I went to stand up, but my legs were shaky, so I sat back down. It was still early. A short nap wouldn't hurt. I lay back, pulled the comforter over me, and closed my eyes.

    I woke to the sound of someone moving around my house and the smell of Lysol.

    "She's alive," Erica said cheerfully as soon as she realized I was awake.

    I pushed myself into a seated position. "What time is it?"

    "Noonish. When I drove the kids to school, I noticed a certain car was no longer parked out front, so I figured it was safe to come in."

    The kids . . . I groaned. "I meant to call Ava before she went to school. How was she?"

Lysol can still in hand, Erica sat on the arm of a chair across the room. "She was fine. She always is for me. She slept in Charlotte's room with her. Who, by the way, is now convinced that she wants a sister, so thanks for that."

"Sorry?" I looked around. My living room and kitchen counter were sparkling. "You're a saint, Erica. I will babysit for you anytime. Just drop your crew off. I owe you."

She dismissed my gratitude with a shrug. "It was nothing. What you owe me is every last juicy detail about last night." She frowned as she looked at me. "I'm assuming you didn't get laid, but you two were looking pretty cozy when I walked in."

I chuckled and covered my face with my hands. "You wouldn't believe it if I told you."

"Wait. You *did* have sex?"

I lowered my hands. "No. No. After what came out of my mouth yesterday, I'm sure there wasn't a part of him he wanted near it."

She rolled her eyes. "You'd be surprised, but go on. What did happen?"

I took a sip of water, enjoyed that my body didn't immediately send it back up, and started from our phone call and how we'd shared a beautiful moment during it.

She made a face. "Gross."

"Right? Can you believe he wanted to come over after that?"

She tipped her head in concession of how unlikely it was that many men would have. "So he drove over and what?"

I told her about how I'd showered and still been wet when he'd arrived.

"I'm sure you were," she joked.

My shoulders shook as I laughed. "You're so bad. Anyway, he told me I should change."

"How deliciously commanding of him."

I blushed, then met her gaze. "I did kind of like it. Is that wrong? I don't like being told what to do, but I might want to try it for a night."

Erica hooted. "Who wouldn't with a man like that? When I saw the way he was carrying you, I decided to drop ten pounds and test my husband's back. He used to do shit like that, but then the kids came along and we've gotten . . . uncreative. I think we need a weekend away for a wall-banging good time like we used to."

"Like I said, I owe you. I can watch your kids here any weekend or at your place."

"Our house might be safer. That way, if the boys break something, I don't have to feel guilty."

"Sounds like a plan."

"No sex, but he undressed you and carried you around. Interesting."

"He didn't dress or undress me. He stepped out of the bedroom while I changed."

"Shame, although I guess that makes the whole thing less creepy."

I took another sip of water as I thought about that. "A little voice in my head did question whether it was safe to let a man in the house like that, but when he was here it didn't feel weird."

"I wouldn't have asked him to leave either."

I tossed a pillow at her.

She sprayed it with Lysol.

"So how did you leave it? What did he say as he left?"

"He said he'd call."

"Has he yet?"

I looked at my phone. No messages. No missed calls. "No."

"Hey, don't make that face. He probably didn't want to wake you."

"Maybe." I didn't like how disappointed I was that I hadn't heard from him. "This is a bad idea, Erica. Ava and I are happy. My business is solid. Life is good. Why would I want to mess with that?"

She shook her head.

I continued, "He was probably just being polite when he'd said he'd call. I mean, look at me. I looked worse last night. What's more likely? That he came, saw me in this state, and decided he couldn't live without me? A man who looks like that? Or would it be more realistic to think that since losing his wife he feels a certain compulsion to help women in need, but after playing nursemaid to me all night, he returned to his life with a sense of relief?"

"Wow, you have him all figured out, don't you? You're right; he's way too fucked up for you to date. Let me call some of my other friends to see if any of them are interested in him."

"Funny."

"Oh, you were being serious? I had no idea you were this insecure."

"I'm not insecure."

"You're also not ugly, but FYI, even ugly people hook up. The world is full of couples no one can explain."

I processed that one for a moment.

She sighed. "Sure, right now you look like shit, but normally you're not bad."

"Thank you? I think?"

"You should call him."

"No way."

"You're right. You should just sit here, wait for him to come around, and sulk. Let the man make all the moves, just like he probably always does. That won't bore him into finding someone else."

"I can't call him."

"I know you have his number. You said he called you. So there is no can't . . . unless you're admitting you don't have the balls to do it."

"Technically I don't."

She rolled her eyes.

"What would I even say?" I asked.

"Check with Teri to see if she's free to watch Ava for a few hours this weekend, then pick a place and tell him to meet you there."

"You mean ask him."

"Do you want to have great sex or something not worth sharing with me? I've known you a long time and I've never seen you *glow*. You know what I mean?"

"I can't just sleep with him. I have Ava to think of."

"Ava won't be there."

I hugged the blanket closer. "Aren't you supposed to warn me he won't respect me if I rush this? Tell me to take it slowly?"

"When was the last time you had sex?" Horror filled her expression. "Don't even say before Ava."

I made a pained face.

"Hon, you need to call that man, fuck his brains out, then worry about a relationship later."

I shook my head, thought about what she'd said, then picked up my phone to send a text.

Teri, could you watch Ava Saturday night?

Teri: Sure.

I dropped my phone on my lap. "She said yes." I looked down at my phone again. "Oh my God, she said yes."

After the enormity of it sank in, the wheels in my head started turning. *If I'm going to do this, I'm going to do it right.*

I'm a modern woman.

Strong.

Bold.

Success in any endeavor doesn't come from doing it halfway.

Time to be clear about what I want.

CHAPTER FIFTEEN

SEBASTIAN

"This was exactly what I was looking for, Miss Steele," I said after glancing over a report my assistant had handed me when I walked through her office. I was feeling good after a productive morning, a workout, and a quick lunch. "You did good work on this one."

"Thank you," Miss Steele said in polite response.

I smiled as those two words reminded me of another conversation. I'd held off calling Heather all morning because I'd wanted to let her rest, but I was about to walk into my office, close the door, and rectify that.

Miss Steele tentatively smiled, then rushed back behind her desk, looking confused.

"Hold my calls." I tucked the folder she'd handed me under my arm.

"Absolutely, Mr. Romano."

I was still smiling when I closed the door of my office and took out my phone. It rang in my hand.

Christof. "Do you have a minute?" His tone was serious enough that I became instantly concerned.

"Yes. Sure. Is something wrong?"

"No, but I'm hoping you're free on Saturday. Remember Gian saying he'd been accepted to Johns Hopkins in Baltimore?"

"How could I forget when we all celebrated how the youngest of us is determined to be a doctor?" I joked.

"He might be, but I think he's worried if he moves away he won't see us anymore."

"That's ridiculous."

"Is it? We don't know what it's like to have a mother ditch and run. No matter how much he says it doesn't affect him, you know it does. Worrying about what will happen with us is all that's holding him back. I spoke to Mauricio, and he agrees—we should go down there with him this weekend. We'll fly down together Friday night. It's less than a two-hour flight, which will show him how easy it would be to come back for the weekends or for us to go there. He needs to find housing, and we can scope out a couple of places with him. Mom and Dad are on board. We'll get a place for the weekend, check out the school grounds with Gian, then come back on Sunday night. We want to show him we support the move, and we're not going anywhere."

"I'm in."

"You are? Great. Your opinion has always carried weight with Gian."

Although I hadn't done much in the past few years to earn that honor, I knew it was true. Everything else Christof had said was also sadly true. Mom and Dad had always been tight lipped whenever it came to anything related to Gian's biological parents. When asked, they'd assured us that not asking was the kindest thing we could do for Gian. No one knew what that meant, but Gian was one of us no matter how it had happened.

Heather would understand that, since that was how she seemed to feel about Ava.

I was not a perfect man, but one of my strengths was my family. They had always been what mattered most to me. "Send me the details. I know how important this is to Gian, and it sounds like a good way to show him we're not going anywhere."

"Will do. Hey, how is your girlfriend feeling today?"

"She's not my girlfriend—not yet, but if you're done, I'll finally be able to call her and see what I can do about that."

"I look forward to meeting her."

"We're a long way off from that, brother, but I'm hanging up now." He was chuckling as I did.

I walked over to the window of my office and took a moment before calling. I wasn't used to a woman occupying so much space in my head, nor was I used to my family being involved in my dating life. If pressed, I doubted they could name anyone I'd been with since Therese.

Heather and I were still circling around each other, not quite sure how to move forward, and my family not only knew her name but wanted to meet her. It was unsettling. It also supported the sense I had that this wasn't something I wanted to rush.

Part of me, everything below my belt, wanted to sweep her off somewhere soon and explore just exactly how intense the heat between us could get. My cock made a convincing argument that there would be plenty of time to get to know her better—afterward.

I normally would have agreed, but this felt too important to treat like every other relationship I'd had recently. My girlfriend? I groaned. The term was juvenile. Dating, the kind that involved more than a few expensive dinners followed by sex, was something I was out of practice with.

Did men still send flowers?

I wanted to do this right.

The buzz of my phone interrupted my thoughts. "Speak," I barked, annoyed that I'd fielded another call before speaking to Heather.

"Sebastian? Sorry. Is this a bad time?"

Heather. "No. Not at all. I was about to call you."

"I'm glad, because I've been thinking about you all day." Her voice was low and sexy.

I was instantly on. "Have you? I'll admit to the same affliction."

"Good," she purred. "Because I'm going to rock your world this Saturday. Text me your address, and I'll send a car for you. Don't ask where I'm taking you. I want to surprise you—in oh so many ways."

I loosened my tie and fought to concentrate as all my blood left my brain. "This Saturday? I'm not going to be in town—"

"Right. Of course you won't be. I'm such an idiot."

"Heather—"

"Forget I called. This was stupid."

The call ended while I was still trying to wrap my head around what had just happened. I tried to call her back, but she didn't pick up.

Had my sweet, modest-pajama-wearing Heather just offered to steal me away for a wild weekend? Holy fuck, YES.

Johns Hopkins. My family. Gian.

Mom? Dad? Do you mind if we postpone our trip to Baltimore? Yeah, I know it's important, but Heather just offered to rock my world.

Dammit.

I typed Pick up, Heather, then deleted it, because it sounded like a command.

Please pick up, I wrote, then deleted that as well. Desperate—no one found that attractive.

I absolutely want to fuck you, but this weekend doesn't work for me. I wrote the words in mockery of my mental state and of the irony of the timing.

"Mr. Romano?" Miss Steele asked from my door, and I jumped.

Jumped and accidentally hit "Send."

Fuck me.

No. No. No.

"How do you delete a text?" I growled the rhetorical question.

"I'm sorry?"

I'd already figured out how, but hesitated. Heather had just hung up, which meant she had her phone on her, probably still in her hand. The only thing worse than sending that message was instantly deleting it.

Was there an emoji for shit like this? A smiley-faced eggplant? One that meant . . . just kidding, not actually that much of a dick.

Fuck.

Miss Steele made a shuffling sound that brought my attention back to her. "What? What was so important that you had to tell me when I said I didn't want to be disturbed?" She shrank from my tone, which made me feel even worse. I ran my hand through my hair. "Sorry. What do you need, Miss Steele?"

"I thought you might want to know there's another package for you."

Fine. Whatever. "Bring it in."

She put it on the table inside my office and skittered out, closing the door behind her. I walked over to it. Same wrapping as the one Heather had sent. Too small to be more cookies. I tore open the note.

Hoping you like surprises as much as I do. —Heather

I tucked her note in the breast pocket of my jacket, then opened her gift. Dice for lovers? I read the packaging—*Oh.* One die had parts of the body on it. The other had sexy action words. *Suck. Lick. Blow.*

I groaned.

It was erotic in a sweet, earnest way.

I should have said yes and convinced my family to go to Baltimore another weekend. Her call had taken me by surprise, though.

I pocketed the dice as well, then took another look at the message I'd sent. She hadn't responded.

Shocking.

I could text that I had been kidding, but decided that wouldn't help.

On the plus side, it was pretty clear that she was interested in me.

If I explained to her what had happened, we might have a good laugh about it—something I couldn't do if she didn't want to speak to me.

"What did you do to upset Miss Steele this time?" Mauricio asked as he sauntered into my office.

"Does no one respect a closed door?" I snapped.

"Ouch, you're in a mood. Christof told me you were on board for this weekend. Is that what this is about? Do you think the Bhatt project will fall apart if you step away for a few days? It won't, you know."

"I realize that, and I'm not in a mood."

"Whatever you say." He looked around, then headed toward the table where remnants of Heather's gift remained. Thankfully only the wrapping paper. "Another gift. I'm jealous."

I slid my phone into my jacket pocket. "What do you want? Please tell me it's not just lecturing about my assistant."

"You could be nicer to her."

"She could be better at her job. We all have areas to work on."

"You're a real asshole sometimes."

I expelled a breath and deflated a bit. "Tell me about it."

Mauricio's eyebrows rose. "You're not referring to Miss Steele. What happened that I don't know about?"

"Nothing I can share. I just messed up with someone, but I'll fix it."

"A woman. *The* woman?"

"Yes."

"You made a move on her while she was sick?"

"No, and I don't want to talk about this with you. Since when are you interested in my social life?"

Mauricio picked up a piece of the wrapping paper, balled it, and tossed it at me. "Since you found someone you might actually like. You spent the night at her house. Was she as amazing as Mom thinks she is? I think we should wait to see what skeletons she has in her closet before any of us endorse her, but you know how Mom gets once she has an opinion on something."

I made a warning sound deep in my throat. "Heather is not a topic for family debate. I went to see her because she was sick. That's all anyone needs to know until, and only if, there is anything else to share."

"But you do like her, right?"

I sighed. "She seems like a very nice woman . . . who might want someone who is less of a dick."

Mauricio came over, chucked me in the arm, and joked, "Don't be so hard on yourself; you're a catch."

"Thanks. Now can I get back to work?"

"Sure you don't want any advice? I have a keen understanding of the female mind."

"I'll pass," I answered with heavy sarcasm.

He shot me his winning smile. "Come on, you know you want to tell me."

"I don't."

"Did she see you out with someone else?"

"No."

"Did you punch someone she's dating?"

"She's not dating anyone."

He shrugged. "I know what this is. You're used to not caring if a woman likes you or not. You're spooked."

"I'm not fifteen."

"Women are not that hard to please. Send her a few little gifts. She'll forgive whatever you did."

"Wow, with such deep insight into the female psyche, you must be considering writing a book on the subject."

"Fine. Make it more complicated than it has to be." He sauntered back toward my office door.

"Mauricio?" I hated that I didn't have a better plan than the one he'd tossed out.

"Yes?"

"What's a good first gift to send?"

CHAPTER SIXTEEN

HEATHER

I absolutely want to fuck you, but this weekend doesn't work
for me.

Over the phone I read the text to Erica, because there was no way
I was going to let her talk me into behaving rashly again.

"Hey, on the positive, it wasn't a no." Her tone was light, but I
knew she felt bad.

As we spoke, I walked my blanket back to my bedroom. Ava would
be home in a couple of hours, and I intended to have everything back
the way it had been. The house. Me. "I know you're trying to help, but
does he sound like someone you can imagine me with?"

"No," she admitted grudgingly. "I'm sorry. It's just that I've seen
you meet and turn away so many guys. I wanted this to work out for
you."

"I know. I'm not upset. I just feel like an idiot."

"He's the idiot for saying no. You would have rocked his world."

I chuckled without much humor. "That's pretty much what I told
him."

"What did you end up sending him?"

I told her, and by her silence I knew it wouldn't have been her first choice. "I'm sorry, I don't cook."

"Do you know if he got it?"

"The service said it was delivered."

She choked on a laugh. "I'm sorry. Is it wrong that I hope he's sitting there with those dice, realizing that if he wasn't such a douche he'd soon be having one hell of a weekend?"

"You saw him. You think it's hard for him to find my replacement?" I read his text aloud again. "Who even talks like that? And what did he think I'd write back? 'Oh, then, please, sir, if it's convenient for you, could you see if you're free next weekend?'"

"He might actually have plans he couldn't get out of."

"I'm sure he does."

After a pause, Erica asked, "So, since your weekend is pretty open now—how would you feel about watching my crew?"

"Like you said—my weekend is wide open." I straightened my shoulders, refusing to wallow. There was too much in my life to be happy about. "What I meant to say is that I would love to. I know Ava will be thrilled."

Another pause. "I'm sorry it didn't work out, Heather."

I wiped down the kitchen counter as I answered. "It's okay. Really. Things don't always go the way we hope they will, but I have to believe they work out the way they're supposed to."

"You're a good friend, a good mother, and you would make some man a great wife."

I folded the towel and pushed it aside. "Not everyone is meant to be in a relationship, Erica. I'm fine."

"I want to punch that douche."

"What douche?" I asked. People came and went. Wishing things were different was an exercise in futility that led nowhere good.

"Exactly."

After picking up Ava from preschool, taking her to a tumbling class, feeding her dinner, giving her a bath, and reading her a story, I was exhausted. When my doorbell rang at eight o'clock, I cursed whoever was risking waking Ava. I was done for the day. D-O-N-E.

I sprinted to the door before they had a chance to ring the bell again. A courier handed me two bags. I tipped him, then took the bags into my living room.

For several minutes I sat on the couch just looking at the bags. Were they from Sebastian? If so, did I really want to know what he'd sent?

I had closed the door on him—once literally and today figuratively. What would a man send after writing what he had? Probably something wildly inappropriate that I'd have to stash or dispose of so Ava wouldn't find it.

Whatever was in the bags—was it meant to be an apology?

We hadn't even been on a date yet, and we were already at the gifts-as-an-apology stage? What did that say?

I peered into the first bag, and as I did caught a whiff of something delicious. I pulled out the first item: focaccia bread wrapped in white linen. The next was a thermos that was warm to the touch. I opened it. Just a hot broth soup.

It was such a considerate gift I didn't want it to be from Sebastian. Then I found the card.

Ever write something stupid, then hit send by mistake? I have. I hope you're feeling better tonight. —*Sebastian*

P.S. There is also something for Ava.

It was a touching gesture that had my head spinning. He'd not only made a mistake and acknowledged it, but his peace offering was exactly what I'd been too tired to make for myself.

But to send something for Ava? I wasn't ready for him to be part of her life in any way yet. Maybe ever.

The second bag was lighter. I poured out the contents on the table, and my eyes misted. Eight small stuffed wolves: the puppies Ava had said were certain to come now that Wolfie had his Wolfina.

I sat back on the couch, shaking my head. It was such a thoughtful gesture, but one that only confused me more.

It was clear that he regretted what he'd said, but even if we put that behind us—did I want to open myself up to more disappointment? For all I knew this was his way of making sure there would be no hard feelings between us. He didn't say he would call me. He didn't ask me to call him.

He just hoped I felt better.

Right then I was wishing I felt a lot less of anything. These were exactly the kinds of gifts the kind of man I wanted would give.

That didn't make him the man for me.

Nor did it give me "the balls" to call him again.

I leaned forward and picked up a piece of bread and dunked it in the soup. "What do you want from me, Sebastian? We agreed that I should stop thanking you. What do I do with this?"

The next day after work, I left my office a little early to stop at the supermarket before picking Ava up. Nothing against my little one, but shopping was a much faster experience without her.

Erica and her husband were only going away for one night and would have food, but I wanted to have all the extra toppings for crepes. Chocolate sauce, blueberry pie filling, whipped cream.

I scanned my small pile of purchase choices and was temporarily transported away from the busy aisle into a tantalizing scene of how I might have been using the whipped cream for an entirely different reason if Sebastian had said yes. Did food and sex live up to the hype? As I'd proclaimed the day before, I'd had sex—what I hadn't mentioned was that none had been worth mentioning. My first time had been with a boy I'd hooked up with at a party my freshman year. The rest had been with one of my housemates when I lived with Brenda and that gang. We'd never officially become a couple, and I don't really know why sex temporarily had become something we did.

Looking back, I think I liked having a warm body beside me as I slept more than I enjoyed the sex. Not that he was bad, but Erica would have been disappointed if she'd seen us together, because he'd never left me *glowing*.

I smiled as I remembered telling him that he must have been forgetting to do something because I was better at bringing myself to orgasm. That hadn't gone over well—not everyone can handle my level of honesty. Even though we'd continued to live in the same house, we didn't have sex again after that.

I shrugged. The man I wanted would have seen that conversation as a challenge. *I bet Sebastian knows what he's doing.*

My hands tightened on the handle of the shopping cart as I thought about the dice I'd sent him. He hadn't mentioned them. I winced. Probably because grown women don't send things like that to men.

I might as well have sent him a meme of me on my knees begging him to have sex with me with the words "It's been so long I need the dice to help me remember what to do."

Pathetic.

My first attempt at being a seductress? Fail.

I replayed the brief phone conversation I'd had with Sebastian before he'd sent that final text. Calling him, propositioning him, attempting to sound sexy had been so far outside my comfort zone that I'd shut down as soon as I didn't get an instant yes.

And I'd been angry.

But it wasn't him I was really upset with—it was me.

"Hey, Heather." A male voice broke into my reverie.

I looked up and smiled at the familiar face. "Levi. Hi. What are you doing in town?" He and I had gone out on one date a year before—set up by Erica. He owned a manufacturing company in Hartford.

"Up for the weekend to see friends." He looked me over as I did him. Still tall, blond, good looking. Younger than Sebastian. His hazel eyes sparkled when they met mine. "We should get together while I'm here."

I wanted to feel something, but I didn't. "I'd love to, but my weekend is packed."

He looked down at the contents of my basket. "Hot date?"

I almost said, "I wish," but decided that would give him the entirely wrong impression. I defaulted to my most common excuse. "No, I have Ava. This is for crepes. We're doing a big sleepover with some of her friends, and they love them. Parenting fills all my free time."

"I remember." He nodded slowly. "If you change your mind, you have my number."

"If I don't get going, I'll be late to pick her up." I gave him that awkward smile women do when they know there is nowhere a conversation can go and pushed my cart forward a foot. "It was nice to see you."

I walked away and let out a relieved breath. An image of Sebastian came to me before I'd even rounded the corner. A smug one, because he knew if he'd asked me to find time for him that weekend I would have.

I wasn't just craving sex—I was craving a toe-curling, wall-banging, "leave me in a glowing puddle" fuck. Levi wouldn't give me that.

Sebastian's intense gray eyes promised that and so much more. Just thinking about him had my stomach clenching and my sex tingling in anticipation.

I pushed my cart through the pharmacy aisle and discreetly threw a box of condoms in my carriage. I might never see Sebastian again, but the prepper in me prevailed.

In the checkout aisle, I placed my interesting assortment of purchases on the belt and didn't look the cashier in the eye. My eyes flew to hers, though, when she said, "Don't forget to say no to Romano."

"I'm sorry? What did you say?"

"The Romano Superstore that is up for public vote. They already bought the property next door like it's a done deal, but it's not. We can stop it."

"Romano Superstores." I'd forgotten that connection. I'd heard of them. Did Sebastian work for them? Was it his family's business? "Do you know a Sebastian Romano?"

"Know him? He's the head of Romano Superstores. If you meet him, tell him we don't want him here. I hear the first thing he'll do is run this store into the ground—there goes my job. After it closes, he'll swoop in and get everything for pennies without a thought of whether any of us could pay our rent. But we can stop him. Just vote no on the proposal to allow the Romano store to be built."

"I will, thanks," I said, because . . . well, what else could I say?

That evening, I was in the middle of a game of Twister at Erica's home when my phone rang. I would have answered, but it was my turn to be on the mat rather than run the spinner, and I was holding my own. Ava picked up my phone. "It's Sebastian." Since she had a boy with that name in her class, it made sense that she could read it. Then her eyes lit up and my hand slipped, but I righted myself. "My hero."

"Don't you dare answer that," I said in what I hoped was a sufficiently stern tone. Hard to pull real authority off while bent into a pretzel position with three kids. I made a move to straighten.

Charlotte's face crumpled. "Don't quit! I'm finally doing it right."

"You can keep playing," I said gently.

"Please." Oh, she knew how to get me.

I looked back at Ava. "Put my phone down."

"But it's Sebastian." She swiped to answer it. "Hi, Sebastian. We're playing Twister. No, she's busy. She's playing too."

I stood and shot an apologetic look to Charlotte. "Hold my spot. I'll be right back." Then I walked over to where Ava had my phone and held out my hand.

"Bye, Sebastian," Ava said before handing my phone to me.

"Bad timing?" he asked with humor in that yummy voice of his.

"A little. I'm watching Erica's kids for the night, and everything goes better if I tire them out."

"With Twister? I've never played. You'll have to show me how it's done." My face warmed, and I turned away from the children. Talking to him again was as exciting as it was embarrassing. The kind of women he dated probably would have parried with their own innuendo, but I couldn't think of one and wasn't willing to say much with the audience I had. He broke the awkward silence. "I don't know what you thought I was saying when you called me the other day, but I wasn't turning you down. I had just committed to going to Baltimore with my family to check out a school my brother has been accepted to. And my comment? I wrote it to be funny with no intention of sending—"

"Stop," I said, not wanting to relive it in such detail. Behind me I heard Charlotte calling my name. I turned. Her brothers were getting restless. Ava was refusing to spin until I returned to the game. "I have to go, but could we start over?"

"I'll be back Sunday night. I have business in Durham. Come to lunch with me on Monday."

"Mom, Kevin is cheating."

"I am not," Kevin protested.

"He always cheats," his brother complained.

My heart was beating wildly as I considered Sebastian's invitation. Lunch. Safest meal of the day to share with a man. "Sounds great. See you Monday. I'll text you a place to meet."

"Until Monday, then," Sebastian said.

"Mom, Tyler just kicked Kevin."

"My foot slipped," Tyler claimed.

"I quit," Charlotte declared.

"Yes," I said quickly and ended the call.

As soon as I was back in the mix, civility returned. Apologies were encouraged and delivered all around. I retook my place on the mat, and Ava called out the next move . . . a move I almost messed up on when Kevin asked, "Are you getting married?"

"Are you, Mom?" Ava asked. Did she even know what that meant? I wasn't sure.

"No. Sebastian is just a friend."

Charlotte added. "Mom said he's hot. Dad didn't like that, but he went for a run this morning, and he hasn't done that in a long time. Mom says she's not sorry she said it, because she's married but she's not dead."

I coughed back a pained laugh. Did Erica realize how much her little one overheard? I hadn't. Kids saw and knew everything. I'd put the box of condoms in my bedroom, but I told myself to hide them better when I got home.

Ava picked up my phone again. "Smile. This is for Sebastian. He said he wanted to see it."

Thankfully she didn't yet know how to send messages.

Or read much. But it would be just my luck if she chose that moment to show me she'd learned how to open my messages as well. I pretended to slip and fall. "I'm out."

This time Charlotte was happy. She didn't often beat her older brothers at such games, but, since they were stealthily sabotaging each other, she just might.

I took my phone from Ava and grimaced at how I looked with my ass high in the air, hair hanging down in my face. Not my most flattering photo. I laughed, though, at the antics of the children around me and how one photo had caught Kevin in the act of trying to tip his brother over. It was not a surprise when I heard the two boys hit the floor and Charlotte cheer that she was the winner.

On impulse I sent Sebastian the best of the photos and wrote: Charlotte won.

A moment later his answer came back: No, I did. Best photo ever.

I blushed down to my toes. Best photo? For laughs, maybe.

"The winner always does the spinner," Charlotte said as she grabbed the board from Ava.

Ava grabbed it back. "You didn't say please."

It was a tug of war that meant only one thing in my eyes—game over. "Who is ready for some popcorn and a movie?" A round of cheers erupted, and the board fell to the ground, forgotten. The boys surprised me by cleaning up the game. Charlotte and Ava settled onto the couch, side by side—perfectly happy to be together again.

A short time later I was breathing easier while watching an animated action film we'd all seen before. The kids were sprawled out, content, munching on popcorn.

In the peace of the moment, I was able to think again.

Sebastian had asked me out.

And I'd said yes.

Monday felt very far away.

CHAPTER SEVENTEEN

SEBASTIAN

Seated beside Mauricio on my family's plane, I was glad I hadn't backed out of the Baltimore trip—even while looking at the photo Heather had sent. Gian had been damn near tears when all of us had surprised him with our plans.

He was such a good kid. He deserved moments like that.

Still, holy fuck, I couldn't tear my attention away from Heather playing Twister. First, yoga pants must have been invented by a man, because the way they clung to her ass was breathtakingly sinful.

Second, the children in the photo were all laughing. The warmth of the scene pulled at me—I wanted to be there. I wanted to hear the squeals of delight as well as witness whatever tussle had occurred when the boy who was trying to knock his brother over actually did.

"What are you smiling at?" Mauricio asked, leaning over from his seat beside me. "Interesting photo."

I pocketed my phone. "It's nothing."

"Was that Heather? I thought Mom said she had *one* kid."

"She's babysitting three more this weekend."

"Impressive. I get what you like about her."

My eyes narrowed. If he so much as mentioned her ass, I was going to slug him. "Do you?"

"You've always wanted a family."

The comment didn't hurt as much as it once would have. "Yeah. I'd given up on that happening, but lately . . . it's at least a possibility again."

"With Heather?"

"I honestly don't know, but she's different. She makes me laugh."

Mauricio nodded. "But can she cook?"

I had no idea, but her kitchen hadn't been stocked like that of someone who could. "Not important to me."

Mauricio patted his stomach. "To you. But I want to be fed when I visit. Someday Mom will want to pass that torch to someone. You're our best hope for marrying."

I chuckled. "You could learn to cook. Or find your own wife."

"I totally would," he joked. "But so far I haven't found a woman who wants to clean my house while I fuck her friends."

I shook my head. "You're an idiot."

He shrugged. "We can't all be the superserious head of the family. Some of us have to find our joy in other ways." Without missing a beat, he added, "Hey, instead of passing judgment on my lifestyle, you should be thanking me. I told you the right gifts would have her answering your calls again. Which of my suggestions did you take? The diamond earrings or the bracelet? I haven't encountered a problem the right jewelry didn't fix."

"I didn't send her jewelry."

"Okay, you went rogue. Hang on, don't tell me. Let me guess." He tapped his fingers on the arm of his seat. "Roses—white. Something traditional."

"No." I liked that he didn't know me as well as he thought.

"Tickets to an opera or ballet."

"Not even close."

His eyebrows rose and fell. "I've got nothing. What did you send her?"

For him to understand my choices, I had to share the first time I'd met Heather and her daughter. "So I sent a broth soup and fresh focaccia because I figured she probably couldn't keep much else down, and I sent eight mini stuffed wolves for Ava."

"Oh, you're good. Get in with the kid and you're golden."

"It wasn't like that. I knew Ava would like them."

Mauricio gave me a long look, then smiled. "All joking aside, I like this Heather. I like the side of you she brings out."

I relaxed back in my seat. "Me too."

Me too.

Monday couldn't come soon enough.

CHAPTER EIGHTEEN

HEATHER

It was nearly impossible to concentrate on work Monday morning. Since erotic fantasies don't pay the mortgage, I pushed through a bulk of the backlog created by my time away the week before.

Ten minutes before I was scheduled to leave to meet Sebastian, I walked into Teri's office. "How do I look?"

She glanced up from typing. "Like you always do?"

I smoothed a hand over my skirt. I'd chosen it and a simple blouse because I didn't want to look like I was trying too hard.

Did I look like I wasn't trying at all?

I walked over to the mirror. My hair was neatly tied back, as it always was at work. Take it down? Leave it up? I leaned closer to the mirror. More makeup? Less?

I groaned.

"Relax," Teri joked. "It doesn't matter what you're wearing on top as long as what you've got on underneath kicks it."

"Underneath. You mean my bra and undies? I'm only going to lunch."

Teri and I shared a painful moment in which I realized she wanted to say something, but wouldn't, and that we had both wandered into a conversation we weren't meant to have. I excused myself to my office and called Erica.

I quickly filled her in on what Teri had said, then asked, "You've seen my work clothes. Can you tell what I'm wearing beneath them?"

Erica sighed. "You wore grannie panties, didn't you?"

"I wore what I always wear. Functional. Cotton briefs."

"Lord save me. Did your mother never teach you—" She stopped and swore. "Oh, I didn't mean to mention your mother. It's an expression."

"It's okay. You're right, though. I didn't grow up with a woman in my life I could ask about stuff like this. What am I doing, Erica? Sebastian is so out of my league. I should call him and tell him I can't meet him."

"Stop. Just stop. He is not out of your league. There is no league. He's a man. You're a woman. That's it. Forget everything else."

"You're right."

"And lose the underwear."

"What?"

"Take them off. Stash them in your drawer, or better yet throw them away."

"And go—commando? I couldn't. I don't—I've never."

"You're not going to sleep with him today, right?"

"Right."

"But you want to."

"No—okay, not today, but yes, I hope this leads in that direction."

"Then throw those damn things in the trash."

"I don't understand. If he's not going to see them, why does it matter?"

"It'll matter. Just trust me."

I chewed my bottom lip for a moment, then slid off my panties and stuffed them in the trash near my desk. "Okay, this bird is flying free."

Erica burst out laughing. "Then you're ready for your first date. Now get going. I don't want to be the reason you miss out on one moment of it."

Head held high, I walked through Teri's office and told her I'd be back in an hour. I felt the material of my skirt move against my bare ass and a slight breeze tickle my sex as I stepped out of the building.

Like a caress.

Oh.

I checked my expression in my rearview mirror when I got in. My cheeks were flushed, and there was a spark in my eyes I wasn't used to seeing. I felt sexy and like I had a naughty secret I could share or not—it was up to me.

I finally understood.

Underneath my conservative clothing—I was *kicking it*.

The confidence it gave me stayed with me all the way to the restaurant, where I parked my car beside the spot where Sebastian was leaning against his. It buoyed me all the way to him.

One long, hot look.

Without even exchanging a word, he pulled me closer and lowered his mouth to mine. It was the kiss I'd waited my whole life for. I melted into it, gave myself over to it. Hot and demanding, talented and teasing. I let him in, tasted him as eagerly as he tasted me.

His tongue taught me the true wonder of what a French kiss could be. I felt claimed, adored . . . wanton.

When he raised his head, I was wet and ready—hungry, but not for a salad.

His hard breathing told me he was as affected as I was.

"Hello," he said in a husky voice.

"Hi," I said in a similar tone.

"Full disclosure, I had to see you today. I can't stop thinking about you."

"Full disclosure, I ditched my underwear in the trash." He gave me an odd look, and I tensed as I thought of how he could have taken that. "Not because I'm still sick. Nothing like that."

He looked as if he was holding back a laugh, and I groaned. "Can we rewind? I can't believe how bad I am at this. I just wanted to be more like the women you usually date."

Whatever else I might have added flew from my mind as he claimed my mouth again. His hands went to my ass, grinding me against his excitement. I moaned with pleasure. Oh God, yes.

He kissed his way to my ear and growled, "Don't. I like you just the way you are." With that, he plundered my mouth again and kissed me until I was ready to spread my legs for him right there in the parking lot. His hands tightened on my ass, and he broke off the kiss long enough to say, "But I love that you're bare for me. Love it too much. If we're actually having lunch, we should go in."

Lunch?

Oh yeah, lunch. Right.

This was how I'd always yearned for it to be—uninhibited, wanton. I didn't want the moment to end.

I pulled his head down for one more deep kiss, savored the shit out of it, then stepped back and smoothed my skirt. "Okay, now I'm ready."

He pushed off his car, offering me his arm like we hadn't just mauled each other. I took it and loved the feel of his muscles beneath my hand. A quick check of my hair confirmed that it was still reasonably in place.

His attention on me as we walked electrified me. I'd never felt so desirable—or desired. Young. Sexy and on the arm of a man I would have written off in the past as out of my league.

No leagues. I remembered what Erica had said. Just a man, a woman, and sexual tension so palpable I could only stare blankly at the hostess when she asked how many we were. My thoughts spun. Now that I'd seen Sebastian again, my choice of restaurant was disappointing. The way I felt would have been better matched to a more intimate setting—dim lighting, quiet tables. Instead, we were seated on opposite sides of a booth in a bustling dining room. The promise of a free meal if we weren't served our food in twenty minutes or less reminded me that my hour-long lunch would be over too soon.

We both ordered light sandwiches and water. I would have eaten sandpaper without complaint as long as he continued to look at me as if I were the only one in the room. I fought an impulse to grab his hand, drag him out of the restaurant, and proclaim that I had a menu of things I wanted and none of them were food.

Exciting.

Terrifying.

Amazing.

After the water was delivered and our server walked away, Sebastian asked, "So is your house crazy now with all those puppies?"

I spun my glass of water between my hands as I bought time before answering. Ava and I had sent him a gift. It made sense that he would send her something. "I didn't give your present to her."

Those intense gray eyes of his gave little away. He searched my face for moment, then said, "Too soon."

"Yes." I struggled to come up with a way to explain it without making it awkward. "She's never seen me with anyone . . . men, I mean. Not that I've dated women. Not judging that choice, just saying that I've never." I took a sip of water to shut myself up.

He had that half smile back. "You're careful with who you introduce her to. I respect that."

Feeling calmer, I chose my next words more carefully. "She already likes you because you returned Wolfie to her. I don't want her to get attached in case—"

"In case this goes nowhere."

We sat there in silence for a moment—long enough for me to kick myself for my obvious talent for killing a mood. A moment ago we were all over each other. There had to be a way to bring that back.

Feeling inspired, I slipped my foot out of my shoe. I'd read about frisky feet happening below tables. The booth would provide some cover. I raised my foot with enough enthusiasm that when my little toe connected with the leg of the booth I swore. "Fuck. Fuck. Fuck."

"Are you okay?" He leaned toward me in concern.

I shook my foot beneath the table and pressed my lips together as I pondered if I'd broken it. "Yeah, I just smacked my foot."

He gave me that look of his, the one that said he was intrigued and confused at the same time. "Do you want me to look at it?"

"No," I said quickly and slid it back into my shoe. No way was I telling him what I'd just done. I didn't want to amuse him; I wanted that hungry fire back in his eyes. "I'm fine. Forget it."

Thankfully our sandwiches arrived.

I dug right into mine. After not eating much the last couple of days, the meal was heavenly. Only when I realized he was watching me did I rethink how quickly I had scarfed down my lunch. Habit. Mostly I ate at my desk—time was money.

He hadn't touched his, and I was done. One corner of his mouth curled in a hint of a smile. "Would you like mine as well?"

"Don't be an ass," I tossed back, even though I was still hungry. I wasn't big on exercise, but I also wasn't big on sweets or carbs. Having Ava kept me active. I guessed the women he normally took out ordered salads and then picked at them.

It's called pre-eating, buddy. Plenty of women I knew did it when they first met a man, but I'd never bought into why. Were women not supposed to be human? Not eat? Not fart? Hide that they also had bodily functions until . . . when? On which glorious anniversary was it acceptable for a woman to finally admit she wanted a whole damn sandwich?

"Tell me about Ava," he said, his question taking me by surprise and pulling me down off my mental soapbox.

"She's my world," I said honestly and without hesitation. "Her mother never made it out of the hospital after having her. While she definitely wasn't in my plan, I can't imagine my life without her now."

"So she's adopted."

"Yes."

"Does she know?"

"Yes. Brenda and I were housemates in college and good friends. I feel that it's important for Ava to know she was loved." I glanced away, getting lost for a moment in the memories. "I was there when Ava was born. Brenda was scared—of motherhood and all that came with it— but she was happy about it too. She died so suddenly. The doctors said the cause was complications from an infection. But to me that was their way of saying they didn't understand it any more than I did."

"I'm sorry to hear that."

Oh, look, there goes the last bit of sparkle from his eyes. What the hell am I doing? He lost a wife and child, and I have to work death into the first real conversation we have.

"And her biological father?" he asked.

"Not interested in the responsibility."

Sebastian's expression darkened. "I don't get how anyone could see a child that way."

I shrugged. "Me either. I heard he got married soon afterward, though, so he probably didn't want to explain Ava. In the end it worked out for the best, I guess. She's fully, legally mine. My name is the only one on her birth certificate."

Sebastian gave me another long look, then took a bite of his sandwich. It gave me a moment to simply watch him. Nothing about his mannerisms implied that he felt out of place, but he didn't look like a man who normally ate at restaurants where you could pay with a credit card at your table on a device you could also play games on.

I glanced around and caught several men and women watching him. Did they know who he was? "How was your weekend?" I asked, because I was more comfortable when he was talking than when I was.

The smile returned to his eyes. "Good. My whole family—my three brothers and my parents—flew down to scope out a school my youngest brother, Gian, has been accepted to. What you said about Ava is something my family understands. Technically, Gian is my cousin, but his mother wasn't stable and asked my mother to take him in. The way he came to us has left him with . . . concerns that we might one day not be there for him as well. This past weekend we wanted to show him that that day will never come."

"That sounds like an amazing family."

"No family is perfect, but I wouldn't trade mine."

"What is your mother like?" I wanted to know everything.

"She's a traditional Italian mother with wooden-spoon ninja skills when necessary."

I laughed.

"We fear her wrath, but in a good way. My father follows the 'happy wife, happy life' philosophy. We moved to the US when Gian was still very young, because she thought we would have better opportunities. My family had one store back in Italy, or 'the old country,' as my father calls it. We've come a long way."

"Romano Superstores."

He smiled. "You've heard of us."

"There's a local buzz about you coming to the area—I heard it's up for public vote."

He leaned closer. "What do *you* think of us coming in?"

I wished I were the type of person who could lie. "I don't know enough about the details yet to have an opinion one way or another."

"That's a safe answer." One eyebrow arched. "I can see someone like you voting against the proposal. I bet you don't like change."

I swallowed hard. "You have no idea what I do or don't like—yet."

A grin spread across his face. His eyes lit with challenge—and heat.

The waitress broke in to remind us that we could pay through the device on the table, or she could bring us a check. I wasn't ready for lunch to end, but I reached for my credit card.

Sebastian was faster. "I've got this. I asked you."

"I just don't want you to think . . ."

He paid the bill and stood. *No, I don't want lunch to end.*

Since stomping my feet and announcing that would have been awkward, I let him guide me back to the parking lot. Standing between our cars, I practically hummed with sexual anticipation. *This is happening. It's really happening.*

Will he ask me to go with him or just pull me back into his arms, whisk me into his car and off to somewhere private? I've made no secret about what I want. Hell, I sent him erotic dice.

I've never had hotel sex.

Right now I'd take back-seat sex.

I should tell Teri to cancel my afternoon appointments.

Shit, why didn't I put condoms in my purse?

I swayed closer to him. He took both of my hands in his.

Okay . . .

"The next few days will be busy for me."

Wait? What? Had I imagined the sizzle? He was frowning at me again, the way he had the first night I'd met him.

I groaned. I had put that look there. It wasn't really shocking considering my choice of topics. Death. Death. Death. Why couldn't I stop talking about it? *Your wife. My friend. Oh, for a real turn-on, let me remind you I don't want you around my kid.*

My hands tightened on his. He couldn't leave if I didn't actually let go of him, right? A memory of the first time we'd met and I hugged him out of gratitude came back to me. Did I really want to relive the feeling of being pried off him? I released his hands. "Me too. I'm swamped after missing so much time last week."

He leaned down until his mouth hovered above mine. Honestly, it made me want to slug him. *What does a woman have to do around here to get a little action? You're making me crazy.*

"How about this weekend?" he murmured.

"I have Ava." My automatic response—mostly because I couldn't think straight with him standing so close. Wait, did his eyes just spark with interest at my refusal?

Maybe, just maybe, this would go better if I didn't rush it.

I counted to ten and pretended that having his lips close enough that I could flick my tongue across them was not affecting me.

"I'm a patient man when it comes to something I want," he said in a voice that definitely belonged in my bedroom. I'd never thought talking dirty was much of a turn-on, but I was pretty sure I could masturbate to him reading a dictionary. "And I want to see you again."

I swallowed hard. I was tempted to cave right then and announce I'd find a babysitter, but what had Erica warned me not to do? *Bore him into finding someone else?* That was how she'd convinced me to pursue him, but the look in his eyes made me think Erica might have gotten it wrong. People did best when they played to their strengths. I wasn't a very good seductress, but if playing hard to get turned him on—hell, I was the queen of saying no. "Then you'll find a way to make it happen," I said and stepped back. "I really need to get back to the office. Thanks for lunch."

I turned, opened the door of my car, and slid in. *Breathe.* I waved at him as if we'd met for a business lunch. I didn't know what to make of the smile he shot me. It made my heart race, though. Maybe I wasn't so bad at this flirting thing after all. I tried to give him a similarly enigmatic smile. A series of beeps returned my attention to the parking lot and the fact that I was about to back up into another car.

I didn't look back at him again until I was just about to pull out into traffic. He hadn't moved from his spot, watching me go. If I could have pulled it off without him knowing, I would have loved to have taken a photo of him like that.

When Erica asked me how we ended our date, I didn't want to muddy my retelling of it. I wanted to say—Oh, yeah, I left him wanting more.

And a photo of him like that would have been glorious proof. *See that beefcake of a man? I'm the one he's looking at that way. And pointing.*

Wait, why is he pointing?

I looked forward again and realized another car was cutting in front of me. A young woman. Jerk. Couldn't she see that I was having a moment?

When our eyes met, she flipped me off.

Me—a person who is known for being a considerate and careful driver.

I threw my hands up in the air.

She peeled out onto the road.

I glanced back at Sebastian. Come on, lady, tell me you would be in a rush to drive away from that.

Sebastian was still watching me. He had his arms folded across his chest, and he looked angry. Angry?

Because I'd let that woman go first?

No. That couldn't be it.

I waved again. He didn't wave back.

With a shake of my head, I drove off.

CHAPTER NINETEEN

SEBASTIAN

I had never come so close to pulling someone out of a car and demanding they not drive. Once again, Heather had revved my engines, made me smile, and left me in a tangled mess.

The rational side of me knew she was probably a safe driver. She didn't come across as someone who would speed needlessly, and she hadn't ordered so much as a glass of wine with lunch. Still, my heart was pounding painfully in my chest.

One's entire life could be changed forever with one misstep.

The official report of Therese's accident said the fault was an impatient driver who had run a red light—an act that had ended his life as well. No way she could have avoided him.

That accident was completely unrelated to Heather almost backing into a passing car or waving at me while pulling out onto the road.

My gut was clenching, though, and I was fighting a demon I thought I had beaten. What the fuck? Why was it rearing its ugly head again?

Heather.

Did I really want to go back to caring about someone if this was how it felt? I got into my car and headed to my meeting with the son of the owner of Bhatt Markets. The purpose of the meeting was still a toss-up. He'd asked me to meet him away from his family's office, and I'd agreed only because I was already going to be in the area anyway.

Did he intend to threaten me? Beg me to reconsider? Neither would sway me. Emotion had no place in business.

"Full disclosure, I ditched my underwear in the trash." I smiled as I remembered how Heather had blurted that particular gem out. How was a man supposed to concentrate on anything else after hearing that?

God, how long had it been since anyone had left me smiling—wishing we'd had more time together?

Heather had made what she wanted clear, but although the idea of spending an afternoon driving her wild was deliciously tempting, I didn't want to fuck her—not *just* fuck her. I tapped the breast pocket of my suit coat, rattling her dice.

Full of bold promises, yet somehow innocent at the same time.

Like Heather.

I smiled again.

She'd turned me down, and I'd liked it. Therese had loved me, but had I made her happy? I'd never know. I couldn't go back and change the man I'd been for her, but I didn't want to be that man again.

Was I capable of better? I wanted to think so.

The night Ava had been sick, Heather had said, "I'm a good mother. I don't have to prove myself to you. I don't require your approval. If you're looking for someone who will tiptoe around your moods, that's not me."

Good. I wanted to know when I crossed a line.

But did Heather need a man like me in her life? I wasn't asking myself if I was good enough for her. My ego was too robust for such a question.

There was no denying, though, that we were very different people. Was a traditional man with relationship PTSD a good fit for a modern woman with a child?

A child.

Fuck.

Heather had been right to not give the stuffed baby wolves to Ava. I had no business getting involved in that child's life until—I corrected myself—*unless* things worked out with Heather.

"I want to see you again," I'd said.

"Then you'll find a way to make it happen."

Yes, I will.

CHAPTER TWENTY

Judy

It wasn't like Alethea to avoid her.

Since texting her hadn't gained Judy more than evasive responses, Judy had executed escape plan 19—playdate bait and switch. She'd asked her mother if she could go over to her friend Grace's house after school, receiving an easy yes since it was something she'd done many times in the past.

Her mother didn't need to know she and Grace weren't friends anymore.

Friends don't gloat that their family tree came out better than yours.

Friends don't laugh along with everyone else when you cry at school.

Judy told her driver she saw Grace in her backyard. With a quick promise that she'd text him when she wanted to go home, she took off down Grace's driveway, then between the houses, and hid in the bushes. Only then did she text Win to meet her. He lived a few houses down from Grace, and although they'd been friends for years, Judy wasn't supposed to play with him, since he'd been caught shoplifting a few months earlier.

He was also not supposed to leave his house because he'd punched a boy who happened to be the son of someone his father worked with. He'd only done it to stop a boy from calling Judy a crybaby at recess.

Unlike Grace, he was a good friend.

Sure, he got into fights at school, but if his parents hadn't wanted their son to constantly get into scraps at school, they shouldn't have named him Winston. He'd been Winnie the Pooh to the school bullies ever since preschool, and that taught a person to stand up for themselves.

His mother had no desire to control him. She worked out, went shopping, and worked out again. As far as Judy could tell, that was all she did.

Win thought she might also be dating her personal trainer.

Disgusting.

His father traveled for work all the time, but Win thought that was a good thing.

"All clear," Win said from the driveway.

Judy stepped out. "I ordered an Uber. He should be here any minute."

"Hey, Grace is looking at us through the window. Should I flip her off?"

Judy turned and frowned at her ex-friend. "No, don't waste the energy. Come on, let's get out of here."

Win jogged down the driveway beside Judy to keep up. "Aren't you worried she'll out us?"

Without glancing back, Judy said, "She won't. I already told her not to mess with me again."

"Didn't she apologize?"

"She did."

"But you're still mad?"

Judy spun on him. "She laughed—*laughed* when I was crying. I'm not mad. I'm done with her."

"Then why did we meet in her yard?"

"So she could see how done I still am."

Win whistled. "I'm glad I'm not a girl. Brian and I are already friends again, and I punched him."

"Brian? He laughed at me too."

"But he got punched for it, so it's done."

Shaking her head, Judy checked her phone. "My ride canceled. Now what do we do?"

Win pointed at the car that was pulling up beside them. "Isn't that your father's bodyguard?"

Marc Stone. Judy's shoulders slumped. "He owns a whole security company, but yes, he works for my father."

The passenger-side door opened. Dark suit. Dark glasses. Built like a football player. Marc could intimidate simply with his presence, but Judy had grown up with him in the background. "Hi, Marc," Judy said in resignation.

He removed his glasses, pocketed them, and folded his arms across his chest. "We've talked about this, Judy."

Judy rolled her eyes and sighed. "Before you pat yourself on the back for finding me, I was on my way to your office."

"Is that the tone I use when I speak to you?" Marc asked in his quiet, firm way.

"No," Judy said in a much more respectful tone. Marc had always been kind to her, but having him around was like having another parent in the mix. "Sorry."

"Good to see you, Win," Marc said.

"You too, sir," Win replied. Judy was pretty sure Marc was Win's fantasy father. He looked a person in the eye when he spoke to them, seemed genuinely interested when they spoke, and didn't take crap from anyone.

"I thought you were grounded at home."

"I am, but . . ." Win nodded toward Judy.

Marc's gaze returned to Judy. "If you wanted to go to my office, why didn't you simply ask to?"

Judy looked away. "I wanted to see Aunt Alethea—alone."

"Why?" Marc pushed off the car and walked to just in front of Judy, crouching so their eyes were level. "You can talk to me, Judy."

When Judy didn't answer, Win said, "You're going to make her cry again."

"Again?" Marc sounded concerned this time. "What's going on?"

Feeling cornered, Judy said, "Forget it. It doesn't matter. Win, thanks for trying. Marc, I'm ready to go back to prison."

"Prison? You mean home?"

"Same thing."

"Really?" Marc straightened and cocked an eyebrow. "I'm sure there are a lot of free people who would love to switch places with you."

"Let them," Judy snapped. "Then maybe I could finally do what I want to."

"What do you want to do?" Marc asked.

Judy blinked back tears. "You wouldn't understand."

"Told you," Win said as he gave Judy's back an awkward pat.

"I definitely won't understand if you don't explain it to me."

"I want to see Alethea," Judy said firmly. "I know she knows something. Why won't she tell me?"

"What? Ask *me*. I might know the answer."

"No, I asked her not to tell anyone."

"I'm her husband. She tells me everything."

Judy would bet she didn't. Like a magician, Alethea lived among smoke and mirrors. "Did she tell you she's pregnant?" Judy regretted asking when she saw Marc's face go white.

"Pregnant?" Then he smiled and slapped his thigh. "That explains a lot."

"You're not mad?" Adult relationships still often baffled Judy.

"I love Alethea and all her layers. No, I'm not mad." His grin grew as he spoke. "I'm going to be a father. A father." He shook his head as if still trying to wrap his head around the wonder of it.

Marc would be an amazing dad. He was strong and brave, and, like Judy's father, he had a softer side to him that had made him part of so many of her memories, like teaching her how to ride a bike without training wheels. Her mother's hovering had made Judy nervous, and Judy hadn't wanted to fall in front of her father. Marc had shown her how to take the wheels off herself. He'd picked her up each time she'd fallen. When she'd skinned her knee and had been just about to give up, he'd said, "You know what fear is? It's God's way of saying try harder." That and a Band-Aid had been enough to get Judy right back on her bike. She'd ridden her bike with confidence after that day. As much as it could be annoying that Marc was always in the background, it was also reassuring. "What did you want to see Alethea about?"

"I need help with a project for school." It was the truth, just not the whole truth.

Marc took out his phone and sent a text off, smiling as he did, then returned his attention to Judy. "Hang on." His phone binged with a message. He read it, and another huge grin spread across his face. "You're right; she's pregnant. I really am going to be a father."

Win lowered his voice and asked Judy, "So do you want to try again tomorrow?"

"No. I'll find another way." Judy watched Marc reduce to a giddy mess. He stepped away, but his happy exclamations carried.

"Do you think your parents were that happy when they found out about you?" Win asked in a subdued voice. "I don't think mine were."

Judy put an arm around his shoulders. Her problem could wait. "I'm sorry, Win."

"My dad said if I screw up one more time, he's sending me to a boarding school in Europe."

Turning him toward her, Judy said, "Is that why you stole the watch?"

Win shrugged. After a moment, he said, "I'm sorry you got a bad grade on your family tree."

129

"I don't care about the grade," Judy said. "I didn't want to hand it in because it wasn't done. I thought I would have something to add to it."

"Judy," Marc said, interrupting, "Alethea wants to talk to you."

Judy took the phone and guessed at what her aunt wanted to hear. "I'm sorry. I shouldn't have said anything to Marc."

"I'm the one who's sorry. I should have told him. I was waiting for the right time, but I'm glad he knows." She let out an audible breath. "Marc said you were coming to see me."

"You found my dad's family, didn't you?" Judy demanded.

"I did."

"I knew it. And?"

"And I don't like what I've discovered so far. My gut tells me they're hiding something, and my gut is never wrong."

"You were supposed to tell me when you found them, and we were supposed to watch them together—to make sure they're okay."

"You're nine, Judy. I know you feel like you're old enough to handle anything we might find, but you're not."

Judy handed the phone back to Marc.

Even though he was still beaming, he did notice she wasn't. "Are you okay, Judy?"

All she'd wanted to do was make her father smile, but all she'd done so far was cry when she'd handed in an eraser-torn-up project, cry again in front of her class, break up with her best friend, get Win in trouble, and spill a secret. Not okay at all.

Judy shook her head, turned, and gave Win a hug. "Don't go away to boarding school."

He hugged her back but didn't promise he wouldn't.

Marc held the back door of his car open. "Come on, Judy. Go home, Win."

Win nodded and headed back toward his house.

As they pulled away from the curb, Judy said, "Do you have to tell my mother about this?"

"It's my responsibility to keep you safe, Judy. You're too young to understand that the world is a dangerous place."

"Being nine sucks." Judy slumped in the back seat.

Marc glanced back at her through the rearview mirror. "That bad?"

"Worse."

"Want to tell me about it?"

After letting out a long sigh, Judy did just that. She told him all about the project, her father's reaction to it, hiring Alethea, crying, Grace's betrayal, Win's situation, and how instead of making things better, she was afraid she'd made them worse. "Now I'm probably grounded too."

"Sounds like a mountain of problems to me."

"It is."

"Do you know how to conquer mountains?"

"No."

"One step at a time. Is there anything you can make better? Like with your friend Grace?"

"She laughed, Marc."

"Everyone makes mistakes. Maybe even you. Could you have handled it differently?"

"I could have punched her. Win says that works better."

Marc coughed. "You know that's not what I meant. Did you tell her she hurt your feelings?"

"I told her she was dead to me. Is that the same thing?"

He made a pained face. "Not really. Why not call her and see if she feels as bad as you do about what happened?"

Judy took out her phone but didn't call Grace. "Marc, why don't you get mad at Alethea when she keeps things from you?"

He sighed. "Everything Alethea does, she does out of love. But you're asking because you're angry with her, aren't you?"

"I'm not too young to hear whatever she found, Marc. It's not fair that she won't tell me."

"Do you believe she loves you?"

"Yes."

"And that she loves your family?"

"Yes," Judy said with less patience.

"Then trust her, Judy. You won't be nine forever. Let her protect you while you are."

How could she argue with that? "Thanks, Marc." Judy glanced down at her phone. "I don't hate Grace, but she hurt me."

"Tell her all that."

"I don't know if I can trust her."

"Then proceed with caution."

Judy nodded. "What about Win? I don't want him to go away to school."

Marc drove without speaking for a few minutes, then he said, "Judy, all you can do is be a friend to him. That starts with not encouraging him to sneak out of his house to be with you."

"Yeah."

"You can't do anything about his situation with his parents, but I promise you—he won't be nine forever either. Neither will you. Before you know it, you'll both be all grown up and driving your own children crazy."

"No way," Judy said with a laugh. "Me and Win? Never."

Marc frowned back at her. "I didn't mean together. Don't even think about boys. You are not allowed to date until you're at least thirty."

That was fine with her. Most boys were annoying anyway. Judy looked down at her phone again. *I do miss Grace. I'm ready to "proceed with caution."* Before she made the call, though, Judy said, "You're going to be a great dad, Marc."

"I hope so," he said, his attention back to the road. "I sure hope so."

CHAPTER TWENTY-ONE

SEBASTIAN

A week later I called for a morning meeting with Mauricio and Christof. They sat at the table in our boardroom as I paced back and forth in front of it.

"What's on your mind?" Christof asked with concern.

"Wait, I know this one. She lives in Durham and her name rhymes with . . . weather." Mauricio leaned back in his chair, looking confident and smug.

I stopped pacing and frowned. "This isn't about her."

Mauricio slid a twenty-dollar bill across the table to Christof and shot me a sheepish grin. "Hey, it was a good guess."

Christof accepted the money with an equally guilty smile. "I still think it might be, but since he said it wasn't, I'll take this."

"Are we done?" I snapped.

Mauricio leaned closer to Christof. "Double or nothing he cracks and confesses the truth before this meeting is over."

"Deal," Christof said, then slapped a hand down on the table. "How can we help you, Sebastian?"

I inhaled a deep, calming breath. Brothers were a double-edged sword when it came to being helpful. "I've hit a snag with Bhatt Markets."

The smiles fell away. Mauricio straightened in his chair. "What kind of snag? Everyone I've spoken to thinks we'll win the votes we need.

Our lawyers don't see a problem with getting the permits. Christof ran a scenario of how long it should take to shut Bhatt down. Less than a year. Am I right, Christof?"

"That's how I see it going. Their liquid cash is low. They've sold off enough of their private investments to make them ripe for bankruptcy," Christof interjected. "The more I looked into it, the more impressed I became with your ability to sniff out an easy kill, Sebastian."

"I met with Rakesh Bhatt."

Mauricio shrugged.

"Does he have cash stashed we've overlooked?" Christof asked.

I shook my head and pocketed my hands. "No, they're in an even worse situation than I knew about. Their father is battling cancer and losing."

"Hey, maybe we'll get a quick sale instead. Even better," Mauricio said.

His words cut through me even though I'd said something similar countless times over the past few years. Weakness was something I'd had no patience for, had shown no mercy toward—but this time I was asking myself why. "Normally I would agree, but when I was talking to him I thought . . . what would I do if Dad were sick? How much would I be willing to give up to get him the best care?"

"Are you thinking we should lowball them now?" Christof asked.

I've taught them well—too well.

"No, I'm—I don't think—Mauricio, you need to take the lead on this one. Or we should pull out. I don't want this blood on my hands."

"Wait. What?" Mauricio stood and walked over to me. "Did you just suggest that we not acquire a store chain because you feel *bad* about doing it?"

"We've already invested a significant amount of cash into making it happen," Christof warned as he also joined me at the head of the table.

I rubbed a hand over my forehead. "I realize that, Christof. We could recoup some from taxes if we donate the land to the town."

Looking genuinely concerned, Mauricio leaned in. Normally, I would have been offended that he was checking my breath for alcohol, but I didn't sound like myself. "So which outcome are you looking for today? That I agree to take over or that we walk away from this?"

"I don't fucking know," I growled. "All I know is I haven't been able to sleep since I met with Rakesh Bhatt. I went into the meeting with no expectation of caring what he said. I did, though. I care that his family story sounds so much like ours. His family came from India. His parents' goal was to make a better life for their children, and they achieved that. Now the father is ill, and the children are trying to save him as well as his legacy. I don't want to be the man who made neither possible for them."

"But you're okay if I am?" Mauricio challenged.

"Stop, Mauricio," Christof said firmly. "That's not what he's saying."

I turned and slammed a hand on the wall behind me. "Dad had one store, and he was happy. We dominate in the region, have more money than we could spend in our lifetimes, and I'm fucking miserable."

Mauricio looked from me to Christof and back. "I'm pretty happy with how things are going, but I hear you. You haven't taken a vacation in years. It's time."

Christof put a hand on my shoulder. "Mauricio's right, Sebastian. You've made the Romano name your first priority for too long. That's all this is—burnout. You may feel like our welfare falls on your shoulders alone, but we're all in this together."

I laid my hand on his. "You both covered for me when I couldn't . . . when . . . when I . . ."

"You would have done the same for us. This is different. This is you wanting to find something that brings joy back into your life. It's a good sign—and well past time." He nodded and dropped his hand.

"Into your life . . . into your bed . . . whatever." Mauricio winked. "Remember, I'm always here with advice if you need it."

"Don't joke about her that way." I tensed. "Besides, I told you—this isn't about Heather. I haven't even spoken to her since our lunch."

"A week ago?" Mauricio shuddered. "You're playing it too cool—like cold, even."

Cold. I ran my hand through my hair. I'd had every intention of calling her. Even though she'd said she couldn't see me over the weekend that had just passed, I had put some serious thought into how to woo a yes out of her.

Flowers.

Cards.

Phone calls that lasted into the night.

I'd changed my mind, though, after I'd met with Rakesh. He'd laid out his situation and his torment for me, humbling himself for the sake of his family, and it had left me cold at first.

Cold—that was what I had become.

His anger hadn't surprised me. Everyone is angry when they discover they can't stop us from taking over. Every ugly thing he said to me had been said a hundred times before.

At the end of our conversation, he'd looked like a man who had sacrificed himself for what he considered the greater good—and still lost. Angry. Confused. Desperate.

Disgusted.

For a moment I saw myself through his eyes, and I didn't like the view. What kind of man could listen to a story like the one he'd told and be completely unmoved by it?

And what business did such a man have courting a woman like Heather? What did I think she was going to do—wave a wand and transform me into the person I'd once been?

He was dead and gone.

In his place was a man who enjoyed nothing, cared about no one beyond his immediate family, and destroyed the lives of others without remorse.

Was this shell of a man really what Heather and her child needed?

There was a good chance that rather than her buoying me up, I might drag her down. What if, while I was testing if I could feel anything for her, she fell for me?

And I felt no more sympathy for her than I'd felt for Rakesh.

It was an unacceptable possibility.

One that had kept me awake several nights in a row. She deserved better than that.

The financial empire I'd built for my family felt like the only thing I'd done right. And now I was jeopardizing that because . . . why? Did I think pulling out of one deal would redefine who I was?

I'd been partially honest with my brothers about why I didn't want to move forward with the Bhatt Market takeover. They believed it meant I didn't want to feel guilty, but the truth was I was more afraid of feeling nothing.

And of what that would say about me.

None of this was anything I could share with my brothers without causing them to worry about me. So I said, "I *am* tired. A vacation sounds like exactly what I need." A glance at the clock said this topic had dragged on long enough. "On that note, I'm going to answer some emails and plan my escape."

After reassuring me that they were capable of moving forward without me, we headed toward the door. Behind me, Christof said, "Cough up another twenty, Mauricio. He admitted to nothing."

"Fine," Mauricio said, "but a hundred bucks says he marries her."

I walked away as if I hadn't heard them.

My only hope was that Mauricio's business instincts were better than his choice of bets. There was no reason for me to see Heather again.

CHAPTER TWENTY-TWO

HEATHER

I was soaking up some sun on a bench in our neighborhood's playground, watching Ava go down the slide for the hundredth or so time. Her face lit up when Charlotte and her brothers bounded onto the sandy area.

Erica sat down beside me. "So did you hear from him?"

I sighed. "Could you stop asking that every time you see me? If he called me, you'd be the first one I'd tell."

"Sorry. After the way you described your date, I thought for sure he was interested."

"Me too. Maybe I was too aggressive. I mean, I sent him sex dice and told him I was going commando on our date."

"No, Bob says neither would turn a guy off."

My eyes flew to hers in horror. "You told him?"

She shrugged. "He's my best friend."

I groaned. "I'm never going to be able to look him in the eye again."

She waved a hand in dismissal. "Bob doesn't care. I did ask him for his opinion, though, and he thinks you should call Sebastian. Maybe something happened to him. Wouldn't you feel bad if he was in the hospital or something?"

I hadn't thought of that. "Wouldn't we have heard about it?"

"Bob knows everyone, and he said the day after the vote came in positive, two Romanos met with the town administrator, but he wasn't one of them. Sebastian came to take care of you when you were sick. I don't think it's unreasonable for you to offer to do the same if he's under the weather."

"I'm not calling him."

"Because you're playing hard to get."

"I'm not playing at all."

"And how is that working out for you?"

I spun toward her. "He's not sick, Erica. He's just not interested. And I don't care either way."

Eyes wide, she raised her hands in surrender. "Then there's no need to chew my head off, is there?"

I rolled my eyes skyward. She was right. "Okay, I liked him. Of course I wish he'd called. But I'm not going to chase him."

"I wouldn't describe a phone call to make sure he's not in a coma as *chasing*."

Relenting a little, I checked the time on my phone. "It's only six o'clock. He's probably still at work. I don't want to bother him."

She took the phone from me and scrolled for his number, then hit the phone icon. "Bother him."

"Hey—don't—you can't—" The phone was already ringing. Even if I hung up, he'd still see a missed call from me.

"Hello?" he answered in a groggy voice.

Oh my God, maybe he was sick. "It's Heather. Just calling to see if you're okay."

"Heather." He repeated my name slowly. "Yeah. Sorry, I was sleeping."

"Sleeping? Are you sick?"

"No, I'm in Italy."

"He's in Italy," I mouthed to Erica. "Not sick. Told you." I cleared my throat. "I'll let you get back to sleep."

"Wait," he said.

My heart jumped in my chest. "Yes?"

139

"I meant to call you, but—"

"Don't worry about it. I'm not." No way I was letting that conversation happen. I was perfectly okay with sparing myself the fun of listening to him make up excuses.

"You're upset. I can understand that without an explanation, breaking things off might have—"

"There was nothing to break off," I said as my pride kicked in. "I said no to you."

"Yes, you did," he agreed far too easily.

I couldn't help it; I had to know. "Why did you ghost me? Because I didn't jump when you asked me to? Well, sorry if I have a life of my own. You might be used to women who fall all over themselves simply because you show up, but I have higher standards than that." I stopped to take a breath.

Erica dragged my hand over and put him on speaker. I slapped at her, but she was too fast. "Don't worry, I'll still watch the kids," she whispered, as if that was why I thought she shouldn't hear his side of the phone call. She leaned toward the phone while facing the playground.

Whatever.

Let her hear this. Maybe then she'll stop asking me about him.

His voice thickened in his next words. "You're hurt. This is what I didn't want to happen. You're an incredible woman, but I have some things I need to work out before I can think about getting serious with anyone."

It's not you; it's me. I hate that line.

"Then isn't it fortunate that I said *no*?"

He chuckled, and I wanted to smack him. "Yes, it is."

"You think this is funny?"

Humor left his voice. "Far from it. I'm laughing because I am so fucked up. A moment ago we were naked and tangled up in my dream. Now I'm on the phone, trying to convince myself I made the right decision, but all I want is you here beside me."

My breath caught in my throat. "Don't do this . . ." *Don't get me thinking there is something where there's nothing.*

"That's what I keep telling myself. You have a child—"

"If Ava has anything to do with your decision not to see me, let me say this up front—there is nothing in my life more important than she is. Nothing. If having her means I don't have sex again until I'm fifty, I'm fine with it."

Erica touched my arm. "You might want to lower your voice."

I looked around. There were only a few other parents in the area, but they were all looking at me. Thankfully none of the children seemed to have heard. In a much lower tone, I said, "I don't need you, Sebastian Romano. So enjoy Italy."

I still shook after ending the call.

For once Erica kept her thoughts to herself.

I stuck my phone back in my purse. Ava was still blissfully swinging next to Charlotte. No matter how chaotic I felt on the inside, nothing else in my life was affected. And that was the way I needed to keep it.

A few minutes passed before I broke down and said, "Go ahead. Tell me what you're thinking."

Erica cleared her throat. "You're sure? Okay, then, you need to chill."

I tipped my head back and looked at her through the corner of my eye. "Too much?"

She pinched the air. "Just a little. I'm not used to seeing you like this. You're usually the calmest person in the room."

Ava ran up for a drink of water. I held my response until she was once again out of earshot. "I'm not used to this side of me either. When I hear his voice, a part of me comes to life and I get . . . giddy? I guess that's the only word for it. I feel this connection to him. It's so real I can't stop myself from getting excited . . . then *whoosh*, it takes a dip like a roller coaster, and suddenly I've had my feet knocked out from beneath me."

She gave me a long look. "You do realize you didn't give him time to say how he felt about Ava. Bob and I went to a counselor when we first got married because we would fight in circles about the same things over and over and over. She said we were talking at each other instead of to each other. I think you're doing that with Sebastian. He's talking. You're talking. But do you have any idea what he's saying?"

I watched Ava move to the sandbox with Charlotte and sighed. "I guess I don't. You're right. I jumped in without giving him a chance. I couldn't hear him because I was so busy defending myself against what I was afraid he would say. I talked at him."

Erica slapped her hands on her knees. "I should do this for a living. It took our counselor weeks to get us to see what we were doing." She snapped her fingers in the air. "Five minutes. One session. Where should I send my bill?"

I smiled. "Well, Mrs. All-Knowing, tell me, what do you think Sebastian was about to say?"

"I have no idea," Erica conceded. "Looks like you'll have to call him back."

I moved my purse to the other side of me. "No way."

"Fine. Text him."

"I'm sure he's asleep again."

"I'm sure he's not. Give me your phone."

"Absolutely not."

"Were you serious about being okay with not having sex until you're fifty?"

My mouth went dry. "No."

"Then give me your damn phone and let me show you how it's done."

I didn't budge.

She arched an eyebrow. "Afraid I'll ruin your otherwise beautiful relationship?"

I tossed my phone at her. "Here."

She placed it on her lap and cracked her knuckles before texting him.

Sorry. When it comes to my daughter, I get defensive.

Nothing.

"See, he's not going to answer. Give me my phone back."

Just then my phone dinged with an incoming message. You're not the one who should apologize. I do have a rule about not dating women with children. It used to be because being around children reminded me too much of what I'd lost. I read the message and moved to take the phone. Erica held it out of my reach.

"He's so broken," she said, putting a hand over her heart. "I totally get what you see in him." She texted: But now?

Sebastian: I'm realizing I'm not the man I was before.

Erica wiggled her eyebrows. "I hope he doesn't mean the elevator no longer goes to the top floor."

"His elevator?"

Erica motioned toward her crotch. "You know—his *elevator*. How disappointing would that be for someone who hasn't had sex in—"

"Mom, I'm hungry," Kevin said, and I went three shades of red.

"Me too," Tyler added.

"We just ate," Erica said.

"I'm growing." Kevin flexed both arms like a bodybuilder.

Tyler mirrored his stance. "Me too."

"I'm doing something important for Heather. Go play. We'll go home in about fifteen minutes, and I'll feed you again, I guess."

Appeased, they trotted over to where Charlotte and Ava were playing.

"They'll never make it fifteen minutes. We'll have to do this fast. Now where was I? Oh yeah, we were hoping all his parts were still functioning."

"You were hoping," I corrected.

She rolled her eyes. "Honey, we don't have time to work through your chronic denial syndrome. I need to think up the perfect answer."

"You could ask him what that has to do with me having a child, because I doubt he's talking about his elevator."

"Good one." She texted: What were you before?

He answered: Kind. Funny. Hopeful.

Erica: Then life dick punched you.

I gasped. "I would never say that."

She shrugged. "If he's afraid of the word *dick*, he's too uptight to be any good in bed anyway. Don't worry. I know what I'm doing."

Sebastian: That's exactly what life did. And I didn't handle it well. When I met you I thought I was ready to care about someone again, but I don't want you to get hurt if I realize I have nothing left to give anyone.

Erica: Why did you bring up that I have a child?

Sebastian: Because she's important. You look so happy together. I don't want to be what changes that.

Erica: Then don't be an asshole.

I nodded. "I would actually say that."

Sebastian: You make it sound so simple.

Erica: It is. Listen, we all have shit to deal with. I'm not perfect. You're not perfect. My daughter is a priority, but let me worry about protecting her. I like you and I do want to have sex before I'm fifty. So step up or step off. Your move.

Erica tossed the phone back to me. "Bam, and that's how it's done."

"How what's done?" I read over her last message and shrank a little in embarrassment. "He's not answering, and I don't blame him. Erica, I had already tried being obvious. Remember?"

She held up her hand and studied her nails. "He'll be back tomorrow."

"I can't believe I let you text him." I shook my head, read all the messages over again, and shook it again. "You're right, though. It's not like there was anything to lose."

"So should I pick up Ava from school tomorrow? How long does first-time sex take? God, it's sad I don't remember."

"Sure," I said with heavy sarcasm. "Pick Ava up because he's scrambling to find a way to get back here so he can whisk me off to his bed."

Erica gave me a look. "Beds are so overrated. Don't be afraid to get a little creative." She motioned toward my lap. "And I don't know what's going on down there, but you might want to consider trimming or waxing or something."

"Like into a little heart?" I was joking.

"Start simple," she said seriously. "Work your way up to shapes."

I flexed my shoulders. "Just because there haven't been hikers in a while doesn't mean I've let the path become overgrown."

Erica hooted with laughter.

I joined in briefly, then sobered. "Okay, answer me this one. If you think you've got him hot and bothered enough to fly back—why didn't he even answer?"

"Because," she said, then lowered her voice, "his next move will have nothing to do with talking."

CHAPTER TWENTY-THREE

Heather

Before work the next morning, I changed my outfit twice. My first choice had been the most practical: skirt and blouse. No different than how I dressed any other day. I'd pulled my hair back in a bun, applied light makeup, and reminded myself that my life was already amazing.

My second outfit was a little black dress I intended to mostly conceal with a conservative jacket. If Sebastian showed up that day, I could slip the jacket off and say, "Oh, this old thing? I just threw it on because it was in the closet." It didn't match with my hair pulled back, so I released my curls and shook them out. I was in the middle of applying what the tutorial video described as a smoky eye when Ava walked into my bathroom and asked if it was dress-up day at my job.

"No, honey, I'm trying out a new look. What do you think?" I applied both fake eyelashes, then turned to her. "Do you love it?"

She made a face. "You don't look like you."

That was the point. "It's still me, just me with makeup."

Her nose wrinkled, and she shot a thumbs-down at me. Not exactly a confidence builder. I took a long look at myself in the mirror and decided she was right—that wasn't me. A few swipes of makeup remover and I was ready to start again.

Ava joined me at the mirror. "Can I do your makeup?"

I glanced at my phone for the time. "Oh, honey, we have to get you off to preschool and me to the office."

"Please." Those damn blue eyes of hers. When she turned them on me in a certain way, I couldn't help but melt.

"Let me change first," I said. The dress wasn't me either. I donned my usual attire again, but this time I impulsively layered in a pair of lavender lace panties and a matching bra. Not for Sebastian, I assured myself. For me. Sexy came from within, or so the articles I'd read myself to sleep with the night before said.

Man or no man, from now on I'm going to always "kick it" beneath my work clothes.

Ava was still in my bathroom when I returned. She'd organized my makeup and lowered the toilet seat cover. "Please sit down," she said.

I sat.

She looked me over. "Welcome to Ava's Salon. Do you want half of your face done or the whole thing? I'm the owner."

"Hello, Ava," I said as if speaking to an actual salon owner. "My name is Heather. What is the difference between a full or half?"

"One eye or two."

"Oh. Then the whole face, please. I need to match."

She nodded. "Close your eyes."

I did. This wasn't our first makeup session. Ava loved to apply it—to me, to herself, to her dolls. We'd all been customers at her salon before.

"All done. That's one million dollars."

I laughed and opened my eyes. "Wow, that's quite a price hike."

"I used special eye shadow. With glitter. Glitter is expensive."

Yes, that was what I'd told her many times when she'd poured it too generously on an art project. She handed me a mirror. My eyes had definitely acquired a sparkle—so had parts of my cheek. I tried to wipe some of it away, but the glitter only seemed to multiply and spread onto my hands. *Looks like one more face wash for the road.* I checked the time. We were still okay.

"I love it." I handed her an imaginary stack of bills. "One million is a bargain. Thank you." I stood and began to wet a washcloth.

Her bottom lip jutted out, and her hands went to her hips. "You can't wash it off."

"Oh, Ava, I can't go to work like this."

"Yes, you can. You're the boss." Those big eyes again. Dammit.

I almost said I wasn't worried about my clients when I stopped myself. Hang on one dang minute. If I weren't secretly hoping to see Sebastian that day, what would I have done?

I would have kept the damn glitter on and laughed with Teri about it.

The glitter stays.

I crouched down to her height. "Just this one time. Now let's get going or we'll have to eat in the car again."

"I like eating in the car," Ava said.

"I know, but I'm a better parent than that," I joked, but the humor was lost on Ava. Single parenting had its ups and downs. On one hand I didn't have to justify any of my decisions to anyone. On the other hand, there was no one there to share the wonder of the early years with. One day, probably before I was ready for it, Ava would be applying her own makeup and thinking more about her friends than about what I looked like.

One day the bathroom salon would close.

"Don't forget Erica is picking you up today. You get to have dinner with her tonight."

"Yay!" Ava did a little dance. "Can I sleep over?"

"No, honey, it's a school night." *And I'll probably be eating dinner right beside you at Erica's.* I blushed when I remembered Erica's question about how long first-time sex took. Honestly, I couldn't remember either.

Thirty minutes?

Fifteen?

If he even shows up.

I checked my phone. No message.

He's not coming. I'm torturing myself over nothing.

I should have just said yes to Levi.

No, the only thing worse than no sex was mediocre sex.

"Mom, can I take these to school? We have to bring one hundred things, remember? It says one hundred on the box." My delightful little daughter was waving the gift Erica had brought me the day after my date with Sebastian.

I snatched the box of condoms from Ava. I'd stashed them under the sink next to the smaller pack I'd bought myself, completely not thinking that Ava kept her extra salon supplies down there. Okay, breathe. "Yes, that does say one hundred, but Mommy needs these for . . . work." I walked to the kitchen and stuffed the box into my oversize purse.

That bottom lip stuck out again. "Then can you send Cheerios? I need them."

"Of course." I poured a bunch of Cheerios into a plastic baggy, checked the time, saw we were running late, and poured more. God, I hoped it was a hundred. As I did it, I remembered doing something similar earlier in the year. "Are you sure you need these? I thought we did this in February."

Ava shrugged.

I felt horrible that I didn't know. I went through her backpack and looked over my stack of papers from the teacher. Nothing. "I don't have a note saying you need a hundred things."

Ava's eyes widened. Her hands splayed at her sides. "We learned to write one hundred yesterday."

"Okay."

"And we counted to one hundred."

"Gotcha. Take the Cheerios. If you don't need them, use them for snack." There probably was no note. Ava just liked to count to one hundred.

My cheeks warmed. But there would have been a note had she made it out of the house with her first choice.

That would have been bad.

Ava looked up at me with sad eyes. "Are you mad?"

"No, honey. Come on. I have an apple, yogurt, and a water for you. We're eating in the car."

"Your face is red."

"I just don't like being late. Let's go. Grab Wolfie."

She returned with him and we were out the door.

Her with Cheerios she probably didn't need and me with a lifetime supply of condoms I definitely wouldn't.

A short time later, as I walked past my secretary's desk, she joked, "Hot date?"

I tripped and came to a spinning halt. "What?"

She pointed toward my face. "You're all glittered up."

I took a calming breath. She didn't know anything about the conversation I'd had with Sebastian the day before. I laughed with relief. "Ava."

"I figured. It looks cool, especially with your hair down."

"Thanks." Forcing myself into a lighter mood I struck a pose. "You should see what's underneath."

Teri gave me a look, then turned away.

I dropped the pose. I hadn't meant that the way it had sounded. "Underwear. Just nice underwear."

Teri looked up from her computer. We had another one of those awkward moments where I felt like I should apologize but was pretty sure I'd cross a whole different line while doing it. I hurried into my office before she asked why my purse was bulging.

We hadn't had embarrassing conversations before Sebastian.

After an initial period of disappointment when he didn't call, I hoped I would soon go back to normal. Several of my clients were on edge because of the announcement that Romano Superstores had been approved for construction.

I sat down at my desk, dropped my purse into the deep drawer on the side of it, and turned on my computer. One hour became two as I lost myself in work.

"Knock, knock," Teri said from the door. "There's someone here to see you. Do you have a minute?"

"Sure." I smoothed my hands down my skirt and stood. *It's not him. It's not him. Don't get all excited. It's not him.*

The man who filled my doorway was well dressed, clean cut, but no, not Sebastian. I did, however, recognize him. "Mr. Bhatt, come in."

"Call me Rakesh. Thank you for seeing me, Miss Ellis."

"Heather, please." I moved to the front of my desk. "Why don't we sit down?" We each took a seat in front of my desk. I took a moment to appreciate the contrast of his brown skin, dark hair, and light-blue eyes. Truly a handsome man who looked about my age.

So why did I feel nothing?

Where was the zing?

I didn't like what that said about Sebastian, because I didn't want him to be special. All he'd done since I'd met him was insult and disappoint me.

Okay, maybe that wasn't entirely accurate.

He'd taken care of me when I was sick and could kiss me right out of my clothes, but that didn't make him any more suitable for me than any other professional man.

Like this one. I looked him over again.

Nothing.

I did note, though, that he seemed agitated, and I realized he'd said something while I wasn't paying attention. "I'm sorry," I said. "Could you repeat that?"

He braced himself with a hand on either knee. "It wasn't easy to come here."

I didn't gossip, but that didn't mean I was deaf to what others said. If the rumors of his financial situation held any truth, he was probably asking for advice on how to avoid bankruptcy as his company dissolved. I could see how that wouldn't be easy.

But why come to me? Surely he had lawyers and accountants of his own.

I waited.

He continued, "You've been seen in town with Sebastian Romano. Do you know him well?"

Warmth spread up my neck. Depending on if his source mentioned seeing me inside or outside of the restaurant, they would have given him a very different account. "We've recently become acquainted."

Rakesh said, "If I had any other recourse, I wouldn't be here."

"Okay."

"I have people relying on me—my parents, my siblings, my employees. With Romano Superstores getting the okay to build, there is nothing to stop him from putting my entire family out of business."

"I'm so sorry to hear that." I really didn't know what else to say.

"Perhaps you could speak to him, convince him to give us a little more time. I can't fail now, not while my father is so ill. The doctors say he may have only a month left. The last thing he sees before he dies cannot be his legacy being torn down." Tears filled the man's eyes, and he leaned forward, covering his face with his hands. "I'm sorry. I've made peace with a buyout, but not yet. Just not now while my family is losing my father." His intense sorrow showed in his eyes when he looked up.

I fought back my own tears. "I wish I knew Mr. Romano better. If I did, I would take your request to him, but . . ."

"I understand. I shouldn't have come here. My father is a proud man, and I used to be. Funny how quickly pride became unimportant when the doctors told me he was dying. I've tried everything I know, pulled in every favor owed to me. All I want is for them to not start to build until my father passes. I know the fight is lost. I don't have the resources to win against a man like Romano."

"Have you contacted him yourself?"

The man's face tightened. "Yes. Empathy is not his strong suit."

My heart was aching for the man before me and confused by the one I'd hoped to hear from that day. "If I hear from him again, I'll talk to him about your situation. He may not care what I think, but I'd like to believe compassion for a fellow human would have him hold off for a bit on building. It's a business, though, and he has people to answer to as well."

We both rose with a handshake. "Thank you," he said. "Even though coming here changed nothing, I needed to know I had done all I could."

"I understand." I walked him toward the door.

He nodded at Teri and left without saying another word. I wiped a tear from the corner of my eye, then reached for a tissue off her desk. After blowing my nose, I asked, "Is it possible to like someone, hate them, want to sleep with them, and also want to throttle them all at the same time?"

Without batting a lash, Teri picked up her phone, pressed a button, and said, "Erica's on line one in your office."

I nodded and chuckled. "You called her? Good choice."

CHAPTER TWENTY-FOUR

HEATHER

Later that day, I munched on a chicken salad sandwich at my desk. Speaking to Erica always made me feel better. I told her she didn't need to pick Ava up, but she said the kids were looking forward to the playdate, so I told her I'd put in an extra hour at work, then head over to have dinner with them.

She didn't say I was giving up too easily, because we both knew I wasn't. I hadn't received so much as a text from Sebastian.

And that was okay.

I was haunted by what Rakesh Bhatt had said about Sebastian. He lacked empathy? That wasn't my impression of him, but then again, I didn't actually know Sebastian very well.

Being attracted to him, indulging in a few sexual fantasies of what it would be like to be with him . . . some while I was awake . . . some in my dreams . . . didn't make us close. It meant I was a woman in my prime. Maybe the reason he was sent to me was to remind me I wasn't dead from my waist down.

Do I really want a man whose response to hearing a heart-wrenching story of a father dying is to head off to Italy? I feel your pain; pass the pasta.

No. I want a man with more heart than that.

"Knock, knock," Teri said. "Looks like you have another visitor. Do you have time to see him?"

I stood and stretched. "Sure. Who is it?"

"He said his name is Rob Smith?"

"Never heard of him. Send him in."

I met Rob at the door of my office. A young, nervous man, he was dressed in a black suit with a white shirt. We shook hands, and I asked him to come in, but he stayed where he was.

"Miss Ellis, I'm here to take you to Mr. Romano."

I checked to see if Teri had heard the same thing I did. Her eyebrows arched in surprise, and she looked about to back away, but I implored her to stay with the same look Ava used on me. "I'm sorry, what did you say you were here for?"

Rob cleared his throat and squared his shoulders. "I'm Sebastian Romano's driver."

"And?"

"And he sent me to retrieve you."

I laughed, more from nerves than humor. "*Retrieve* me?"

Sweat beaded on his forehead. "I'm sorry. I've never done anything like this before. I thought Mr. Romano called me in to fire me. This is my chance to get back on his good side. I'm supposed to look professional and not tell you where we're going."

"Why would I get in a car with you, someone I don't know, especially since I have no idea where you're taking me?"

He nodded and started patting his pockets. "Hang on. I have a note for you." He pulled one out of his trouser pocket and read it aloud. "Pick up flowers on the way." He grimaced. "Shit. I forgot the flowers."

I exchanged another look with Teri while Rob continued hunting through his pockets.

"He's not going to be happy. This was supposed to be romantic. Hang on. I really do have a note from him somewhere." Rob looked more and more nervous as he searched his pockets for a second time. Eventually he stopped and met my gaze. "I could take a good guess at what it said."

"No, thanks—" I started. I was already confused enough.

"Please do," Teri said, cutting me off. "I think we should hear what Rob believes Mr. Romano wrote in his note."

Teri was enjoying watching the poor young man squirm. He went white, then red.

Rob rubbed his hands together as if warming them and said, "Dear—"

When he hesitated, Teri interjected, "Heather."

He started again, "Dear Heather. It would be my . . . pleasure . . . if you accompanied my driver to an address he's not allowed to share with you because I made him swear he wouldn't, so please don't ask him for it."

This time I did laugh. "And then you were supposed to hand me the flowers?"

"Yes."

Teri put a hand on one hip and said, "A tempting proposal—right up there with 'I have beer in my trunk, want one?'"

"I could totally go for a beer right now," Rob said, then stopped and went bright red again. "But I would never drink and drive."

At a loss for how to respond, I looked across at Teri. "I'm not getting in a car with, no offense, Rob, to go somewhere he won't tell me. How do I even know you were sent by Sebastian?"

"That's a good point," Teri concurred. She wagged a finger at Rob. "You are not allowed to abduct my boss. I love my job."

I smiled. "You do? You love it? Not just saying that?" I really could never tell.

"You're funny," Teri said. "Even when you don't mean to be. I leave here smiling every day. I'd never find another job like this again."

I turned to Rob. "See why you can't abduct me? I'm a great boss."

Rob opened and closed his mouth as if he were struggling for what to say next. "I have to take you with me."

Now it was my turn to put a hand on my hip. "Do you mean he didn't give you a plan B in case I said no?"

Rob shook his head.

"He just assumed I'd hop in any car he sent for me? Oh, that's a little overconfident, wouldn't you say, Teri?" I looked around. "Teri?"

The phone on my desk beeped. I picked it up. Erica. "Although I appreciate Teri looping you in, I don't need your advice on this one. There's no way I'm getting into that car."

Erica went off for the next few minutes without taking a breath—if I wanted to have romance in my life I needed to embrace it when it appeared. She went on to assure me this was an incredibly sexy move on his part.

Still holding the phone to my ear, I said, "I guess I'm going with you, Rob."

"Before you do, though, make damn sure you take a photo of him and send it to me." I took out my cell phone and did just that.

Erica cooed. "Oh, he's so cute and looks so scared. He's not a killer."

"I'm going to text Sebastian."

"No, you're not," Erica said firmly. "Don't suck the fun out of this for you or for him. For once, don't plan—just go."

"Just go," I repeated, then told Erica I'd see her either at dinner or soon after. "I think."

She assured me Ava would be fine and said she couldn't wait to hear about my date.

After ending the call, I grabbed my purse out of the drawer. One handle got stuck. I pulled harder. It came flying out, and the box I'd stuffed inside it flew up in slow motion before coming to a tumbling stop on the floor before Teri and Rob.

I scrambled to get it but couldn't think of a single way to explain it.

To Rob, Teri said, "Do you see why I can't lose this job? It gives me so many great stories to share with my friends."

I shot her a glare, but she was laughing, and I couldn't keep a straight face while holding a box of a hundred condoms. "Erica gave

them to me, and Ava found them. I couldn't leave them at my house."
I groaned. "I should leave them here. I can't take them with me."

"Unless you say they're a gift," Teri said, laughing so hard she had
to wipe tears from her eyes.

"I wish every woman I knew brought me some." Rob's shoulders
shook with laughter he was holding back, and he looked away.

"You're both jerks," I said with no bite. I stuffed the box of condoms
back in my purse and walked toward the door of my office. The prepper in me wouldn't let me go to Sebastian unprepared. Teri returned
to her desk.

Rob hovered behind me.

"Jerks," I said again.

They both burst out laughing.

A few minutes later I was in the back seat of a Bentley as we pulled
out into traffic. "Hey, Rob?"

"Yes?"

"Do you know what type of bouquet it was?"

"Something lavender, I think."

I smiled and settled back into my seat. Lavender was my favorite
color.

With a start I remembered something and texted Teri: Clear my
afternoon.

Teri sent me back a string of emojis, which I interpreted as "Okay."

CHAPTER TWENTY-FIVE

HEATHER

About twenty minutes later Rob pulled up to a large gate between two stone pillars. The gate opened, and I tried to not look as nervous as I felt. I didn't do much breathing as we made our way up a long, tree-lined driveway.

The trees fell away to reveal a towering three-story mansion with two massive chimneys and enough ivy climbing the stone facade that I felt transported back in time. Scenes from historical movies where a woman was brought to meet the wealthy hero she would fall for flashed through my mind. Had Elizabeth felt this way when she'd first arrived at Mr. Darcy's manor? I had assumed that Sebastian had money, but my house could have fit into this one about six times—more if the footage of the three-car garage was included.

No leagues, my ass.

Rob parked and rushed around to open my door, offering me a hand, with a much more professional air than I'd seen from him so far. I glanced up at the door of the mansion and saw why—Sebastian was coming down the front steps.

I started to move away from the car but stopped when Rob called my name. "Your purse," he said, handing it to me with a straight face but a twinkle in his eyes.

"Thanks," I said with a slight smile. When I turned back toward the house, Sebastian filled my vision . . . all six feet something of broad shoulders, expensive suit, glorious black hair that shone in the sunlight, and a look in his eyes that made my thighs quiver in anticipation.

Oh yes.

He looked me over as if he were as hungry to be alone with me as I was to be with him. Unlike me, though, he didn't appear anxious about it.

Me. Sebastian. And a hundred condoms.

I didn't know whether to turn and run home or race him to the nearest bed.

Okay, no way in hell was I going home.

"You can go, Rick," Sebastian said in a curt tone.

Rob didn't correct him. "Should I come back in an hour?"

When Sebastian's expression darkened, Rob quickly added, "I'll stay in the area, ready for your text."

Sebastian nodded once, then turned his attention back to me. "How did you like the flowers?"

I hated to lie, but I felt real sympathy for Rob. No wonder he was afraid he was about to be fired. Sebastian looked completely annoyed with him. "They were lovely," I said with enthusiasm. "A beautiful touch that convinced me to come."

Rob let out an audible sigh of relief.

Sebastian's eyes narrowed. "And my note? Did you like it?"

It was a strange question to ask in front of Rob, but I found the second lie came easier than the first. "Yes. Who knew you were such a romantic?"

Even before Sebastian reached into his jacket pocket, I knew what was coming. I saw it in his eyes.

"I'm so glad both pleased you, considering the flower shop called to say no one had picked up the bouquet. Oh, and I found this on the floor of my office." He held a folded note in the air before stuffing it back into his pocket.

My temper rose.

He was totally ruining my fantasy.

"Stop, Sebastian," I said, propping my hands on my hips, which banged my heavy purse against the side of one leg. "You're scaring Rob."

"He should be scared. I have no tolerance for incompetence."

My chin rose. "He might do better at his job if you bothered to learn his name."

Sebastian's eyes flashed with irritation and something more.

I stepped closer, going nose to nose with him. "Before you tell me it's none of my business, let me make something very clear . . . this house? I couldn't care less about it. I love my home. I'm not awed by wealth. I love my life. I don't need to be saved, and I'm not even sure I want to be *retrieved*. I came to see you because I like you, so don't be a jerk."

"A jerk? You just lied to me," he said, still not looking happy.

He had a point, but that didn't mean I had to like it. "Okay, so maybe I shouldn't have done that, but I didn't want you to fire him. Can we move on, because I'm beginning to question if coming here was a good idea?"

Sebastian held my gaze. "Because I hold my employees accountable?"

"No, because you're not kind while you do it. You can reprimand someone and leave them with their dignity."

"What she said," Rob chimed in, then flushed when we both turned to look at him. His hands went up. "My bad. I'll be in the car." He stopped before walking away and nodded to me. "I won't leave until I see you go in the house. You know, in case you change your mind."

"Thank you," I mouthed. Unless I saw another side of Sebastian soon, there was a chance I might take Rob up on the offer to leave. I could picture this Sebastian refusing to help Rakesh Bhatt when he asked for a short reprieve. Amazing in bed or not, I would regret sleeping with such a man.

The man I wanted was the one who had bent down and let Ava hug him as long as she needed to. The man who had fallen asleep in the chair beside me because he didn't want to leave while I was ill. Where was that man?

Alone, Sebastian and I stood there, glaring at each other. "This isn't how I imagined today going," I muttered.

"Me either," Sebastian said, a wry smile curling one side of his mouth. "I'm an ass."

"You are, but they say the journey back begins when you acknowledge it," I joked to lighten the mood, then winked for good measure.

His expression sobered. "I've been angry for so long I don't know if I'm capable of anything else."

Goose bumps.

This was the connection I had sensed, the one that kept drawing me back to him. He wasn't an arrogant man looking to control me; he was a man who'd lost his way and wanted to be the kinder person I'd glimpsed in him.

This wasn't all about sex.

What he'd said about not being the man he was before finally made sense.

He's afraid to care again. He's not sure he can.

I knew that feeling. When a social worker had met with me at the hospital to ask me if I was willing to take on the responsibility of Ava—I'd said I was, but I'd been scared. Not of the legal process that followed, but of myself. My own mother had walked away from me. What if I was like her? What if I took Ava home and discovered I was incapable of truly loving her?

I'd learned, though, that as scary as it was . . . love always won if given the chance. I wasn't my mother. My past, my pain, had not destroyed me—nor did it have the power to scare me anymore.

No matter what life threw my way, I now would always choose love.

I prayed Sebastian found his way to that same place.

Filled with compassion, I wrapped my arms around him and gave him a tight hug. Resting my forehead on his strong chest, I breathed in his pain.

His arms came around me, and I felt a shudder pass through them; then he kissed the top of my head. "Every time I think you can't surprise me again, you do—in ways that make me wonder what the hell you see in me."

I tipped my head back so I could look into those beautiful, tormented gray eyes of his. "You don't have to wonder. I see me. We've walked different paths, but I know what it's like to be angry about something I could do nothing about. I've asked myself the same questions you're probably asking yourself."

"And what conclusion did you come to?"

I caressed the side of his proud jaw. "That I am not a quitter. No matter what happens, I won't let it change me. I won't let it win."

He nodded slowly. "Ava is one lucky little girl."

I smiled. "I know."

He chuckled. "So humble."

Still tucked against him, I joked, "Why deny the obvious? I'm a catch."

"Yes, you are." This time he swung me up into his arms. I cried out only because the move surprised me. Rob popped out of the car and called out for confirmation that I was okay.

I waved him away.

Please, if there is a God in the heavens, could I have this moment go uninterrupted?

Sebastian took the steps two at a time, swung the door of the house open, then slammed it shut behind him with his foot. The foyer was probably impressive; I couldn't say. The moment his mouth claimed mine, we could have been anywhere.

I dropped my purse. He lowered me almost until my feet hit the floor, then hiked my skirt up to my waist. No further encouragement needed, I hopped up and wrapped my legs around his waist while digging my hands into his hair.

Utter abandon. His hands gripped my ass and ground me against him. I opened my mouth wider for him and writhed against him.

My back hit the wall, and I gave myself over to the sheer joy of his touch, his scent, the way he bent me to his will while adoring me at the same time. As he kissed his way down my jaw, I closed my eyes and arched closer, loving how hard and ready his cock was as it strained to be freed. So big. So needed inside me.

There was no gentleness, and I loved the roughness.

He pulled my blouse free from my skirt and yanked it over my head rather than unbuttoning it. My pretty little bra hit the floor seconds later. But, oh God, I did not miss either. His tongue was sinfully talented. He teased my breasts, licking, circling, nipping at them gently until I thought I might orgasm from that alone.

One of his hands slid forward, pushed beneath the lace of my panties, and dipped inside my folds. I was wet and ready, but he wasn't rushing. He moved up and down, deeper into my slit until his fingers found my clit.

If his tongue was talented, his fingers were pure magic. Classes should be taught on this subject. Really, men would get a lot more time behind the wheel if they knew how to drive like this. When I thought it couldn't get better, he slipped a finger inside me, so, so deep inside me, and did some circular motion with it that sent a wave of heat through me.

"Open your eyes for me, baby. Look at me when you come."

Our eyes met, and I gasped for breath as one of his fingers swirled inside me while his thumb teased my clit. He raised his head from my breasts and kissed his way back up to my mouth. Our tongues intertwined. My sex clenched around his finger, and the strongest orgasm I'd ever felt rocked through me.

"Fuck. Fuck. Fuck," I cried out as I climaxed.

"Oh, we'll get to that," he promised in that deep voice that was a caress all on its own.

I clung to him as I came back to reality. He shifted a few feet over and set me on a marble tabletop. I braced myself, hoping I hadn't knocked the mirror off the wall behind me, then stopped giving a shit about the mirror when he slid my shoes and then my panties off.

Right there, only a few feet inside the door, Sebastian spread my legs, sank to his knees, and showed me what oral sex could be. There was no embarrassment, no awkwardness. He dove into my sex like a man who loved every part of a woman and, in loving those parts, had learned what to do with them. He spread my lips and tickled at my clit with his breath. He suckled, plundered, used the stubble on his chin to drive me even wilder.

And then, when I was certain I had died and moved on to a better place, his fingers returned—two this time. Oh God. So deep. So confident.

I was climbing that wonderful crest toward another orgasm, but I savored my trip back to it. Nothing that good should be rushed to. Especially if rushing meant he would stop doing what I'd waited my whole life for someone to.

Then . . . oh . . . I couldn't hold back. I came again, and it was so fucking good I cried out triumphantly like someone making their first touchdown. He was smiling when he raised his face. "I hate to do this, baby, but we have to finish upstairs. I wasn't thinking when I put the condoms in the master bedroom."

"I have some," I said in a breathless rush.

His eyes burned hotter. "Where?"

"My purse," I said, not caring about anything past having him inside me, filling me, taking this where we both were dying for it to go.

My bag had opened during the drop, and the large box of condoms was prominently displayed through the top of it. "One hundred," he murmured. "I like the way you think."

"Shut up and fuck me," I growled, then laughed at the surprised look on his face. "It's been a long time."

He gave me a deep, toe-curling kiss that brought a flush to my cheeks. Then he stepped back, ripped open the box, claimed what we needed, undid his belt, released his huge cock, sheathed it, and stepped back between my legs.

Fully clothed.

Porn-movie hot.

Dirty Dancing if it had been porn hot.

He hauled me up so my legs wrapped his waist again. Two orgasms in, I melted in his arms. I gave myself completely over to him. When he drove into me, it was with a force that made me gasp, then cry out for him to do it again, deeper.

It was wild. It was violent. I don't know if he knocked the small table over or if I did, but the crash of it to the floor just made it more exciting. This was how I'd always dreamed of being taken. Back to the wall, I clung to him as he pounded into me. He turned so his back was to the wall, and I rose and lowered myself onto him with a force that took him so deeply into me it almost hurt.

We turned again, and he controlled the depth and the pace.

His mouth was rough on my breasts.

His grip fierce on my ass.

I dug my nails into his shoulders and begged him not to stop. God, don't stop.

We rolled again and again until finally I wanted the release that was beginning to lick through me once more. "I'm going to come," I exclaimed.

He increased the speed of his thrusts and came as damn near close to when I did as humanly possible. We swore in unison; then our ragged breathing was the only sound in the foyer of the mansion.

For a blissful few minutes, neither of us moved. Still connected, we simply held each other. Finally he gently pulled out, lowered me to my feet, and said, "So how do you like the foyer?"

Without looking around I answered, "Very nice. Impressive. Is the rest of the house like this?"

He laughed.

I laughed.

And suddenly I wasn't embarrassed that I'd brought a hundred condoms to our second date.

CHAPTER TWENTY-SIX

SEBASTIAN

Just when I thought I was too old to have my world rocked by a woman, Heather took sex to the next level. I realized as I stood there grinning that no matter where things went with this woman—I would never be the same.

I collected myself enough to clean off, put my junk away, and pick up the table one of us had thrown onto its side.

She picked her clothing off the floor and held it in front of her. My personal preference would have been that she never put her shirt on again; her tits were too damn perfect to cover up. A hint of shyness, however, after what we'd just done was endearing.

This wasn't the last time we'd be together. With that certainty in mind, I helped her back into her bra and shirt. At twenty I didn't understand that dressing a woman could be as intimate as undressing her. At thirty-eight, I found pleasure in so much more than just getting my rocks off.

I picked up her purse, tucking the open box of condoms back into it. "You're a woman who believes in being prepared."

She accepted her purse with a blush and a smile. "I am a closet prepper, but they were a gift from my friend. I don't want you to think . . ."

I dug my hand into the back of her hair and pulled her to me for a deep kiss. "What I think is that we now have enough to stash some all over this house. I don't usually have a problem making it to the bed, but I can see with you I'm going to have to step up my game."

She smiled against my lips. "Yeah. I'm a wild one."

The wry note in the way she said it made me wonder how she saw herself. Was it possible that she didn't know how sexy she was? Did she believe sex was always like this for me?

No man would correct that assumption, but, honestly, it had been a long time since sex had shaken me. It could be good, even very good without being mind-blowing. My enjoyment of everything had waned after Therese, and somewhere along the way I guess I had begun to expect less.

Heather said she saw herself in me—her struggles reflected in my own. I didn't know how to begin to explain to her how much her words had touched me. She was right; she didn't need to be saved. She was a strong, independent woman with a loving heart.

How could she not see how sexy that was?

Just then, it struck me that we were still standing in the entrance of the home. "Before we go, there's something I need to tell you."

Her mouth rounded. "Oh?"

"This isn't my house."

Her eyes widened. "Whose house is this? Tell me no one else is here."

I chuckled. "We're alone. And technically, I guess, the house belongs to me. Romano Superstores acquired it as part of a buyout. The family needed cash, and it's a twenty-million-dollar home, so we gave them half of that and took it. What we didn't know at the time was how much money the family had poured into *personalizing* the home. Once you see the inside, you'll understand how they lost their business. Not only did they waste a fortune renovating this home, but they did it in an unmarketable fashion."

Interest sparked in Heather's eyes. "You've piqued my curiosity."

My heart thudded heavily in my chest. She'd piqued more than that in me. "Up for a tour, then?" I offered her my arm.

She looped her arm through it. "Absolutely."

I wiggled an eyebrow at her. "Bring your purse."

She rolled her eyes, but her blush was telltale.

Just inside the second door, the house opened up to a large white marble two-story room that was dominated by a spiral staircase that wrapped around a glass elevator.

"An elevator," she exclaimed. "I've always wanted to have sex in one of those. I mean, the books make it sound incredible."

My cock was back at full mast, and we'd hardly made it into the house. "I'll have to remember that." Then a thought came to me, a fun, lighthearted one that I shared. "Hey, we should stash a condom in there. For future use."

"Like hiding Easter eggs but more fun."

"Definitely more fun."

Laughing, we stepped into the elevator and checked it for the perfect hiding spot. There was a slot on the side of the control panel. She edged one in, met my gaze, then tucked in a second one.

Lord, was it possible to fall for a woman after just one fuck?

We took the elevator to the second floor, where the bedrooms were. "I could describe the first room, but it's better if you experience it for yourself."

Her eyebrows met, forming the cutest line between them. "Is it . . . like a *red* room?"

"You could say that."

I threw open a set of white double doors. The room was indeed red, but only because it was Mickey and Minnie Mouse–themed from top to bottom. A big red polka-dotted slide swirled down from a loft to a huge red tufted pillow. Icons of the famous couple filled every corner of the room in one way or another, from ceiling to floor to the twin-bed comforters. "I have no desire to have sex in this room," she said.

I hugged her to my side. "If you don't make it as a tax accountant, you should do a show on home decoration. Stylish? Who cares. Could you fuck in it? Now that's the question every homeowner should ask themselves."

"That show would get great ratings."

I kissed her cheek. "I bet it would. Ready to see more?"

"Lead away."

The next room was twice the size. The carpet and walls were varying shades of green. A queen-size bed was built into the trunk of a large tree. Thick branches sprawled out from the trunk. "It even has a wooden swing." A second later she was on it, testing if it could take her weight. "This is so cool."

Knowing that the house was equipped with the latest voice-activated everything, I gave the wake word and said, "Night light." The room instantly darkened except for lights that came on in the ceiling and in strings that decorated areas of the room. Crickets chirped from the corners. "Okay, this room is amazing. Now that everyone has a cell phone, I would be too paranoid to have sex outside, but this . . . this would be just like that."

I held out my hand. "Condoms, please."

She tossed me two.

I quickly assessed the room and decided the stash had to be somewhere near the swing. One cluster of leaves made the perfect spot.

She watched me, and her expression turned serious. "Are we just having fun, or are we really saying today isn't a onetime thing?"

I crossed to where she was standing and pulled her to me. "This house is halfway between where you live and where I do. It's vacant. No one else comes here. We could use it whenever we want to."

"That's not what I'm asking."

Another man might have rushed to assure her of more than he was certain of. I wanted whatever we had to be based on honesty. If I could give her nothing else, I could give her that. "I want to see you again.

Here. In Durham. I don't care. I like you, and I like who I am when I'm with you. If you need more than that—"

"I don't. I like who I am with you too." She went up onto her tip-toes and kissed my lips.

I made love to her in that room, under the flickering stars. It was slow; it was sweet and ended with us naked and entangled on the bed. We didn't use the swing, but we could the next time we went there— and that was a tantalizing, but also unsettling, realization.

I wanted there to be a next time.

And a time after that.

We napped briefly. When I woke and checked the time, I knew the rest of the tour would have to wait as well. "Heather, it's time to go home."

She snuggled tighter to my side.

If it weren't for Ava, I would have let her sleep. I wanted to wake with her beside me, but part of what I loved about her was her devotion to her daughter.

I selfishly gave myself a few extra minutes of her in my arms, then woke her. "It's four o'clock. When do you pick Ava up from preschool?"

She blinked a few times quickly. "She's with Erica, but I did say I'd meet them for dinner."

"Do you want me or Rob to take you back?"

"Rob can do it. I'll probably head straight to Erica's, and with Ava there . . ."

Right. "Rob it is."

I rolled so I was above her. "So when do you want to come back and see the rest of the house?"

She chewed her bottom lip. "The next couple of days are tough. I could probably get Teri to watch her for a few hours on Saturday morning."

A few hours would have to do. "Lunch tomorrow?"

She wiggled beneath me. "*Lunch* lunch . . . or *lunch*?"

"Wait, is the second one on the menu before Saturday?"

"If we choose somewhere close to my office, I can still have a sandwich."

She caught my smile. "Hey, I get hungry."

A rumble of laughter rolled out of me.

Sex and a sandwich, now that was worth driving an hour for. "I'm technically on vacation, so I'll hunt around for the perfect place."

Her eyebrows furrowed again. "Vacation?"

It wasn't something I was ready to discuss with her yet. "I hadn't taken one in years. Sometimes you have to step away to regain perspective."

She looked like she wanted to say something, but whatever it was, she changed her mind. "I really do have to get going. Could you text Rob?"

I rolled off her, hunted for my phone, and did as she'd asked. She gave me a half smile that instantly had my radar tuning in to the change of mood.

Things had just been warm and sexy. Suddenly there was a tension between us, but I didn't know what was causing it. While we dressed, I kept looking over to her. There was definitely something on her mind.

"Are you okay, Heather?"

The smile she gave me looked forced. "Of course I am."

I pulled her back into my arms and tipped her face up so our eyes met. "If you want to take it slower, just tell me."

"It's not that."

"Then what is it?"

She studied my face for a moment. "If I had an opinion about something, would you want to hear it?"

"Yes."

"Even if it was about your business?"

"Just say it, Heather."

She took a deep breath and said, "Rakesh Bhatt came to see me. He told me about his father and how he'd gone to you, but you hadn't even considered his request to postpone the start of your construction."

"Wait, Bhatt came to you?"

"Yes. He heard I knew you. I promised I'd say something to you if I saw you again. I know, it's not my place to ask this, but maybe if you met with him one more time?"

If there was one thing I hated, it was anyone who tried to use my personal life to affect my business dealings. "Is that why you slept with me? To plead his case?"

I regretted saying it as soon as the words left my mouth. I'd gone to Italy to clear my head about what my role in the company should be, and I hated that I was no longer sure. I couldn't lead if I couldn't be decisive. As much as I felt for Bhatt, my duty was to provide for my family.

So, yeah, the takeover was a sore spot for me, but I couldn't explain why my response had been with something as unlikely as what I'd thrown at her.

She pushed out of my arms. "Yes. That's exactly what this was. So tell me, did it work?"

I deserved that jab. "Heather—"

"Don't." She grabbed her purse off the floor. With that she stormed out of the bedroom.

I was hot on her heels. "It was a stupid thing to say."

"Yes, it was," she said between gritted teeth.

She strode to the front door and stepped into her shoes. I followed her, hating that I'd taken something as good as what we'd shared and fucked it up.

"Heather—"

She spun, wagging a finger at me. "I feel for you, I do, but I am not going to be your emotional punching bag while you try to decide what kind of person you are. If you want to be in my life, and I still can't figure out if you do, I have to know I can trust you to be kind all the time. Not just when things are going your way. Not just when you want something. Ava depends on me. Right now my first priority is her. I don't know what your priorities are."

I would have answered her, but that was exactly what I was still figuring out.

She opened the door and walked to where Rob was standing beside my car. Head high, she slid in without looking back.

I wanted to rush down to the car and apologize.

I wanted her to drive off and for this to be over.

Only after the car had disappeared around the corner of the driveway did I turn and slam my fist against the wooden door. Time away from work hadn't given me the answers I sought.

Time with Heather hadn't made me a better person.

She was right to keep me out of her life.

I jumped into my own car and drove off, not caring where I was headed, half hoping it led to somewhere I couldn't come back from—because in some ways that was where I already felt I was.

CHAPTER TWENTY-SEVEN

Heather

Walking into Erica's house to see Ava and Charlotte laughing while Kevin and Tyler crashed cars on a racetrack that was sprawled across the living room floor made me feel a little better. As soon as Ava spotted me, she yelled, "Mom!" and bolted over to hug me.

Life was good.

Confusing and frustrating, but good.

"Having fun?" I asked as I ran my hand over the top of her head and hugged her back.

"You have to see the crashes, Mom. Big crashes. They don't even care about their toys. It's awesome," Ava said.

"Those kinds of cars were made to crash," I assured her. "They care about their toys as much as you do."

One car sailed across the room and hit the wall. Well, maybe they cared a little less. "Tyler, be careful, or you'll break it."

He frowned. "It's already broken. I'm trying to fix it."

Ava left my side to march over and inspect the car. "The wheel is coming off." She fiddled with it, pushed the bent wheel against a corner of a table, and held the repair up with a grin. "All better. When I grow up I'm going to be a veterinarian of cars."

"Veterinarians are animal doctors, dummy," Kevin said.

I was about to tell Kevin that calling anyone names wasn't nice, when Ava held the car up and said, "Dummy? I fixed it. You know who calls people dummies? Dummies. Say you're sorry." She put the car down on the track. It took off.

Yes, indeed, Ava was my daughter.

"Sorry," Kevin grumbled.

Ava seemed to accept his apology. She settled back onto the couch with Charlotte, and peace returned to the room.

I sat down next to them and in a low voice asked Ava if she should apologize to Kevin as well. "You did call him a name too."

"He said it first," she countered.

"You're not responsible for what he says, but you are for what you do. I did like, though, that you accepted his apology. That's a good friend."

Ava shared a look with Charlotte, then called out, "Sorry, Kevin."

"It's okay," he answered absently. He was already playing with his brother again.

Was it an ideal resolution? Could I have done more? Should I have done less? Parenting felt like a series of on-the-fly best guesses. Later I'd think of things I could have said, but right then I was just happy to see the storm had passed.

Rising, I headed toward the kitchen. Erica looked up from setting the table in the dining room. "Hey, you didn't have to rush back. The difference between three or four children is so marginal I sometimes forget she's here. I just listen for yelling or any prolonged quiet—that's never good."

I chuckled and started placing silverware near the plates for her. "I do the same. Although, with one kid my house is often quiet. I think that's why Ava loves to come here."

"And we love to have her. It's like having another parent in the house. I never have to worry about what my boys are up to; she'll either tell them to stop or she'll tell me to tell them."

That was Ava.

I paused from setting the table. "We don't have to stay for dinner. I have food at home."

"First, Bob is working tonight, so please stay so I can get my daily dose of adult interaction." Erica waved one finger, then two. "Second, there is no way you're leaving without telling me how your second date went. He sent a car for you. Swoon. I may have to role-play that out with Bob . . . that was hot."

I took a seat with a sigh. "It started off good. Really, really good."

"So his elevator is still functioning."

"Oh yes." My cheeks warmed. "That was the good part. And the house he took me to was amazing."

She sat down across from me. "Then why so glum?"

I fiddled with a paper napkin as I spoke. "He made me glow, Erica. And things were so easy between us. I thought I'd be here telling you that he and I were diving into something wild and amazing."

"But?"

Discussing it wasn't easy, because it required unpacking what I'd already stuffed away in a mental box. "I didn't tell you that Rakesh Bhatt came to see me this morning."

"The one who owns the store Sebastian is buying out."

"His family owns it, but yes. His father is very ill, and he asked Sebastian to postpone construction on the new store until after he passes away. They don't think it will be long. Sebastian refused to even consider it, and Rakesh asked me to see if I could sway him. All I did was ask Sebastian if he'd consider meeting with him again."

Erica blew a hair out of her eyes. "That was what you chose to discuss right after you rode his elevator?"

I shrugged and looked at the plastic plate before me. "I promised Rakesh I'd say something to Sebastian if I ever saw him again."

"Girl, I have to teach you about timing. Let me guess—he did not take that well."

I swallowed and met her gaze. "He asked me if I'd slept with him to sway his decision."

"Idiot. Him, not you. Men say stupid shit when they're cornered. Bob once bought an antique car without asking me. When I say *antique*, I mean old, beaten up—someone should have paid him to take it. He hid it in the garage . . . like I wouldn't notice it. When I asked him about it, he accused me of switching laundry detergent and giving him jock itch. How does that even make sense? My point is, he really wanted that car, and instead of talking it out with him, we had a yelling match about itchy balls and who does which house chores. Thankfully, we've learned to circle back after a cooling-off period and ask for clarification. He doesn't splurge on many things for himself, and he was already feeling guilty about getting the car—that's why he went off the deep end when I confronted him about it. He brought baggage to the talk. And me? I actually do care about his junk's comfort, and I was okay with the car. I just wanted to be included in the decision to buy it. So what I'm saying is that I brought my own baggage to our itchy-ball fight."

I shook my head, trying to dislodge the mental image of her husband scratching himself while arguing for his antique car. "I could have chosen a better time."

"Um, yeah. So after he asked you if you were pimping yourself for his competition, did you stick around and try to talk it out?"

I looked away again.

"Let me guess—you told him off and stormed back here?"

"I was angry."

"And scared. My guess is mostly scared."

"No."

"Heather, I adore you, but I've seen you with him. I've also seen you with your father."

My head snapped up. "You've never seen me with my father. He's not part of my life anymore."

"That's what I mean. I've seen the way you avoid him."

"He has no interest in me or Ava."

"You've told me that he used to call to check in on you."

"Too little, too late."

"I'm not a psychologist—but I wonder if being left by your mother hasn't made you a little . . . proactive when it comes to cutting people out of your life. Do you think pushing them away is better than being afraid they'll leave you?"

"You're right, Erica. You're not a psychologist. I'm past being affected by anything my mother did."

"Are you? Before you deny it again, I just want you to consider that everything we do teaches our children something. Ava has a grandfather she doesn't know. I hope she doesn't one day have children who don't know you."

I gasped as if sucker punched. "That would never happen."

Erica just held my gaze.

My eyes misted. "My father didn't approve of me adopting Ava. You think I'd want him around her after that?"

"You want to protect Ava; I get it. People make mistakes, though. They say things they regret. I just hope that if I ever say something stupid, I won't be the next one you refuse to talk to."

"I promise you, if we ever argue, I will come back for advice on how to make up with you." I sniffed. Erica knew me better than anyone else did. If she thought she was one argument away from being cut out . . . what did that say about how I was living my life? And about what Ava was learning from me?

I'd told myself that I'd left the past in the past.

Maybe I hadn't.

Maybe I was still as confused as I accused Sebastian of being.

"If we ever do fight, I'll leave my door open for that talk." Erica leaned over and gave one of my hands a pat. "Just don't accuse me of making your junk itchy. Apparently that's a trigger for me."

I chuckled.

"Now"—Erica lowered her voice and leaned closer—"tell me about this house he took you to . . ."

CHAPTER TWENTY-EIGHT

SEBASTIAN

After a restless night, breakfast with my mother wouldn't have been my first choice, but she wanted to hear about my trip, and I had told my brothers they wouldn't see me back at the office that week. Time out of work was supposed to be relaxing, but I had only been back in my apartment for a day, and I was already climbing the walls.

As I entered my parents' home, my mother rushed over. I ducked down so she could give my forehead a big hand-on-either-side-of-my-face kiss. "Morning, Mom."

She stepped back and looked me over. "You look tired."

"Jet lag."

"Are you hungry?" she said as she led me toward the kitchen. I wasn't, but she would fill a plate with food for me regardless of what I said.

"Sure." I settled down at the counter of the kitchen island. She handed me a cup of steaming coffee.

"So how was Montalcino?"

"Nice. I didn't understand much Nonna said, though. My Italian is rusty."

My mother set a heaping plate of eggs in front of me. "She might also not be speaking clearly. She's ninety-two. When you're ninety-two, we'll see how well you speak."

I blew on the coffee. "Did you tell her to fatten me up? I probably put on five pounds from all that homemade pasta."

That pleased my mother. "That's how you know she loves you. I'm glad you went to see her. At her age, every year we have her is a gift."

I nodded. "Curious, though, I didn't see any table wine while I was there. Not once. No after-dinner digestif either."

My mother sat on a stool on the other side of the island. "That is curious."

"It was almost as if they'd been told I couldn't be around alcohol." When my mother didn't deny her involvement, I added, "Mom, I'm okay. You don't have to worry about me."

"A mother's job is to worry about her babies. I don't care how old you are, Sebastian; you'll always be my baby."

I smiled down at my coffee. Parts of my life had gone very wrong, but I knew how blessed I was that other parts were very, very right. I could imagine Heather saying something similar to Ava. She was a good mother, a good person.

I groaned.

My mother sighed. "Sebastian, you have always been my most serious child. You've also always assumed responsibility for things even if they weren't your fault. When you were little, if your brothers fell, to you it was your fault for not keeping them safer. You're not God, Sebastian. You can't control the twists and turns life takes."

"I know."

"Talk to me. What were you hoping to find in Montalcino?"

I shook my head, then admitted, "Some of who I used to be. I don't like who I've become."

She bustled around the kitchen, then placed a freshly baked piece of bread next to the plate of food I still hadn't touched. "You're too hard on yourself, son. We've all made mistakes. We all have things we wish we could go back and do differently. You can't let that define you. Who is this Sebastian you don't like? The one who married a woman he loved? Worked hard to provide for her? Do you dislike the loving son, the one who put his pain aside to build a good life for all of us? I look at you, and I don't see anything I would change."

I ran a hand through my hair. She wouldn't see my faults. Still, because I needed to get it out of my head, I told her about the conversation I'd had with Rakesh Bhatt, along with my response to him. This situation had haunted me, and I shared the conversations I'd had with my brothers that had led to me taking this "vacation." My mother had always been able to look beyond what I said into the heart of what was bothering me.

She came around to sit closer to me. "This man's situation with his father is not your responsibility."

"I know."

"And your brothers are perfectly capable of filling in for you. You deserve time off."

"That's why I left."

"But you want to help him, don't you?"

"I do. But there's a cost to agreeing to push back the construction. We have employees to pay. Compassion doesn't pay our bills."

"But nor does a little of it topple a business like you've built. Sebastian, when I was younger I thought there was a right way and a wrong way. It brought me a lot of grief. Eventually I realized that the only right way is the one I can live with. And the only wrong one is the one my heart cannot tolerate." She laid her hand over my heart. "The answers you're looking for are not in Italy. Your heart is telling you everything you need to know."

Although I wasn't sure what that would mean as far as my business decision, her words struck home. "That helps, thank you."

She smiled and kissed my forehead again. "Now tell me, why do you have glitter in your hair?"

My hand went to my head. Glitter? Oh yes, it had started on Heather's face, then slowly spread all over both of us. I'd thought I'd washed it all off. "A friend of mine has a child."

"A friend. Do I know this friend?"

"Mom."

Her eyes went wide with innocence. "If a mother can't ask her son about who he is spending time with, what can she ask him?"

"If there was something to tell you, I would."

"Mauricio said you've been talking to the woman you returned the stuffed animal to. She has a child."

"Yes, okay? I've seen her a few times. She's a very nice woman."

"You've gotten close, no?"

I wasn't about to say.

My mother waved a hand at my hair. "Glitter doesn't jump. So why haven't I met her?"

I rubbed my hands over my face. "Could we drop this? I'm reasonably certain it's over anyway."

"What did you do?"

"Why are you sure I did something?"

She arched an eyebrow. "A mother knows. So have you apologized to her yet?"

"It's a little more complicated than that."

"It's never more complicated than that. My sources say only good things about her. I'm sure she'll forgive you."

"Your sources? Since when do you have sources?"

She waved both hands. "Since my children have all decided to stay single. I am not getting younger. Don't focus on me; think about you and this woman. You need to fix this."

Speaking of having sources made me remember something. "Mom, when I was at Nonna's, she said there was a red-haired American woman asking a lot of questions about you and your sister."

My mother went pale. "Did Nonna tell her anything?"

"It didn't sound as if she did. Is there something *to* tell?"

My mother stood. "It's better to look forward rather than back, Sebastian. Now eat and think about what you can do to get back in the good graces of this Heather woman. I know my vote doesn't count, but her daughter is adorable. After so many boys, I would love to spoil a little girl."

I allowed my mother to change the subject, because I understood how sometimes the only way a person could deal with something was to close a door on it. What was the past my mother refused to face? What was she afraid someone might uncover?

I could have told her that no matter what she'd done, nothing would change my love for her—but she knew that. My mother wasn't one to keep secrets or pretty up the truth. If she was hiding something, she had a reason to.

From concern, not curiosity, I sought out time alone with my father before leaving that day. I told him about the red-haired woman who'd been asking questions about our family in Montalcino and about my mother's reaction to hearing of her.

My father sat down in his favorite leather chair and took a moment before answering. "A man could draw a thousand pictures and never create one as perfect as your mother. She was a beauty who stood out in our town like a rose in a field of wildflowers. Her older sister was a beauty as well, but not like Camilla. Theirs is a complicated story that's not mine to tell, but I love your mother more for every choice she made. We've had our good times and our not-so-good ones, but I'm a better man because she pushed me to be."

It was the most my father had spoken on the subject. I paced beside his chair. "Does this have something to do with Gian? Is Mom's sister looking for him?"

"She knows where he is. She's always known."

"Why have none of us met her, then? Is she dead?"

My father's eyes darkened. "To me, to our family, she is. Once, perhaps, she acted selflessly, but she chooses to live in a state of crisis to justify putting her own needs above those of anyone else. I don't hate her. I refuse to waste any emotion at all on such a person. If Gian never meets her, I think he'll be better for it. She is neither strong nor loyal like your mother."

I didn't know quite what to say in the face of that. "So who do you think is interested in our family history?"

My father stood and placed a hand on my shoulder. "I couldn't be prouder of my four sons. Sebastian, you have always protected your brothers and done what's best for the family. For that reason, I will give you a name. What you do with it is up to you."

"Dad, is the mystery really necessary?"

"I am a man of my word. Age has not changed that."

I didn't push my father to say more, because I knew he would say only what he felt he had the right to. Although it meant I wouldn't receive an easy answer to my questions, it confirmed his loyalty to my mother, and the beauty of that was undeniable. "What is the name you think I should know?"

After giving my shoulder a final squeeze, he said, "Corisi."

Somewhat in jest, I asked, *"Dominic Corisi?"*

My father nodded. "That's the family I'm referring to."

"The billionaire?" As if there could be two. The Corisi name dominated the news, revered as American royalty, respected predominantly out of fear. His tech companies spanned the globe. When watercooler conversations turned to companies or individuals with so much power they were dangerous, his name headed the list. Anyone with that much money or influence was a potential threat to global welfare. Some said his business holdings were too big to fail—that the economies of many countries would topple if he withdrew from them.

People said that, but the news never did. The positive spin on any and all of his endeavors was a testament to how pervasive his influence was even in the media.

"Why would Dominic Corisi be interested in our family?"

"He may not be. I pray he isn't. My father used to say that if you turn over enough rocks, something bad will crawl out from under one of them."

"Dad, you're not making sense. Did you give me his name because you think I should contact him or not?"

"I can't tell you what to do, Sebastian. You're a good boy, though. I know that whatever path you choose, it will be the one that is the best for our family."

It was a lot of faith to put in me, considering I had no fucking idea what we were talking about.

CHAPTER TWENTY-NINE

HEATHER

My stomach grumbled, reminding me that I'd skipped breakfast. Even though I was my own boss, I kept myself to a schedule—or at least I had before Sebastian.

Sebastian.

I didn't know what to do about him. I wish I could go back and stop myself from talking about anything after sex beyond how great it had been. Or when he'd asked me if sleeping with him had anything to do with Rakesh Bhatt, I wish I hadn't gotten so defensive. I knew the two were completely unrelated. How differently it might have gone had I brushed off his comment or asked him why my question upset him.

After leaving Erica's, I'd gone home, given Ava a bath, read to her, put her to bed, then done something I hadn't done in years—I'd called my father. Our conversation might have been strained and short, but I closed by asking him if he'd like to meet Ava, and he'd said he would.

Erica was right; everything we did taught our children something. I lectured Ava about forgiveness and talking things out, but that wasn't how I lived. How would she ever believe that forgiveness was important if she didn't witness me forgiving anyone?

How could I justify calling out Sebastian for not being kind, when I slammed the door on him each time there was a hint that things might not go well with us? How kind was that?

I took out my phone, pulled up his last message to me, and texted: Sorry about yesterday.

His answer was immediate: I'm sorry too. I want to see you again.

I'd like that. When?

Five seconds? Open your office door.

I dropped my phone to my desk, sprinted across my office, and threw my door open. "Sebastian." I didn't even try to hide how happy I was to see him.

He held out a bag from a local sandwich shop. "Hungry?"

I wove my arms around his neck and let desire sweep me away. He held me to him and kissed me back with the same fervor.

When he raised his head, we were both breathing heavily. He glanced at Teri's desk and said, "We may have scared her out of here."

"I don't care," I said, feeling giddy from head to toe. "Yesterday I said a lot of things about you without thinking about the baggage I was bringing to this. I care about your feelings. You were trying to tell me your junk itches, and all I could think about was that I wanted to be asked."

"Huh? I am not itchy," he said with an arched eyebrow. "Are you . . . itchy?"

As I replayed what I'd said, I realized out of the context with Erica, the analogy didn't sound as good. "No. No. What I'm trying to say is that I may have issues left over from the way my mother left. Sometimes that makes me defensive, and instead of asking someone for clarification, I assume the worst and bolt. It's easier to leave someone than to wait for them to leave me."

"But nothing that requires an ointment is bothering you." He cocked his head.

I smacked his shoulder. "Are you listening? This is me apologizing."

He grinned. "Oh, I thought the apology was in the kiss and the text." He held up the bag. "Mine was in a chicken salad sandwich. Teri said it's your favorite."

"It is." I took the bag with a happy sigh. "And I'm starving."

He followed me to my office, and we took seats at the small conference table in the corner.

I dug into the bag. Warm bread too. Heaven. "I can't believe you did this for me. Thank you." I probably should have waited for him to take his out, but when my stomach rumbled again, I took a bite and closed my eyes as I savored it. "Delicious."

He was smiling when I looked at him. Smiling, but not eating. "Aren't you hungry?"

"No, I had a large breakfast."

"But there are two sandwiches."

"For you. I know you enjoy them."

I narrowed my eyes at him but didn't argue that point. People said the way to a man's heart was through his stomach. I would argue that such a method was universally effective. Show me a woman who doesn't love a good carb now and then, and I'll show you someone lying through their skinny teeth.

Half a sandwich in, I slowed. He was still smiling, which made me wonder if I had food on my face. "What?"

"I can't help where my mind takes me whenever I'm near you."

I paused. "Wait, so stuffing my mouth with food reminds you of . . . oh. Really?"

He shrugged.

I purred, "So it would turn you on if I ate it really slowly . . ." I held a piece of it up, opened my mouth, and licked at my lips in what I hoped was an extremely sexual manner. A big chunk of chicken fell and bounced off my eye. Thankfully, I'd closed it just in time, but I raised my hand to wipe mayonnaise from my eyelid.

A laugh rumbled out of him.

I gave in to one of my own. "I am so not sexy."

"Come here." The command in that voice sent licks of desire straight through me.

I put my sandwich down and stood.

Don't need to ask me twice.

"Have you ever fucked on a desk?" he asked, standing.

"No," I answered in a strangled voice.

"Does your door lock?"

I nodded.

"Go lock it."

I did and returned to him on autopilot. He moved to clear a corner of my desk with a sweep, but I jumped forward and grabbed the papers. "It would take me forever to organize these again." I placed them on the shelf on the side.

He stepped closer.

I backed up until I bumped against the side of my desk. Oh yes. Desk sex. Messy. Primal. Desk sex.

Messy.

I leaned back and took my coffee from where it sat and moved it to the floor. "Can't spill that on the keyboard."

The corner of his mouth twitched. "Anything else?"

I glanced back. My twenty-seven-inch monitor had cost a mint. "We should just move that—"

He reached back and released my bun, twining his fingers into my hair to pull me forward for a kiss. As soon as our lips met, I stopped caring about collateral damage. I could afford another computer.

I tugged his shirt out of his trousers.

He undid the buttons on my shirt.

His belt fell away with ease. He stepped out of his pants.

My skirt hiked up in a flash.

His mouth adored my nipples through the thin material of my bra. My hands sought and pumped his shaft. His fingers pushed aside the material of my panties and dove in to make their magic. "You're so wet for me already."

I could only mew my agreement.

He pumped his fingers in and out of me, teasing, kissing, driving me wild.

Then he stepped back, and I sank to my knees before him. I took him deep in my mouth as he fisted his hands into my hair.

He was so big, I strained to take all of him in.

So hard.

His moan of pleasure gave me the confidence to get daring with my tongue as well as my hands. I wanted to drive him as out of control as he drove me.

In and out, deeper and faster. I cupped the base of his dick with my hand as my other caressed his balls. His hands tightened in my hair. Pain and pleasure. Control and submission. I'd never felt so powerfully free.

When he came I drank him in, loving every grunt of release he made. I was still basking in the knowledge that I could please him to the same level that he pleased me. He hauled me to my feet and carried me to one of the chairs we'd sat in to eat.

He positioned me so I was straddling his lap.

He wasn't at full erection when he slid his cock along my wet slit, but he hardened against me. The tear of a condom wrapper brought a tingle to my sex, and I took over from there. I slid it over him, and as I moved to take him in, he thrust upward.

Oh God, yes.

From there it was a wild dance, with me in charge. His mouth went everywhere. He pushed my bra upward to expose my breasts and then gave them each attention.

I rode him with an abandon I didn't think myself capable of.

I came before he did, slumping against his chest after a mind-erasing release.

He stood, turned me around, and pounded into me from behind. I didn't think I could come again; then suddenly I was joining him for a profanity-filled explosion.

Afterward, he cleaned up and we dressed. I didn't have experience with office sex, so I didn't know what to expect, but when he invited me to curl up on his lap on one of my deep leather chairs, I didn't hesitate.

I sat there, cuddled in his arms as our breathing returned to normal. Safe in his embrace, I told him about what Erica had said and how it had led me to calling my father.

"And?" he asked.

I caressed his muscled forearm, buying myself time before answering. "I don't know what I was expecting, but we didn't actually talk about anything. He asked me how I was doing. I asked him how he has been. We could have been two people standing in line at the grocery store lightly catching up. I don't know if I should move on and pretend we never had an issue or try to talk it out."

He kissed the side of my head. "There is no right way or wrong way. Do what's best for you and Ava, whatever that is. Your father will either come around or he won't. Ava's too young to protect herself, so my only suggestion would be to move forward carefully until you know where your father stands."

I hugged him then. "You're so wise."

He smiled. "I have my moments. Trust me, I don't have all the answers. In fact, sometimes I'm not sure I have any at all."

"Want to talk about it?"

He took a deep breath. "I wasn't sympathetic to the whole Bhatt situation, and that's why I snapped when you asked me to meet with him again. The man I used to be would have helped him, or wanted to. Yet I felt nothing in the face of his distress, and that was a wake-up call for me. Is that who I am now? Is that who I will always be? I went to Italy, back to where our family roots are, hoping I'd find a piece of myself, I guess. I didn't."

"Because it's not missing; it's buried. You went through something that no one should have to. You survived it by shutting parts of yourself off. That's what I think. It doesn't make you a bad person, just one who doesn't want to get hurt again."

His arms tightened around me. "It's that and more. I want to meet with Rakesh again, but I don't know what to say to him. I don't want to cut a deal that has a negative impact on my family."

I raised my head. "Do you have your own money?"

He tensed beneath me. "I do."

"Enough to buy your family's investment out and move forward with the project yourself, allowing the risk to fall just on you?"

"Yes," he said with growing enthusiasm. The kiss he gave me was euphoric. "I fucking do."

To quote a brilliant woman, I said, "Bam, and that's how it's done."

Sebastian laughed. "I don't always understand you, but I'm falling hard."

"Me too," I said and pulled his face to mine for another kiss. "Me too."

We sat there in comfortable silence for several moments. Neither one of us brought up my itchy comments from earlier.

I did raise my head, though, and ask, "Sebastian, what did you write in the note Rob was supposed to give me?"

He smiled. "Your move."

"That's it?"

"Would it have taken more than that?"

I chuckled. "You have a very healthy ego there."

"Thank you."

CHAPTER THIRTY

SEBASTIAN

Three weeks later, my father and I sat in the last place I would have expected us to be, the Bhatt family living room. Rakesh's father had joined us in a wheelchair with a blanket over his lap. Though he was pale and thin, the smile on his face warmed his eyes.

My father was seated on a chair near him. They'd spent the last hour swapping stories of opening their first stores, the long hours, raising children American while trying not to lose too much of their own culture. They'd both married in their hometowns, both moved their families to the US looking for more opportunities for their children. They both had family and friends they still missed from "the old country," but they considered themselves American now.

They might have come from different parts of the world, but they were cut from the same cloth. Rakesh and I stood off to the side, both respectfully quiet, as we'd been raised to be.

No warmth met me from Rakesh's eyes when he looked at me, and I understood. His first impression of me had not been a good one. He didn't know that the offer we'd brought to his family had been initiated by me.

I'd gone from Heather's office to my own and called a meeting with all three of my brothers, as well as my father. I'd offered to wipe the slate clean with my personal income. If loss were to be incurred, it would be by me and me alone. Without hesitation, Mauricio refused to consider my proposal. He said we rose and fell as a family, and if I thought this deal needed changing, that was what we'd do—together. He'd punched Gian in the arm with enough force to make him wince, but smile. His meaning had been clear: all of us. Christof had nodded his approval.

And my father? He'd never looked prouder.

After that, our lawyers had written up the necessary paperwork for a partial acquisition of Bhatt Markets. They would retain their store name and continue on with us in a sort of partnership. For five years, we'd have the deciding vote on how they did business, but with our support we were confident we could grow their brand. It was Heather's idea to add a buyback clause that would be offered only at the five-year mark. The family would have a chance then to buy control back, as long as my family was paid in full along with a healthy percent of the profit. If done right, both families would come out the other side having benefited from the deal. Not charity. Not shark tactics. A mutually beneficial business deal that both families could live with.

"My only regret?" Rakesh's father looked at him. "Not a single prospect for grandchildren in sight. The doctor keeps telling me my days are numbered, but I'm not going anywhere until I look into the eyes of our next generation."

Love for his father shone in Rakesh's eyes. "Then you'll be with us a long time."

"One grandchild." His father looked to mine and waved a hand in the air. "Is that too much to ask?"

"From your mouth to God's ears," my father said. "Four sons and not one grandchild so far."

"I have two, and they both say they have no time for a wife. No time? What else is worth a man's time?" He covered his mouth with a handkerchief as he coughed. "I told Rakesh he should go back to see that sweet accountant woman he met a while ago. He needs a smart woman to keep him in check."

My eyebrows rose, and my shoulders flexed. I'd almost forgotten that he'd met with Heather.

"Dad, please." Rakesh looked almost as uncomfortable as I wanted to make him feel.

My eyes narrowed. "The woman I'm seeing is a tax accountant."

My father scoffed. "Seeing? He says that, but has he brought her home for us to meet? No. If it's the same woman, your son should go see her again; perhaps that would light a fire beneath the dragging feet of my son."

Rakesh held my gaze and shook his head. "I'd never do that."

"Good." I nodded, and as my father continued to lament on my reluctance to bring Heather to Sunday dinner, Rakesh and I commiserated with a look. One day, who knew, we might be friends. For now it was good enough that we respected each other.

As the conversation turned to our siblings, my mind wandered. I thought about the name my father had given me and decided I'd been correct to not look further into it. I had to believe my father's assessment of Gian's mother. If Gian ever asked me to, I would help him find her, but whatever had happened back in Italy was probably best left there.

I needed to keep moving forward.

Heather.

I did want the family to meet her, but I also didn't want to rush her. We saw each other or spoke every day. Her voice was the last I heard before I fell asleep each night and often the first I heard in the morning. She'd put Ava to bed, then call me. In the morning, she'd reconnect as she drove from Ava's preschool to work.

Depending on how our schedules were, we'd meet for lunch. Sometimes we ate at her office, sometimes at the house with the elevator.

I now had a deep appreciation for some of the idiosyncrasies of that house. I'd once considered the tropical island–themed interior pool tacky. Fake palm trees, a sloping sandy beach, and an island with a tiki bar in the middle of the pool. Why would anyone think a house needed such a pool? The cost of maintenance alone was substantial. My opinion changed, though, after Heather and I spent a naked afternoon frolicking in the water and fucking on that island. That was all it had taken to convince me that every house needed a pool like that.

And an adult game room. With the same dedication as they'd covered every inch of the walls of their Disney room, the family had adorned another room with Kama Sutra artwork. Everywhere one looked there was a statue of a couple or a series of paintings depicting some sex act in graphic detail. I thought I was pretty savvy sexually, but touring that room with Heather was educational as well as inspirational for both of us. We'd spent more than one lunch reenacting the artwork. One time with mind-blowing results. Another left us laughing and wondering if that position was physically possible for anyone.

Friends as well as lovers, I was beyond being able to imagine my life without her in it. My father was right, it was time to introduce her to the family.

My phone buzzed, and I realized everyone was looking at me.

My father snapped his fingers. "He's been in a daze since he met this woman. Sebastian, answer your phone."

"Of course." I stepped out of the room to answer it when I saw Heather was the caller. She never called me midafternoon. "Are you okay? Is it Ava?"

"We're both fine. I'm sorry, I know you're busy. I should have waited until tonight."

"Heather, stop, you can always call me—always."

She let out an audible breath, and my heart started pounding in my chest. She sounded worried. Nothing would keep me from her side if she needed me.

"My father called. He'll be in the area this weekend. Cheshire has a strawberry festival. I told him we'd meet him there. Then I started to freak out as I thought about all the ways I could do this badly. I don't want to rehash the past. I want him to see how amazing Ava is and for him to be the grandfather I know he can be. Was the festival a bad choice? Should I have chosen somewhere quieter? Should I meet with him first, talk everything out, or just plow ahead? I need to do this right."

"You will. Stop second-guessing yourself. Meeting at a festival sounds like a stress-free way to introduce them and a nice memory for both."

"Can you come with us?" she asked in a rush, and I swayed on my feet.

My immediate impulse to say yes was tempered by my desire to move forward in a way that was best for everyone. "You want me to meet Ava for the first time on the same day she meets your father?"

She went quiet for a moment. "I didn't think of that. Are you free for dinner tonight? I know this is last minute, so if you can't make it, it's okay. I didn't think seeing my father again would be so hard for me, but I'm freaking out a little."

That was an easy one to answer. "What time tonight?"

"Five thirty? We eat early." Her obvious relief made my heart soar.

"I'll be there." She was strong and independent—exactly what my old-fashioned ass needed. With her, I'd be the man I should have always been.

After telling her I'd call her when I was on my way, I ended the call and returned to the living room. My father said, "See that look on his face? I don't even have to ask who called him."

I shrugged. "I'll bring her home soon, Dad. When I do, I'll have a ring as well."

My father's face lit up.

"Now those are words every father wants to hear," Rakesh's father said to the room in general.

Rakesh groaned.

I felt his pain. If he had a prospect, I had no doubt he would have loved to bring that joy to his father. Dates were easy enough to find, but someone worth bringing home to the parents? In families like ours, no man did that lightly.

I walked over and offered my hand to Rakesh's father. "My plans for this afternoon have changed, so I need to get back to the office."

My father rose and shook his hand as well. "This has been a pleasure."

Rakesh nodded toward the door. "I'll show them out."

He and I fell into step as we walked out of the room. Rakesh said, "It has been a long time since my father has smiled so much. Thank you."

If apologies came easier to me, I would have given one then, but instead I shook his hand and said, "I'm glad we were able to come up with a mutually beneficial deal."

We didn't need more than that.

My father joined us near the door. "Rakesh, you should drop by Sebastian's office."

I tilted my head to the side. "Why?"

A smile spread across my father's face. "Miss Steele is not only intelligent, she's also attractive and, according to your mother, her last relationship ended recently."

"*Dad.*"

My father's answer was a shameless chuckle.

As we made our way down the steps, my father said, "Your mother and I do want to meet Heather, but it's more important to us that you're happy." At the bottom of the steps, he clapped a hand on my shoulder. "You deserve happiness, Sebastian. Therese would want this for you."

Rob opened a car door. As my father slid in, I took a moment to digest what he'd said before getting in myself. I directed Rob to take me to the office and my father home.

After a moment on the road, I said, "When Therese died, a large part of me died with her. Lately, though, I feel like I'm waking from a long sleep. The sun is brighter. Food tastes better. Part of me feels guilty for it."

"You shouldn't. If you had gone first, would you have wanted Therese to live out the rest of her life alone and mourning for you?"

"Of course not."

"She loved you just as much as you loved her. She's smiling down on this. Who knows, perhaps she even placed that stuffed animal in your path because she knew it was time for you to wake up."

As far-fetched as that sounded, I liked the idea of it. Therese was always generous and loving, a better woman than I had deserved. Someone like that wouldn't see my relationship with Heather as a betrayal—she was always looking for a way to make people happy.

If you did bring Heather to me, Therese—thank you. I promise you this time I won't take a moment for granted.

CHAPTER THIRTY-ONE

HEATHER

When I invited Sebastian for dinner, I was thinking about Ava and how it really would be good for the two of them to meet before the strawberry festival. I didn't think about the state of my house or remember that my cooking ability was mostly limited to a simple meat, the occasional pasta, and cookies.

The plus of not being a great cook: Ava was accustomed to eating vegetables raw, thus I could claim my style fit a healthy trend. I would have liked to impress Sebastian, though. It was a beautiful day, and Ava had wanted to ride her bike in the driveway, which meant the time I had after work to cook and clean was drastically reduced, so I settled for what we normally ate.

I'd made time, though, to wrap an important surprise for both Ava and Sebastian.

Sweaty and flustered, I checked my reflection in the mirror after I heard the doorbell. I smoothed a stray hair. Deciding there was nothing I could do about the rest, I rushed for the door.

Ava looked up from playing with her dolls on the living room floor.

"My friend Sebastian is here to eat dinner with us. Do you remember him?" I'd considered preparing her for his visit, but sometimes that made her anxious about things that she otherwise simply accepted.

She jumped to her feet. "Sebastian? My Sebastian?"

"I guess that depends if your Sebastian is six feet tall with black hair."

"My hero?"

I ruffled her hair. "Yes, then your Sebastian is the one at the door. Should we let him in?"

Ava beat me to the door. "Hi, Sebastian."

Hands on knees, he bent to her height. "Hi, Ava. Nice to see you again."

"Want to play dolls?" she asked.

His eyes flew to mine. I laughed. "Dinner still has a few more minutes to cook, so there is a little time."

He mouthed, "Thanks," but he smiled as Ava led him to the living room.

I was glad he hadn't kissed me. I wasn't ready for that in front of Ava. It would happen, but I wanted Ava to be comfortable having Sebastian around first.

"Sebastian," Ava said firmly, "you have to sit on the floor. Here, do you want to be the mommy or the daddy?"

Sebastian tossed his suit jacket on the arm of a chair and rolled the sleeves of his dress shirt up before lowering himself to the floor beside the tree house Ava had set up. His expression was serious. "I've never played dolls before."

Ava brought a hand to her heart. "Never? Don't you have a sister?"

"Only brothers," he said in a solemn tone.

I heard the oven beep, but I lingered a moment longer.

Ava looked down at her dolls, then to the man I was falling more in love with by the second. "It's really easy. Here, you be the mommy. You have to say things like 'Don't touch that. No running around. Be nice to everyone.'" She picked up the male doll. "I'll be the daddy."

"What does a daddy say?"

Ava stage-whispered, "Charlotte's dad says bad words sometimes. Like *stupid*. One time when he was driving he called someone a *stupid dumbass*." She giggled behind her hand.

"Ava, I'm going to check the chicken. Be good," I said as I stepped farther away. Our open-concept home meant I could see them from the kitchen area, but I was less worried about how it was going when I heard Sebastian laugh.

Sebastian and Ava looked more like they were having a conversation than actually playing dolls, but they both looked so happy I hated to announce dinner was ready. Once I did, though, they both came and helped me carry the food to the table.

Chicken breast. Raw broccoli. Raw cauliflower. Ava was excited about it, but I shot Sebastian an apologetic smile.

He gave me a curious look I couldn't decipher.

As soon as we sat, Ava started talking nonstop to him about how her whole class had spent the morning in another classroom because a little boy peed on the rug during circle time, then how she was learning to ride her bike but still had to use training wheels, and finally about how sad she was that she didn't have a pet when everyone else in the world had one. Everyone. Else.

Sebastian met my gaze across the table. Rather than looking bothered by Ava, he seemed to be genuinely entertained. "When I was her age, we had a dog."

I almost kicked him under that table.

"Really?" Ava exclaimed. "See, Mom. What was his name?"

"Digger," Sebastian said. "He was an Irish setter who loved to dig up our backyard. When I was little I used to think his name was Get Out of the Garden."

Ava laughed. "He was a bad boy."

"Sometimes," Sebastian said, then lowered his voice as if whispering to her, "we used to sneak him into the house so he could sleep with us, and my mother would get angry because he was so dirty."

"Mom would be mad too. She said we don't have room for one, but, see, he could use my bed."

I shot Sebastian a look. "Easy there on the sharing. We don't have enough yard here for a dog."

Ava slumped a little and started eating.

Sebastian made a pained face and mouthed, "Sorry."

I shrugged it off. There was no way for him to know that I felt guilty I wasn't superhero single mom. I could handle running my business and raising Ava, but I was afraid of adding another responsibility. The only thing worse than not getting Ava the dog she wanted would be to get her a dog and have to rehome it when we realized we didn't have the time to take care of it properly.

Ava's mood rebounded as soon as Sebastian asked her what color her bike helmet was. He didn't seem to mind that she answered that simple question by telling him all about her helmet, her bike, her knee-pads, and her broken old scooter. She said she didn't just like toys when they worked, but she also liked fixing them. "When I grow up, I want to be a car veterinarian."

"The world needs more of those," Sebastian answered in a serious tone. Ava looked completely taken by him. No wonder. Although he could appear stern when he didn't smile, my daughter wasn't intimidated by that at all. She saw through his hard exterior to the man I'd sensed when I'd first met him.

After both Sebastian and Ava had cleaned their plates, I said, "Ava, Sebastian brought a present for you. Would you like to open it?"

"I did?" he asked.

"You sent it earlier, remember? I thought today would be the perfect time to give it to her."

"It's not even my birthday," Ava said with wonder.

"I'll be right back." A moment later I returned with the present I had covered with purple wrapping paper, Ava's favorite color.

Sebastian's smile was as wide as Ava's. "It's really a present for Wolfie."

Ava's eyes rounded, and she tore off the paper, uncovering a large basket with the small stuffed wolves. "Puppies!" She held each one up to her face and hugged them in turn. Then she bolted over to Sebastian and hugged him.

She ran out of the room, but I knew where she was going. A second later she was back with Wolfie and Wolfina. "Wolfie, you have a family now. You're a daddy." She stopped, turned to Sebastian, and asked, "Are you somebody's daddy, Sebastian?"

He shook his head. The pain I expected to see in his eyes didn't materialize. His expression was somber, but not tortured like it had been the first time he'd met Ava.

Ava looked from Sebastian to me. "I would like a daddy." With that, she went back to introducing the stuffed animals to each other.

"Ava, why don't you take your pack to the living room?" I suggested.

She didn't need more encouragement than that to gather them up and take them to where her dolls were. I smiled as I watched her introducing them all as if they were real.

When I turned back to Sebastian, I said, "I hope you don't mind that I sprang the gift like that. After we talked, I remembered I'd stashed them in my closet."

"This was the perfect moment." He leaned across the table and laced his hand with mine. "You have an amazing daughter, Heather. So young, but so confident. I see a lot of you in her."

That made me smile. "Nature versus nurture. I was always serious, always needed to feel in control. Brenda was a much freer spirit. She believed in things like luck and fate. We were very different people— but in the ways that mattered, we were the same. My hope is that Ava gets the best of both of us."

He nodded. "In the future I have no doubt car veterinarians will exist. With a powerhouse like Ava, how could they not?"

I loved how easily our hands fit together; would our lives blend as smoothly? I wanted to believe so. "Thank you for not pushing to get to know her before I was ready."

He raised my hand to his lips for a gentle kiss. "This is too important to rush."

My breath caught in my throat. The last few weeks had been magical, but we hadn't talked about the future. Nor had he said he loved me.

I understood why. Some men might throw the word around or use it for gain, but Sebastian wouldn't say it until he felt it.

He didn't play games.

"So," he said, "when is this festival?"

"Saturday."

"Do you want to meet there or for me to pick you and Ava up?"

Forward, not back. "Let's all go together."

His smile said it was the answer he'd hoped for; then his expression turned serious again. "What do you think will happen when you see your father?"

I tightened my hand on his. It was a question that took a moment to consider before answering. I lowered my voice. "I'm not sure, but I know I need to give him a chance. In the past when something scared or disappointed me, I closed the door on it. I want to do better—for Ava."

He was quiet for a moment. "When you're ready, I'd like you and Ava to meet my family."

"Your family?" A small panic washed over me even though I knew it was the next logical step.

"We gather at my parents' home every Sunday. You're welcome whenever you're ready for that step."

I didn't thank him for his patience, mainly because I couldn't breathe. *We're doing this. We're taking this to the next level.*

Yes, I'd asked him to meet my father, but that was because Sebastian was more than a lover now—he was also my friend. So far, though, being with him hadn't had a stronger impact on the life I'd made for myself.

Meeting his parents was a big move, especially to a man like Sebastian. Despite my feelings for him, I wasn't sure if I was ready to make that leap.

Everything would likely change.

If things got serious—where would we live?

Would he understand that I still wanted to work?

Would he want children? Would I? How would that affect Ava?

All those questions and more awaited me as soon as I agreed to meet his family. I sat there, slightly hyperventilating, wishing I could think of something—anything—to say.

The front door of my house flew open, and Erica's three children poured in with Erica fast on their heels. She looked uncharacteristically flustered. "I hate to do this, but Bob was in an accident at work. He's at the ER. He got his arm stuck in something. It might need surgery. Could you watch the kids so I can go to the hospital?"

"Of course." I was on my feet in a heartbeat. "Have they eaten?"

Sebastian was at my side.

Erica brought a hand to her mouth. "Yes. No. We were in the middle of dinner when Bob called."

"I'll drive you," Sebastian said.

Still looking panicked, Erica said she was fine, but Sebastian insisted. "Erica, we'll take your car. I'll get a ride back. While I'm out, I'll pick up pizza for the kids."

Relief spread across her face. "Sebastian, you're my hero."

"Mine," Ava chimed in. "He's *my* hero."

"Look! He brought puppies," Charlotte exclaimed.

Erica answered her phone. "I'm on my way, Bob. No, I'm not; Sebastian is driving. Fifteen minutes tops."

I stopped Sebastian near the door and gave him a quick kiss. "No, *my* hero," I murmured against his lips.

He lifted his head and winked. "Save your gratitude for when we're alone."

I chuckled and told Erica to call me as soon as she knew anything. Wrapping my arms around myself, I watched him sprint down the stairs with Erica, and I realized it was already too late. Even if moving forward held uncertainty, I loved Sebastian and I wanted him in my life. Not just on the phone, not only for lunchtime romps.

A few hours later, the children were all fed and finally asleep—Charlotte with Ava and the boys together in my bed. I snuggled against Sebastian's side on the couch.

"Erica said she'll be here first thing in the morning to get her children ready for school. No surgery, just stitches. She's driving Bob home now. She was going to pick the kids up, but I told her they were all sleeping. You don't have to stay."

"I don't mind. I'm glad it turned out less serious than she thought." He yawned. "I can't believe you actually got Kevin and Tyler to go to bed. Those boys don't stop."

It was my turn to yawn. "It helped that we took them to the park after they ate. They're good kids; they just have a lot of energy."

"Four boys, how did my mother do it?"

"I was an only child. One is easier, but when I see the kids all playing together, I wonder—"

"Would you like more?"

"In the right situation, yes."

He cupped my chin and turned my face so our eyes met. "And what situation would that be?"

"It's not something I'd want to do alone, and I could only do it with someone who could love Ava as much as I do . . ."

Sebastian kissed me on the lips gently. "You left something out."

"Did I?" As was often the case, I couldn't concentrate when he looked at me with desire burning in his eyes.

"You'd only want to make that family with someone you loved."

"Ah yes." I traced a finger over his lips. "I might know a man who fits that description."

"This man should be equally, madly in love with you."

Heat surged through me. "Do I know someone like that?"

He nuzzled my neck. "You do."

Even though nothing further was possible, being in his arms was enough—for now. "Sebastian?"

"Yes?"

"This weekend Ava is meeting my father, but next weekend"—I stopped, then took a leap of faith—"next weekend I'd love to meet your family."

CHAPTER THIRTY-TWO

SEBASTIAN

I don't like feeling powerless. Even though Heather was putting on a cheerful face for her daughter, her hand was tense and cold in mine. I wanted to reassure her everything would be okay—her father would show up with presents for Ava and a heartfelt apology for not immediately accepting her.

I didn't fucking know what we were walking into.

At a red light I glanced at Ava in the back seat. She'd brought her entire wolf pack and had given each a distinct voice. If things worked out, I would suggest her father buy an even larger wolf—and call him *Grandfather* or whatever Heather's father chose as his title.

We parked, and although it wasn't an easy feat, Heather convinced Ava that a strawberry festival was too messy a place for stuffed animals. She reminded her daughter that they couldn't go on the blow-up slides or the bounce house . . . and Ava wouldn't be able to either if she had a wolf pack to look after.

Before leaving the car, Heather turned in her seat and said, "Ava, we're going to meet someone today. I think my father is here."

"You have a father?" Ava asked in awe.

"I do. He lives far away, which is why you've never met him, but he's here to meet you." When Ava didn't immediately answer, Heather looked to me for confirmation that she was presenting the meeting correctly. I took her hand in mine and gave it a squeeze.

"I have a grandfather?" Ava asked slowly.

Looking like she was smiling but was also close to tears, Heather nodded. "You do. Would you like to meet him?"

Ava turned to me. "Sebastian, do you know him?"

"This is the first time I'll meet him as well," I answered.

"Are you scared?" she asked.

God, that girl knew the way into my heart. I could tell then that the boys in her future would fear me because I would slay dragons for her—and do worse to anyone who dared break her heart. I raised the hand I had linked with Heather's. "Nothing scares me when we're together."

Heather held out one hand to Ava between the seats.

I held out mine to Ava as well.

She took both of our hands, and a huge smile spread across her face. "Nothing can scare me now."

Heather sniffed, but she was still smiling. "Me either."

We dropped hands and climbed out of the car. As we walked across the grass parking lot, Ava took her mother's hand, then mine. I exchanged a look with Heather. If we were alone, I would have pulled her into my arms and assured her that everything would be okay, but I settled for letting my eyes tell her how much I cared.

I knew the moment Heather spotted her father because her face tensed. He was younger than I'd thought, somewhere in his fifties probably, and conservatively dressed in a white polo shirt and khaki pants. His expression didn't change when he saw us, but he did meet us halfway.

"Hi, Dad."

He looked his daughter over. "You look good, Heather. Happy."

"I am." Heather glanced down at her daughter. "Dad, this is my daughter, Ava, and my, um . . . Sebastian."

"Bill," her father said by way of introduction. The handshake he gave me was firm. I waited for him to introduce himself to Ava, but he didn't. His hands were empty, and I had the feeling it wasn't because he'd stashed a gift somewhere to give Ava later. "There's a booth with fresh strawberries and cream," he said.

Ava lit up. "Can we get some, Mommy?"

"That's what we're here for," Heather said, but her forehead furrowed as she looked at her father. Was she hoping for more from him?

I sure as hell was.

We waited in line together, ordered our bowls, then found a picnic table where we could dig in to them. As we ate, Heather and her father stepped away to speak privately. Although I wanted nothing more than to make sure that conversation was a healthy one for Heather, I had Ava to think of.

I dabbed her nose with whipped cream.

She retaliated with a smear of her own that had us both laughing.

When we finished our food, Ava looked over at the bounce house. "Can I go in?"

I glanced to where Heather and her father were still talking. If Heather had been smiling, I would have walked Ava over to ask if that was what Heather wanted, but I had a feeling she'd thank me for distracting Ava. "Sure. You just have to take your shoes off."

"Will you watch me?" Ava asked.

"Of course." I followed her to the bounce house and paid for a ticket for her. "Go on in. I'll be right here."

She left her shoes by the entrance. I went to stand beside the mesh wall so I could see her. "Watch this, Sebastian," she said. "Did you see that? Watch me, Sebastian." Even though she was doing nothing different than any of the other children in the bounce house, I cheered her on and applauded her attempts at high jumps.

I thought of my first child and how they would have loved the bounce house as well. For once, the thought didn't fill me with despair. I would always feel the loss, but it no longer had the power to overwhelm me. Instead of locking it away and releasing it like a demon once a year, my grief had become a companion who would walk through life beside me—always a part of me, but not defining who I was.

Heather and her father came to stand beside me. With her father there I couldn't ask Heather about their conversation, but their expressions made it clear it hadn't gone well.

Ava popped out of the bounce house and danced over to Heather. "Mommy, I have to pee. Right now."

"Oh, okay, let's find a bathroom," Heather said in a rush and shot me a panicked look.

"We'll be right here," I assured her.

They were well out of earshot when I said, "Seeing you today meant a lot to Heather."

Her father sighed. "Seeing her meant a lot to me too. She's my baby girl."

That didn't sound like a bad foundation to build on. "You seemed to be talking things out."

Bill shook his head. "Nothing to talk out. She's been angry with me since the day her mother left. If you ask me, she's a lot more like her mother than like me. Four years, that's how long she hasn't spoken to me. The apple didn't fall far from that tree."

Even as my temper began to rise, I held my patience. This was Heather's family, and for that reason alone I would be respectful. "It might seem that way to you, but Heather is hopeful the two of you can work things out—that you might be part of Ava's life."

With a shrug, Bill said, "That little girl is not my grandchild. Her mother was a wild one who was always in some kind of trouble. I told Heather my opinion when she said she wanted to adopt her. It hasn't changed. Don't get me wrong, I'm happy to see my daughter doing well, and she seems to like being a mother, but when she has her own children, she'll see how different it is. You can take in someone else's kid, but it's not the same thing."

My hands fisted at my sides. "I'm going to need you to shut the fuck up," I said in a low tone.

He turned to me, anger flashing in his eyes. "What did you say?"

I rose to my full height and took a calming breath, only because there were children present. "I love your daughter and that little girl of hers. I intend to marry Heather and, if they both agree to it, adopt Ava. They will be my family—and Ava will be my daughter regardless of whether or not we have other children. As Heather's father you will be welcome in our home"—I leaned closer to him and growled—"but if I ever hear you talk about Ava like that again, or get any sense that you make either Heather or Ava uncomfortable, it will be my pleasure to throw your ass out."

Before he had a chance to say anything, Ava ran back with Heather at her heels. "Can we go on the slide now? Can we?"

Heather looked from me to her father and back. "Everything okay?"

"Absolutely," I said smoothly. "Your father and I were just getting acquainted."

Ava was tugging on her mother's hand. Heather smiled. "Do you mind if I go down the slide a few times with Ava?"

Ava looked up at Heather's father. "Come watch us."

Bill hesitated. He looked a little less sure of himself than he had a moment earlier. "Okay."

Ava stood there, looking up at Heather's father. "Can I call you *Grampy?*"

In the heartbeat it took for Bill to respond, I came damn close to dragging his ass off somewhere where I could clarify the point I'd made earlier—this time with my fists. Bill looked at Heather for a long moment before leaning down near Ava and saying, "Grandpa."

With that, Ava let go of Heather's hand and took his. "Do you go down slides, Grandpa?"

He shook his head. "Bad back."

"That's okay, you can watch me and Mommy." She started to drag him toward the slide, then stopped and looked back. "Sebastian, are you coming?"

"I sure am," I said, taking Heather's hand in mine.

On the short walk to the slide, I asked, "Everything okay with your dad?"

"I don't know," she said. "I tried to tell him how happy I am with how my life is now, but he kept trying to drag me into old arguments about why he still believed adopting Ava had been the wrong choice. I don't get it. It's like being right is more important to him than being part of our lives." She gave my hand a little squeeze. "I'm not upset, though. I didn't argue with him. I don't have to prove Ava's worth to him. You're right—either he'll come around or he won't. If anything, I feel sorry for him. He doesn't see that *he* is the reason he's alone."

"You needed to see him again."

"Yes, I did." She motioned toward where Ava was happily chatting with her grandfather, completely unaware of his rejection of her. To give him credit, Bill seemed like he'd had at least a partial change of heart. Heather added, "They seem to be getting along. Baby steps, right? He's here. Ava likes him. This might work out."

In that moment she reminded me of my family. Strong and proud, but also loving and forgiving. Only a fool would let a woman like that slip away. I pulled her to me for a tight hug and a light kiss. "I love you, Heather. I never thought I could love again; now I can't picture my life without you in it. You and Ava. If you don't think it's too early, I'd like to ask you a hefty question next weekend when we go to see my parents."

She froze in my arms, and her eyes riveted to mine. "Hefty question? Like *the* question?"

"Unless you want me to wait."

She wrapped her arms around me so tightly I could hardly breathe—or maybe that was from the love for her that was welling within me. "I love you, Sebastian. Even more because you understand that I'm not good with surprises. I have to warn you, though, with you the answer will always be yes."

I wiggled my eyebrows at her. "Oh really?"

CHAPTER THIRTY-THREE

HEATHER

A quick check of the clock confirmed I needed to make a decision soon. I'd told Ava we were going to spend the day with Sebastian's family because I knew she'd be excited rather than nervous. She'd chosen a dress, matching tights, and a sparkly pair of shoes. Last I looked she was attempting to tie ribbons on the necks of her wolf pack before placing each into the basket she said they'd travel in to Sebastian's house. Tying included clear tape rather than knots, but it was keeping her entertained, so I went with it.

Erica called to see how I was doing.

"I'm freaking out," I said.

"I'll be right over."

A few minutes later, she was standing in the doorway of my bedroom. "Charlotte's playing with Ava. I left the boys home—looking at Bob's stitches is their favorite thing lately."

I laughed. Normally I loved to see them, but my nerves were already on edge. "Thanks. Sebastian is going to be here any minute, and I can't decide what to wear. I was fine with dinner. Why did I agree to go early? He said it would give me time to get to know his mother. What if that means in the kitchen? He knows I don't cook."

"Breathe," Erica said before sitting down on the edge of my bed. "He's taking you home to propose to you, not test if his family likes you. Just be yourself."

My mouth dried, and my hand tightened on the dress I was holding. "Exactly. He's going to propose. This is the real deal. What if his family hates me? What if—"

"Stop, Heather. Do you love Sebastian?"

"I do."

"Do you think he'll be a good father for Ava?"

That one was easy. "Yes. He already adores her, and it's mutual."

"Then that's all that matters. I'm not worried about his family. I'm one hundred percent positive they will love you."

I went to sit beside her. "Why do you say that?"

She put a hand on my back in support. "I was here the first time you met him, remember? You brought a smile back to that man's face. What parent wouldn't love you for that?"

I nodded. "He does seem happier than he did in the beginning."

"Because he is. Don't underestimate yourself, Heather. He was one lucky bastard the day he found Wolfie, and he knows it. That's why you're going home with him. So, really, any outfit will work, because I don't see a way today ends without you dropping by my house to show off your engagement ring."

Tears filled my eyes. "This house is so small, I can't see Sebastian living here . . . not if we're thinking of having more children, but I don't want to move away from you."

Erica hugged me. "I don't think you'll be moving farther than that house you run off to with him at lunch. Didn't you say it's massive?"

"It is."

"And halfway between here and his family."

"That's true."

"And you love it there."

I blushed. "I do. Although some of the rooms would need a lock."

She cocked her head to the side. I hadn't shared *everything* with her. "It's not all child appropriate."

Her eyes rounded. "Girl, have you been holding out on me? Oh, we'll be talking more about this house tomorrow. But for right now, stand up. Let me see what you're wearing."

I did. Although I had a dress in my hands, I was wearing nice slacks and a silk shirt. "I get the feeling his family is on the traditional side, so maybe I should wear the dress."

"Which one are you more comfortable in?"

"I wear skirts all week. I prefer slacks on the weekend."

She pulled the dress out of my hands with a smile and tossed it in the air behind her. "Decision made."

And just like that I was smiling too.

"Mommy, Sebastian is here," Ava called up the stairs. "He brought flowers."

"Well, what are you waiting for?" Erica chided. "Get down there."

I rushed halfway down the stairs but came to a stop when I saw him standing just inside the door. He was giving Ava and Charlotte flowers from my bouquet as they laughed and danced around him. When he looked up, the love in his eyes washed over me, and I felt like the bride he was about to ask me to be.

One lost stuffed animal.

One knock on the door.

That was all it had taken to change the course of my life.

Brenda, maybe, just maybe, I'm beginning to believe in fate too.

"Ready?" he asked.

"I am," I said, and suddenly I was. "Erica's here."

"Hey, Erica," Sebastian said. "How's Bob's arm?"

"Better every day. He said he'd love for us to all go somewhere together. Mini golf?"

"I'm in," Sebastian said and actually sounded like it might be something he'd do.

"Me too," Ava said. "Can we go now?"

"Not today," he answered. "We're going to see my family, remember?"

"Oh yes. Do they play mini golf?" Ava circled back to the important part of the conversation.

"Not recently, but I bet they would if you asked them to."

Erica came to stand beside me. Her expression said, *"See."*

I did. She was right; there was no way that day would end without me dropping by her house to show off my ring.

I expected the Romano family home to be ostentatious, a sprawling estate with stone walls and a gate like the home Sebastian and I had made into our romantic getaway spot. Yet though it was a beautiful home set in the middle of a well-maintained acre or so of a yard, it could have belonged to any middle-class family.

We were the only car in the driveway when we pulled in. Clutched in my hands was the bottle of Italian wine I'd brought for his parents.

Sebastian put a hand on my arm. "There's nothing to worry about. They are going to love you because I do."

Ava chimed in between the seats. "You love my mom, Sebastian?"

He chuckled. "I do, peanut."

"I love her too," Ava said cheerfully.

"She's pretty great," Sebastian said, then opened his car door. "Ava, you might not want to bring your stuffed animals in. My mother told me they have something in the house that might chew them up."

"Like a lion?" Ava asked.

He walked around to open my door and Ava's. "Smaller. I told my mother I missed Digger, and she took that to mean it was time for our family to get another dog. I believe they got a golden retriever."

"For themselves?" I asked as we walked up the driveway to the steps.

Sebastian held out his hands as if at a loss. "Hard to say. I told them we don't have room for a puppy right now."

"It's a puppy?" Ava squealed. "A real puppy? For me?"

"Oh, hon, I don't think it's for us. But I'm sure they'll let you play with it," I said.

The door opened, and a tall woman with dark hair waved us in. Sebastian's father smiled at us over her shoulder. His hair was brown rather than black, and I had expected him to also have Sebastian's dark-gray eyes, but he didn't. He looked a good ten years older than his wife but still healthy and active.

"Mom. Dad. This is Heather and her daughter, Ava. Heather, this is my mother, Camilla, and my father, Basil."

My heart warmed when Sebastian ducked down for his mother to give him a kiss on the forehead. His father hugged him as well. It was the kind of welcome I'd always imagined other families had.

I was taken by surprise by the hug his mother pulled me in for. It wasn't unpleasant, just unexpected. She released me before I had time to regain my balance. Sebastian took the bottle of wine from me, which was a good thing because I'd forgotten I was holding it.

His father took my hand between both of his and simply held it for a moment. "We are so happy to meet you, Heather."

Did they know why I was there? It seemed that way.

Sebastian's mother turned to Ava. "I heard you like puppies, and I just happen to have one. Would you like to meet her?" She held out her hand. Ava took it and happily followed her into the house.

We stepped into the house, and it was easy to find Ava. She sat on the floor of the kitchen in a round playpen with a blonde puppy licking her face. "Isn't she beautiful, Mommy? Camilla said I could name her."

"That's a big responsibility," I said lightly. *Especially if they think she's leaving with us.*

Sebastian bent to whisper in my ear. "Dad says the puppy is theirs. They wanted Ava to have a friend when she comes to visit."

Emotion choked my throat, making it impossible to speak at first. "I don't know what to say."

He kissed my cheek. "I'm hoping for a yes."

I laid my head on his arm. "Is this the big question?"

"I'd like to hold off until my brothers are here, but you tell me. Now. Later. I don't care as long as the answer means you become a Romano."

I couldn't resist. I asked, "What is the ring like?"

In my ear he growled, *"Oh, so big."*

I pushed him away playfully. I couldn't go there with him, not with his parents a few feet away. "Behave."

He chuckled.

His mother called my name. "Heather, Sunday is a seven-course meal. Would you like to learn some of our family recipes?"

"Sure," I said, reluctantly leaving Sebastian's side.

The next twenty minutes turned into a sad mockery of a cooking lesson. She rattled off ingredients, half of which I had never heard of. She looked concerned as she watched me cut the vegetables, as if I were a child wielding a knife for the first time.

When she asked me to stir the gravy, I stood there at a loss. There was pasta sauce on the stove, but gravy? I didn't see any.

I was about to admit defeat when Ava joined us. After washing her hands, she climbed up on a stool Camilla set beside the table for her.

"Mommy doesn't know how to cook," Ava announced.

Camilla looked at me with a small smile. "I guessed that."

"She didn't have a mom to teach her. If you teach me, I'll teach her." Ava rolled up her sleeves as if ready to do just that.

I hugged my daughter from behind. "I would love that."

"Me too," Camilla said. She explained to Ava that gravy is what her family calls pasta sauce. I relaxed as they chatted. I might not be a good cook, but my little Ava was turning into a pretty wonderful person anyway.

"Mommy"—Ava pointed at a pot of green beans—"look, it's like at Erica's house. They cook their vegetables too."

I smiled awkwardly at Sebastian's mother.

Her answering smile was kind. "You eat raw vegetables, Ava? They're so good for you. Your mom is one smart woman."

Ava tipped her head back and smiled at me. "She is. She's my second mom. I'm adopted."

"I'm the second mom for my youngest son," Camilla said. "He's my favorite." She ducked down and said in a conspiratorial voice, "Don't tell any of them I said that. They all like to think they're my favorite."

"Am I your favorite, Mommy?" Ava asked.

I kissed the top of her head. "Absolutely."

She climbed down from the stool. "Can I go play with the puppy again?"

Camilla nodded, so I did as well.

Once Ava's attention was back on the puppy, I said, "Thank you, Camilla, for being so kind to her."

Camilla wiped her hands on a towel. "Heather, my son loves you. I know meeting all of us today must be a little scary, but you brought joy back to Sebastian's life—we love you for that already. I don't care if you can cook. Just take care of my son. He's a good man."

"He is." It wasn't just the diced onions that were making my eyes water. "And he's so good with Ava."

"She's a lovely child. If you're here for the reason I think you are, I'd love it if you let her call me *Nonna* one day."

That was it. I started crying happy tears and walked right into the arms Camilla held out for me. I couldn't remember what it was like to be hugged by my own mother, but that thought didn't make me sad anymore. When I stepped back, I wiped my eyes and said, "I'm sorry. I'm not usually a crier. I've always wanted Ava to have more family than just me." I sniffed.

"If I say I hope you call me *Mom*, will you start crying again?" Her tone was gentle.

Tears welled in my eyes again, and I nodded.

Sebastian appeared at my side. "Heather? Everything okay?"

"I love your mother," I proclaimed through my tears, and he relaxed.

He put an arm around my waist. "That's good. I love her too. Mom, everyone is here. Do you need help in here?"

"No," she said. "Introduce Heather to your brothers. Ava can stay with me and . . . Ava, what is the puppy's name?"

Ava called back, "Sara."

"Sara it is," Camilla said.

CHAPTER THIRTY-FOUR

Sebastian

I never thought I'd feel anything this deeply again. Yet all it took was a look from Heather to tangle me up on the inside—in the most amazing way.

I loved seeing her with my family. My parents' thoughts were an easy read—I knew they approved of how she'd taken Ava in. I wasn't sure how a career woman would get on with my mother, but they already seemed comfortable around each other. My father hadn't stopped smiling since we'd walked in.

My brothers overwhelmed Heather when she was first introduced to all of them at once, but as soon as they started giving me shit, she relaxed. For an only child, she didn't seem to mind my loud, chaotic family. Nothing my family could have said would have swayed my decision to ask Heather to marry me, but their acceptance of her was important to me.

During dinner, Heather and I sat closest to my parents. They asked Heather enough questions to write a book, but she didn't seem to mind. On my other side, Ava sat quietly with big eyes while my brothers bantered back and forth. I was considering moving her closer to Heather when I saw Gian motion toward Ava.

Conversation on that side of the table quieted. "Ava," Gian asked, "did you bring Wolfie with you?"

"You know Wolfie?" Her little jaw dropped open.

"We all do," he said. "We met him the day Sebastian saved him from the side of the road. How is he?"

She leaned forward. "He's in the car because of Sara. Wolfie has his own puppies now. Eight. And a wife—Wolfina."

"That's great," Gian said.

Mauricio asked Ava what grade she was in, and her shyness fell away. She told them about her teacher, her friends at school, the boy who pooped himself and tried to hide his underwear in his cubby. My brothers didn't have to prompt her to hear about Charlotte and her brothers. No one would ever have to worry that Ava would run out of things to say.

After dinner but before dessert, my brothers and I cleared the table. In the shuffle, I pulled Ava aside. "Ava, I'm about to ask your mother to marry me. Do you know what that means?"

"Maybe," she said with confidence.

"It means that I'm going to ask her if she wants to be my family. If she says yes, we'll have a wedding, and then you both will live with me. Would you like that?"

"You'd be my daddy?"

I swallowed hard. "If you want me to be."

She pulled on my arm until I bent down, and she gave me one of her tight-around-the-neck hugs. "I want a daddy."

"My parents would be your grandparents. Your Nonna and Papa."

"Really?"

"If you want more grandparents."

"Wow."

"And my brothers would be your uncles."

"A big family." Ava's expression turned serious. "I hope Mommy says yes."

"She will," I assured my little peanut. "But there's something I need you to do. Could you hold on to the ring until I ask for it?" I handed her the box that held a flawless two-carat diamond.

She opened it and said, "It's so pretty."

"You think she'll like it?"

Ava nodded, closed the box, and looked down at her dress. "I have a pocket." She stuffed the small box inside.

"Good thinking," I said. "Now let's go back in, and you take good care of that ring for me until I ask for it, okay?"

She gave me a confident thumbs-up and followed me back into the dining room.

When we returned to the table, cannoli were waiting on dessert plates. Ava rushed to take her seat.

Heather gave me a curious look.

I tried to appear innocent.

Once everyone was seated again, I tapped my fork against the side of my glass of water. All eyes turned to me, and conversation died away.

I stood and took Heather by the hand. She rose to stand beside me. "Heather, I don't know if it was chance or something greater that brought us together, but I'm grateful for whatever it was. You'll probably never know how much meeting you has brought me back to my life. I love you and Ava." I dropped down to one knee. "Marry me and let's be a family."

"Yes. Yes. Yes," Heather said, holding out her hand.

I gave my coat pocket a pat. "Hmm, I had it with me earlier." I felt around the breast pocket of my jacket. "No, just dice in there."

Heather blushed.

I continued, "Where could I have put that ring?"

Mauricio joked, "Small things are easy to misplace. I'm sure you'll find it."

Ava jumped up. "I have it. I have your ring."

Heather teared up when her daughter came to stand with us and handed me the ring box. Ava's eyes rounded as I slid the ring onto Heather's finger.

"Can I have the box?" Ava asked.

"You sure can," Heather said, "because I'm never taking this ring off."

I kissed her then. It wasn't the kiss I would have given her had we been alone, but it held a promise of a future together.

"I'm so glad she said yes," Ava said to the table in general, and there was a round of laughter.

When I rose to my feet, Heather simply hugged me, then put out her arm for Ava to join in. It was a sappy scene, but not one my brothers mocked. They knew the depths of where I'd been and how much this meant to me.

My parents stood and each hugged Heather, welcoming her and Ava to the family. My brothers followed suit. When we took our seats again, Ava asked, "Mommy, can I go get Wolfie? I want him to meet my new family."

"I'll get him," I said.

"I'll go with you," Heather said.

As soon as the front door closed behind us, she was in my arms. Our kiss tasted of forever. I raised my head and said, "I'm not a perfect man."

"Great, now you tell me." She cupped my cheek with one hand.

I laid my hand over hers. "But I'm going to do my damnedest to be the husband you deserve and the father Ava wants."

She went up on her tiptoes and whispered. "News flash, we're not perfect either. On my best day I'm only sixty-five percent certain I know what I'm doing as a parent."

I smiled. "I bet we can get that to at least seventy percent if we put our heads together."

She laughed. "I love you, Sebastian."

"I love you, too, Heather. Now why did we come out here?"

EPILOGUE

Sebastian

May 20—one year later

As I laid a bouquet of flowers at the base of Therese's headstone, I didn't know if she could hear me, but I needed to believe she could.

Look at me, Therese. It's the anniversary of the day you left, and I'm sober.

My eyes misted.

Six years and I can still remember the way you liked your coffee, and I regret every time I complained that your feet were too cold to tuck beneath me as we slept.

I laid my hand on the top of her stone.

I'm not angry anymore. I couldn't stay in that place—it was killing me.

The platinum and gold ring shone on my left hand.

Heather and I are married now. You should see the house we live in. You would have hated it, because you would have insisted on cleaning it yourself. Heather doesn't worry about things like that.

You'd like her—she's not afraid of speaking her mind.

She could have come to work for Romano Superstores, but she likes her independence.

And I don't mind that.

I can't keep flogging myself for what I did wrong with you. All I can do is try not to repeat those mistakes.

Oh, and I know you sent her to me, because when I get out of line, she kicks my ass.

I smiled.

Not saying I don't deserve it.

Mauricio is enjoying the show a little too much. So if I can put in a request, could you please send him someone who will knock a little of that cockiness out of him? Someone nice that my parents will love, but you know Mauricio. His ego could use a trim.

I glanced back at my car. Heather was waiting patiently beside it.

I love her, Therese. I love the life we're making together. Ava is in kindergarten now and growing up too fast. Heather worries that we're spoiling her. But Mom and Dad dote on my little peanut. For her birthday, Gian bought her a puppy, Christof got her a kitten, and Mauricio sent her over the moon by getting her a pony.

Our house is chaotic, but I love it.

I'm happy again, Therese. That doesn't mean I don't miss you. It will never mean I'll forget you. What I'm leaving behind is the guilt.

I can't be a man who hates himself and still be a good husband and father. Did I tell you Heather is pregnant? We don't know the sex of the baby yet, but we will as soon as it's possible to. And I'll be right there with her at every appointment, as I should have been with you.

Remember the bear Mom bought us when she found out you were pregnant? I intend to keep it in the baby's room. Watch over our baby, Therese. In my mind, we're all family.

Heather. Every time she gets in a car, a part of me wants to forbid her to. I'm getting better, though. I couldn't Bubble Wrap her and keep her safe even if I tried. She's an independent woman with strong opinions of her own.

It's good for me.

I called to Heather to join me. She came over and slid beneath my arm. When I told her where I was going that morning, she'd asked me only how she could best support me.

Another woman might have resented Therese.

Some might have jealously asked me to choose.

That wasn't Heather.

She'd once told me she understood loss, and she did.

"Tell me a favorite memory you have together," Heather requested.

I didn't. As kind as she was, I didn't want to do that to her.

She looked up at me with such love in her eyes there was no way I could deny her anything. "If our places were reversed, I would want the best of who I'd been to be remembered. That's what I'd want to live on. I'll come here every year with you, but I think we should leave Therese laughing. So share something she would have told me if she were here. How did you meet?"

I had to reach deep into my memories for that. With Heather in the circle of my arms, I shared a story about Therese walking into my father's store. That was all it had taken. I'd accidentally double-charged her credit card—something she'd always teased me about doing, saying I'd done it on purpose so I could see her again. My defense? How could any man be held accountable for how many times he put a credit card through when he'd just met his future wife?

"A smooth talker back then, huh?" Heather asked with a chuckle.

"I was. She saw right through me, though, and somehow wanted to be with me anyway. She had such a big heart, Heather. I was too young to fully appreciate how lucky I was, but I see it now."

We stood in each other's arms for a long, quiet moment. I hoped what I'd said hadn't been too much for Heather to hear.

She didn't look upset when she turned to Therese's stone. "Thank you for sharing Sebastian with me, Therese. Camilla was telling me about guardian angels. If you're interested, I'd love it if you'd watch over us. This parenting stuff is tough. And now we have a pony. A pony? I've never even ridden a mechanical horse. Sebastian might get nervous when I drive, but I'm a basket case every time Ava takes a riding lesson. I thought ponies were supposed to be tiny."

I chuckled and hugged Heather closer.

She continued, "Oh, and I have a request. If you see my friend, Brenda, could you make sure she pays the utility bills? I'd hate heaven to go dark before we get there."

Hand in hand we walked back to the car. Before driving off, I said, "What should we do now?"

"I'm starving," Heather said, and I barked out a laugh.

I could take her anywhere as long as the trip included a sandwich. *Life is good.*

MEANWHILE . . .

JUDY

"What if we get caught?" Grace asked from the inside of Alethea Stone's office.

"It's a little late to ask that," Judy said with sarcasm. "Watch the door."

"Did I do this to you? Just because I laughed at your family tree last year? I thought it was a joke and you were going to pull out another one. I'll help you this time. Or you could ask your parents if they can write a note to your teacher if you don't want to do another one this year. I don't want to go to jail."

Judy scanned the room for a filing cabinet. Not an obvious one. Alethea would never put anything important where it could be easily found. She also wouldn't have put her notes online—she trusted no one. "No one is going to jail. Alethea works for my father. Worst case, I'll get grounded again. Plus, Alethea is still on maternity leave. Stop worrying."

"Why can't you just ask her what she found out about your father's family?"

"I promised her I'd stop looking, but I can't do it. If anyone would understand, she would." Not those cabinets. Not in Alethea's desk. Judy ran her hand along a wooden panel beside a bookcase until a part of it lit up. A concealed biometric unit? "I bet it's in here."

Grace joined Judy near the bookcase. "That's so cool."

"Predictable is what it is." Judy pulled out a small plastic case. She opened it, revealing rubbery-looking squares. "Luckily I have plenty of access to Alethea's fingerprints. All I had to do was grab a few prints, make a mold of them, add a little gelatin, and voilà. It will even fool a device that blocks inorganic replicas."

"You scare me sometimes," Grace said as Judy began to place the gelatin squares on her fingertips.

"You're the one who said you wanted to come with me," Judy answered as she aligned her hand to the reader. It beeped, went green, then slid to the side. With a huge grin, Judy said, "Best part? Gelatin is edible. How can I be guilty of anything if there is no proof?"

Grace's rebuttal to that was lost to the excitement of seeing a second door open. Behind it there was only one file. Judy pulled it out. The label read "Corisi Family Tree."

Not wanting anything to spill out, Judy laid it down on Alethea's desk before opening it. Her smile faded when she saw that it only contained one piece of paper—addressed to her.

Dear Judy,

If you're reading this it means you sneaked into my office and found my hidden filing cabinet. First, bravo for getting this far. I am one very proud auntie. Second, you know you're not supposed to enter anyone's office without permission. Especially not mine. And don't think I won't know you were here. As soon as you accessed the panel, I was notified.

No, I won't tell your parents.

Although I don't know the circumstances that have made you start looking for your father's family again, I beg you to stop. Not every secret is meant to be revealed. Not every family member is meant to be found.

You won't want to hear this, and I can't believe I'm going to say it, but the truth is sometimes better left buried. Especially if not knowing endangers no one.

I'll call you tonight and tell you all of this again.

Please—stop.

Love, Auntie Alethea

P.S. Don't forget to close up the panel before you leave. It's where I usually hide my chocolate stash.

Judy read the letter aloud the second time.

Grace hovered by her side. "I wish I had an aunt like that."

With a growl, Judy stuffed the letter into the folder and tossed it into the hidden compartment. The panels automatically slid back into place. "I'm not handing another incomplete family tree in. You heard Alethea—my father has more family out there."

"What I heard was that looking for them is not a good idea."

"Why?" Judy paced the office. "Are they dangerous? Criminals? What if they're in some kind of trouble? My father would want to know, and he'd want to help them."

Grace made a pained face. "Wouldn't he be looking for them if he did? Maybe you could just ask him about them?"

"He doesn't know about them, and I can't ask him about any of this because whenever he talks about his family, he gets sad."

"That sounds like a really good reason to listen to Alethea."

"My father didn't get where he is by letting people tell him what he couldn't do. Only in school are we rewarded for being well behaved and quiet. Out in the world it's the brave and daring who make a difference."

Shaking her head, Grace said, "You just want to keep looking."

Judy shrugged. "Wouldn't you?"

Grace looked around the office before answering. "I wouldn't, but I understand why you do. So what's next?"

Judy took out her phone and scrolled through her contacts. "I have other people I can ask for help." She touched on a name of someone she knew wouldn't go running back to her parents if she asked him for a favor.

She texted: Uncle Jeremy, I need your help with a school project.

Less than a moment later his response came back. Absolutely.

Judy: It may require some hacking.

Jeremy: Are you texting using encrypted software?

Judy: Of course I am.

Jeremy: Then what do you need?

Judy: I'm working on a family tree for my father, and it's a surprise. Can you keep a secret?

ACKNOWLEDGMENTS

I am so grateful to everyone who was part of the process of creating *The Broken One*.

Thank you to:

Montlake Romance, for being as excited about this new series as I am. Special thanks to Lauren Plude for encouraging me each step of the way.

My very patient beta readers. You know who you are. Thank you for kicking my butt when I need it.

My editors: Karen Lawson, Janet Hitchcock, and Krista Stroever. As well as all the talented line editors who polished away my mistakes.

My Roadies, for making me smile each day when I log on to my computer. So many of you have become friends. Was there life before the Roadies? I'm sure there was, but it wasn't as much fun.

Thank you to my husband, Tony, who is a saint—simple as that.

And my children, who have given me so many wonderful memories. I hope my love for them shines through in every story I write.

ABOUT THE AUTHOR

Ruth Cardello is a *New York Times* bestselling author who loves writing about rich alpha men and the strong women who tame them. She was born the youngest of eleven children in a small city in northern Rhode Island. She's lived in Boston, Paris, Orlando, New York, and Rhode Island again before moving to Massachusetts, where she now lives with her husband and three children. Before turning her attention to writing, Ruth was an educator for two decades, including eleven years as a kindergarten teacher. *The Broken One* is the first book in her Corisi Billionaires series. Learn about Ruth's new releases by signing up for her newsletter at www.RuthCardello.com.